From the Shadows

Lisa HARTLEY
FROM THE SHADOWS

CANELO

First published in the United Kingdom in 2017 by Lisa Hartley

This edition published in the United Kingdom in 2020 by

Canelo Digital Publishing Limited
Third Floor, 20 Mortimer Street
London W1T 3JW
United Kingdom

Copyright © Lisa Hartley, 2017

A CIP catalogue record for this book is available from the British Library.

Print ISBN 978 1 78863 989 7
Ebook ISBN 978 1 78863 942 2

Look for more great books at www.canelo.co

Printed and bound in Great Britain by Clays Ltd, Elcograf S.p.A.

For my Grandma, Edna Woollas

All nice people, like Us, are We
And every one else is They

                    —Rudyard Kipling, *We and They*

Chapter 1

The bar was packed at five in the afternoon, the early evening crowd making the most of the Saturday happy hour. Catherine Bishop leant forward and tried to catch the eye of one of the staff, attempting to keep her elbow out of the pool of cold beer already accumulating on the bar's surface. She turned her head, and Ellie flashed her a smile from the booth she'd managed to grab. The warm press of the bodies around Catherine was overwhelming, and as the music and the chatter filled her ears, the room blurred. When it was over, she blinked a few times, hoping Ellie hadn't noticed.

'Can I help?' A barman was eyeing her expectantly.

Hugging the beers close, she picked her way through the crowd and over to Ellie, dropping onto the bench beside her friend with a sigh of relief. She slid one of the bottles across the table.

'Cheers.' Catherine took a swig. 'Busy in here.'

'Lots of students around. I suppose they don't all go home for Easter.'

Catherine sat back, her gaze roaming the long, narrow room. The walls had been painted a sickly yellow-white, reminding her of the stained ceilings of the smoke-filled pubs of her teenage years. An enormous flat-screen TV half-filled the wall beside them, the day's Premiership goals floating past in a seemingly endless flow of replays. A few people glanced at the screen, but most ignored it. Why did the bar's owners bother to have it there at all? Perhaps it drew in customers during the week when people saved their money and looked forward instead to Saturday night. She focused on Ellie again, who was checking a text.

'The others are at the restaurant already,' Ellie told her, dropping her phone into her bag. 'We've got to crawl up Steep Hill yet.'

Catherine pretended to choke on her drink. 'Now I know why you didn't tell me where we're eating.'

Ellie laughed, finishing her beer and setting the empty bottle on the table. 'Didn't want to put you off. Come on, I'll race you.'

As they pushed their way through the crowd and out into the street, Catherine caught sight of a homeless man sitting on the pavement, his back pressed against the glass window of a department store. He had a ragged tartan blanket tucked around his legs, but his thin jacket didn't seem to be offering his body much protection. Ellie hadn't seen him, and she was already a few paces away. Catherine was torn for a second, but she rushed over and dropped a few pound coins into his hat. He muttered a thank you but didn't meet her eyes. She hurried away, guilt and shame mingling in her stomach.

–

Mackie pulled the hood of his jacket around his face, hunching his shoulders as the wind bit his cheeks. Glancing at the collection of change in the baseball cap lying on the flagged pavement in front of him, he sighed.

The handful of coins would have to do for tonight. The cold was seeping into his body through his thin coat and jeans, his toes numb, his fingers thrust deep into his pockets. He tugged a hand free, collected the money and pulled back the hood again as he set the hat on his head. It was the end of March, but felt more like December. No signs of spring so far, not in Lincoln at least.

He stood slowly, a dull ache in his hips and knees, pain in his shoulder, his ribs and gut. Stepping back out of the throng of shoppers, he stood under the canopy of a bakery and blew on his hands. He hated this part of town. With its multitude of chain shops and fast food restaurants, he could be anywhere. His city was up the hill – the cobbles and ancient brickwork, the history and heart-break, walking in the footsteps of the Roman legions and medieval monks. Lincoln was old, and you could sense its history if you tried. He looked at the sea of shoppers with contempt. They wouldn't even consider it; obsessed with the latest gadgets, the newest fashions, hurrying towards the next bargain. No, the city was wasted on them. Better they stayed down here.

As he fumbled in his pocket again for some of the change, a plump middle-aged man came out of the bakery and stopped beside him.

'Here you go, mate.' The man held out a cardboard cup and a paper bag with a smile. Mackie took them slowly, like a wary dog being offered a treat by a stranger it didn't entirely like the smell of.

'Thank you.' His voice was quiet, gratingly unused. He didn't have much occasion to speak these days.

'It's only a pasty and some coffee, but I saw you and… Well, you looked as though you needed them.'

Mackie tucked the paper bag containing the pasty, hot and smelling delicious, into his coat pocket, lifted the cup to his lips and took a small sip.

'Thanks. Good of you, mate.'

The man beamed. 'You're welcome. Least I can do. You know there's a soup kitchen in the church over there?' He gestured towards the impressive old building, standing solemnly, penned in by a busy road on one side and the railway line on the other.

Mackie sipped the coffee again, allowing his gaze to wander over the church's sooty stonework. He knew about the soup kitchen, but it wouldn't hurt to let the man imagine he was helping.

'Right.'

'I mean, it's none of my business, but...' He glanced at his watch. 'Well, enjoy the pasty.'

'Thank you, I will.'

Mackie raised the cardboard cup to his mouth again, his eyes following the Good Samaritan as he crossed the street and disappeared around the corner. Kind of him. Most people dropped a few coppers into his hat without making eye contact. He'd had drinks bought for him before, a sandwich or two, but usually, people didn't even see him.

He was counting on it.

–

The restaurant was a warren of small rooms inside an old house, in a row of similar buildings which had been sympathetically modernised. The music was discreet, the clientele prosperous. Smiling waiting staff dressed in pris-tine white shirts with thin black ties stepped carefully across the polished floorboards, moving with practised grace around the tables. Catherine's eyes followed one man, older than the rest, as he hurried across to greet a group of diners. He was tall and handsome, resembling a boyfriend Catherine remembered from her time at university, now a lecturer himself. She had treated him unfairly, frustrated by her own lukewarm response to his advances, not yet knowing herself well enough to understand why he would never be right for her. She glanced back at Ellie, who was pouring wine, and shook her head slightly. Ellie smiled, and Catherine was struck by how well they understood each other, only four months after their awkward, embarrassing first meeting. Ellie knew if Catherine had wine, she would end the evening slumped across the table.

With only half an ear on the conversation, Catherine gazed over her friend's shoulder. Set into the wall behind her was a window, the flame of a tea light in a glass vase on the sill flickering against the darkness outside. The larger panes of glass were clear, but the top two, smaller and square, were stained glass, a red and yellow sun rising against a greenish-blue sky. On a ledge outside two fat grey pigeons huddled together, feathers ruffled by a slight breeze, their bright beady eyes staring back at Catherine. A grubby yellow plastic sign on the wall above them warned CCTV cameras were in operation while an empty ice cream tub, wedged next to the pigeons, overflowed with water dripping from a broken drainpipe above. The water ran down the brickwork beneath, a trail of green slime marking its path. The owners of the restaurant had apparently tried hard to create the right image and ambience inside their premises while hoping no one would notice the cracks they had papered over. Glancing around at her companions, Catherine hid a smile. Who could blame them? *It's what most of us do, after all.*

A young waiter, his red-blond hair standing in improbable spikes, arrived at the table bearing two plates of food. Catherine caught Ellie's eye and consciously brought her mind back to being sociable. In this company, it would be an effort, but they were Ellie's colleagues, and for her sake, Catherine would be polite.

When all the food had arrived, and the wine glasses were filled again, Catherine dug her fork into her pasta, keeping her gaze on her plate. One of the reasons why she'd wanted to avoid this evening soon spoke up.

'You'll have to be careful walking back to your hotel later, you two.'

Melody Grange was in her late thirties, thin with curly blonde hair and viciously pointed fingernails which she kept drumming on the tabletop. Her raucous, braying laugh was making Catherine want to throw things.

Ellie took a piece of garlic bread from the plate in the centre of the table. 'What do you mean?'

Melody gave a smug smile. 'Another robbery last night.' She gestured over her shoulder with her fork. 'Only a few streets away. He always picks on a couple or two friends. Grabs one of them and threatens them with a knife, tells the other to leave their wallets or bags and phones on the ground. Once they've given him their stuff, he lets them go.'

'Sounds risky,' Ellie said.

Melody raised her eyebrows. 'Would you argue with a knife at your throat? I know I wouldn't.'

There was a pause as they all considered it. Catherine kept eating, hoping she could continue to avoid speaking once she had finished her food. Melody turned to her.

'What would the police advice be, Catherine?'

Catherine lifted her head, swallowing a few strands of spaghetti. She raised a linen napkin to her mouth and took her time wiping her lips.

'Sorry?'

Melody's tone was impatient. 'What would the police advise? Do you fight back or do you give him your stuff?'

Catherine hesitated, and Faye Rogers jumped in. Married to one of the officers Catherine worked with, she was also a colleague of Ellie and Melody.

'I know what Chris would say – give him what he wants, get away and report it as soon as you can.'

Catherine took the opportunity to fill her mouth again, making sure she chewed slowly.

Melody shook her head, not satisfied. 'Well, it seems the police are clueless in any case. They haven't caught him yet. And we saw a bloke begging as we walked through town – aren't you coppers supposed to have clamped down on that too?' She held a breadstick between her thumb and forefinger, waving it around as she spoke, jabbing it in Catherine's direction as she made her point. Catherine pushed back her chair.

'I'm going to nip to the loo,' she said.

Ellie glanced at her with a tiny frown, but stayed silent.

–

As Catherine locked the door, there was a clatter and Melody's voice rang out: 'It's only me!'

Catherine closed her eyes as Melody thumped into the next cubicle.

'What are you doing about these beggars? Can't do some shopping without someone asking you for money,' she bellowed. Silence. 'Catherine? Are you listening?'

She shook her head in despair, hoping the noise of the flush would put Melody off. Fat chance. At the sinks, Melody cornered her, hands on hips.

'You're a police officer, aren't you? Can't you have a word with one of your bosses? It's getting beyond a joke.'

'I don't work in the city.' Catherine turned away, hoping Melody's mouth couldn't compete with the sound of the hand dryer.

–

Later, the streets were busy, thronged with people. Catherine relaxed – the sights and sounds of people out for a good time were intoxicating. The night air seemed warmer as delicious smells from the restaurants they passed drifted along with them. Bursts of laughter and snatches of music spilt from the pubs and bars. To Catherine, now more used to nights alone at home with a cup of tea and a book when she wasn't working, the familiar streets felt exotic tonight, as if she were on holiday. She smiled to herself. Her brother would laugh if she told him, call her a hermit, say it was the shock of her leaving the house.

At the top of Steep Hill, the group parted with hugs and promises to meet soon. Catherine fervently hoped never to see Melody again as she and Ellie turned away and the other two stumbled off in search of a taxi.

'I didn't know how obnoxious Melody was after a few drinks,' Ellie said.

The hill stretched away in front of them, sloping towards the modern town.

Catherine laughed. 'She wasn't as bad last time we all went out. Is she charm itself at work?'

'Well, she's loud, but… Is your phone ringing?'

Catherine opened her bag and checked the screen. 'DI Knight.'

'Your boss?'

Shrugging, Catherine answered the call. 'Jonathan?'

Knight's voice was barely audible. 'Catherine, I'm on my way to London. Caitlin's gone into labour. I'll let you know what…' There were three loud beeps and his voice disappeared.

'Is he all right?' Ellie sidestepped a flushed man and woman as they toiled towards them, cursing the hill as they went.

'Caitlin's in labour at last. He's on the train already.'

'Why would he go now, before the baby's even born?'

'I've no idea. If I were him I'd stay away, but who knows how his mind works.' Catherine frowned as she remembered. Knight was a mystery, especially to her.

At the bottom of Steep Hill was The Strait, a sweep of cobbles narrowing to a tiny street with a flagged pavement on either side, lined with shops and a few houses. Catherine paused for a moment and lifted her hand to hold Ellie's arm, silently asking her to wait. They turned. Towering behind the other buildings, the cathedral was still visible, bathed in golden light and seeming to shimmer against the night sky. The cobbles around them were illuminated by old-fashioned street lights, the whole scene reminiscent of a film set. It didn't seem real. For a second they were alone in a tiny pocket of silence, Catherine's hand still on Ellie's arm as they gazed at the picture-perfect scene. Ellie shifted a little, murmuring, 'Catherine?'

As Catherine turned, a group of men rounded the corner from Steep Hill, jostling and singing, arms around each other's shoulders. One man dragged a plastic ball and chain from his ankle and had an enormous pair of inflatable antlers perched on his head. Catherine smiled.

'Shame I haven't brought my handcuffs.'

Ellie laughed, and the moment was gone.

–

It had been hot in the restaurant, warm on the street, but now a cold wind followed them as they made their way to the hotel. Winter wasn't yet ready to give way to spring. Ellie linked her arm through Catherine's as they walked, huddling closer.

'It's been a lovely evening.'

Catherine wrinkled her nose. 'The thirty seconds Melody was quiet for, you mean?'

Ellie laughed. 'She must have swallowed her food without chewing it.'

'If we go out with her again, let's order her a well-done steak. Might keep her busy for a while.'

The hotel was quiet, the bar still open, though there were only a few people dotted around the seating area. They climbed the stairs to the first floor, where Catherine's room was. It had seemed extravagant to book into the hotel when she lived less than twenty miles away, but now she was pleased Ellie had suggested it. An anonymous room suited her mood tonight.

When they found her door, Catherine stopped, fumbling to swipe the key card, conscious of Ellie standing close beside her. As the light on the lock flashed green, Catherine glanced at her friend and Ellie smiled, her eyes bright. She held Catherine's gaze, stroked her hand, still resting on the door handle. Catherine swallowed, panic rising in her belly as Ellie stepped closer, her intention clear. Closing her eyes, Catherine willed herself to relax as Ellie's lips met her own. Hadn't this been inevitable? Hadn't she been anticipating it earlier while she carefully straightened her hair, applied her make-up? She tangled her fingers in Ellie's thick, dark-blonde hair, pushing her doubts away. Ellie was perfect – kind, funny and gorgeous.

And Catherine felt nothing.

Furious with herself, she broke the kiss and fumbled again for the door handle. Half-turning back, she was stung by the confusion evident on her friend's face. 'Ellie, I... I'm sorry. Good night.'

She fled inside, closing the door before she could see Ellie's reaction, flicked on the lights and stumbled into the bathroom.

How long could this continue?

Chapter 2

'All right, Mackie?'

He nodded, lifting the bottle to his lips, swallowing enough to dull the cold in one gulp. He didn't bother to see who had spoken to him. They all knew him, but were also aware he liked to be left alone. Tucking his chin into his scarf, Mackie hunched his shoulders. He hated sleeping here. Too many people knew about it. He'd told some of them – those he liked, trusted – about it himself. But it was a cold night, and there had been drizzle earlier in the day. He knew from experience once you were cold and wet, you would stay that way for hours, even days. There was the homeless shelter, but he couldn't go back there now. Taking another mouthful of vodka, he tipped his head back against the wall behind him. The bricks were cold, as was the bench beneath his backside. The vodka burned his throat, and he drank greedily, savouring the warmth as it reached his gut. He huddled deeper into the sleeping bag, drawing his feet onto the bench, twisting to lie on his side. A cold wind whipped across the open front of the pavilion. It wasn't the ideal place to spend the night, resembling a large bus shelter, with a concrete floor which leeched the warmth from your bones. Still, it was better than being out in the open, in a doorway. Mackie had built himself a shelter using a couple of broken pallets and some plastic sheeting, had spent a few nights there, but it was a risk to stay in one place for too long. Eventually, you were found. Do-gooders trying to nurse you back into society, coppers or maybe people fancying knocking a homeless person around before staggering off to hail a taxi.

Last night, it had been drunks. Not young lads either – older men in their thirties or forties, pissed on cheap lager and wanting to prove they weren't past it. Beating up a tramp, four against one, had obviously seemed like the perfect way to do so. Egging each other on, laughing and boasting, kicking the shit out of someone who could barely stand even before they touched him.

Running his hand across his chin, Mackie winced as he explored the bruising along his jaw. He didn't have many teeth left, but Christ, the bastards had dislodged some of those that remained. Lifting his head, he threw more vodka down his throat. He had managed, eventually, to beg for enough cash to buy something to take the edge off the pain. You had to avoid the police, be on your guard constantly. He couldn't blame them. People didn't want to see the homeless, didn't want to know. Anything that was a reminder of how fragile day-to-day existence could be was a threat. Mackie knew how it went. He had been on both sides of the argument.

His body ached with fatigue, but the pain of the cuts and bruises, each flaming and burning every time he moved, would allow him no rest. His eyes were open, watching cars flit by on the nearby road, headlights cutting through the chill air. What would the people driving them think of him settling here for the night, if they saw him at all? Most homeless folk were invisible, Mackie had realised. It was amazing how many people could simply see straight through them, continuing their day as they passed, turning their heads and focussing on anything but the person huddled on the ground. It had angered Mackie at first, shocked him, though he knew he had been no better. When he'd had a job, a family, a home, a life. Respectability. A purpose, a point. Those were all long gone. His existence now was a drag towards death. No need to dress it up; no wish for sympathy. He would do nothing to hasten his own end, but he wouldn't fight it either. His decisions, choices he had made, his own actions had left him here, alone and afraid. Homeless, drinking and trying to sleep on a bench – what a cliché. In his former life, he would have disgusted himself. Now, it was different. Once you were used to the discomfort, the smell of your own unwashed body, the loss of respect and status, the boredom, the absence of hope, there was nothing left to fear. He could sink no further.

He was punishing himself, and he deserved to.

There were four other benches in the pavilion, and glancing around, he saw all were occupied. The low hum of voices, an occasional burst of laughter. The smell of dope and dog. Sweat. Despair.

Cradling his bottle, he slowly, painfully, got to his feet. He couldn't stay here. There would be no sleep, not yet. He would walk, haunting the streets as he had years before, when he was on the beat.

–

You could still hear the screams. The castle had been a powerhouse, a place of imprisonment, of punishment. The crown court, still in use, stood in the grounds. Mackie

14

stood on the cobbles of Castle Hill, the cathedral looming behind him. He loved the city of Lincoln, the place of his birth. There were a few people around, but not many. Mackie held his vodka bottle close, his rucksack digging into the bones of his shoulders. Carrying your life on your back was hard work. For reassurance, he patted his trouser pocket, where his ancient leather wallet, cracked and faded now, but still serviceable, was held safe.

Soon, it would be filled with banknotes. He would leave the city he loved to make a new life elsewhere.

It was a glint of hope, a glimmer. He turned towards the cathedral, glowing against the night sky. As he approached it, there was a sense of awe. He wasn't religious, not at all, but there was wonder, all the same. The scale of the building, the detail, the love. The splendour, the celebration, while people begged, starved, lived and died on the streets below, as they always had. History could appear to erect barriers between the present and the people of the past, but Mackie knew none truly existed. People didn't change. Human nature, every thieving, greedy ounce of it, echoed down the ages.

Checking his battered watch, Mackie drank the last of his vodka and turned away.

It was time.

Chapter 3

Sunday morning, close to midday. The jangling of her mobile phone shook Mary Dolan out of a restless doze. She turned her head on the pillow, her tongue as dry as one of the horrible brown crackers she'd forced down her throat earlier in deference to the diet she'd started yet again. Her hand knocked a half-pint glass of water from the bedside cabinet to the carpet beneath, and she cursed.

'Where's the bloody phone?' She was talking to herself, but there was a muffled grunt from the other side of the bed, and she froze. Who the hell had she brought home? She ought to know, given it was such a rare occurrence. This was why she seldom drank alcohol these days.

The phone was still ringing, and she ran her hand around again on the floor by the bed. There. She squinted at the display: Collette. Her head ached, her stomach protesting as she struggled to sit upright.

'Coll?' Dolan's voice was more a growl. She moved the phone away from her mouth and cleared her throat, working her jaw to introduce a little moisture into her mouth. Pity the glass of water was now decorating the carpet. She could hear her friend breathing, but she hadn't spoken yet. 'Collette?'

'Mary.' It was a sob.

Dolan stifled a groan. 'Don't tell me. Not again?'

Collette sniffled. 'It's my own fault, I...'

'Provoke him,' Dolan interrupted, rolling her eyes. 'Yes, Collette, you do. It's not his fault at all, it's yours.'

'Mary...'

'Come on, Collette, when will you see it? I can't help you until you help yourself. Pete's a bullying shitbag, and he won't ever change.'

'He loves me.'

'He's got a funny way of showing it.'

'I annoy him...'

'You annoy me, but I don't punch you in the gob, do I?' Dolan had had this conversation more times than she could count.

There was another sniff, followed by a strangled laugh. 'It wasn't my gob, as you put it. It was my stomach.'

'Oh well, okay. Lucky he didn't damage your precious dentures. Wait a minute, Pete's the reason you had to get false front teeth.'

'I don't know why I bother ringing you. I get more sympathy from the gerbils.'

Dolan shook her head. 'Come on, Collette. I want to help, but you won't let me.'

Another silence. 'Mary, please don't arrest him.'

There was more movement in the bed as a hand searched for Dolan's thigh, found it and gave an affectionate squeeze. She blinked as realisation dawned.

'Mary? Are you still there?' Collette's voice was plaintive.

Dolan gave the hand an experimental slap. It squeezed again. 'Yes, though I don't know why.'

'You won't arrest Pete, will you?' Collette bleated.

Dolan settled back against the headboard. 'I haven't decided yet.' Collette made a sound reminiscent of a cat being trapped in a door. Dolan shook her head, patience exhausted. Talking to Collette always had the same effect; her friend's passivity and excuses infuriated Dolan, though she had seen similar situations more times than she cared to remember. 'I'm not going to barge into your house and handcuff him, Collette, as you know. You could find some balls and dob him in, though.' The hand tried to explore further, and Mary shifted, grabbing it and halting the movement.

'Collette, I'm going to have to go, I need the loo. Is Pete still asleep?'

'Yeah.'

'Right, well, I didn't tell you this, but you need to go out to the shed, grab a shovel, take it into the bedroom and—'

Collette hung up. Mary turned to the other occupant of the bed. 'Right, show yourself.'

Laughter. He pushed back the duvet, hair tousled, his face flushed red.

'Charming.' He grinned.

Mary shook her head at him, dismayed. 'What are you still doing here?'

—

Catherine Bishop drove from Lincoln to Northolme, the market town where she had lived and been based since she joined Lincolnshire Police. She turned into her drive, frowning as she saw Anna Varcoe's car parked at the side of the road. Rummaging in her bag, she took out her phone.

'Thomas, I'm home.'

'Yeah, your car appearing in the drive was a bit of a giveaway.'

She could tell her brother was smiling. 'Wanted to warn you.'

'Give us chance to make ourselves decent, you mean?' Thomas laughed. 'Don't worry, we're fully dressed, ankles covered and everything.'

'You're hilarious.'

They were in the kitchen, sitting at the table eating scrambled eggs on toast.

Anna offered a warm smile as Catherine dropped her keys onto the worktop. 'Morning, Sarge... Catherine. I hope you don't mind me staying?'

Thomas squirted more tomato sauce onto his plate. 'She's said she doesn't. Have you eaten, Catherine?'

She filled the kettle, took three mugs out of the cupboard. 'Yes, thanks. Ellie and I had breakfast before we left the hotel.' Catherine didn't want to think about it. No reference had been made to the kiss. It had been a stilted conversation under a fog of awkwardness. She indicated their plates, trying to lighten her tone. 'Your scrambled eggs look better, though.'

'How was your night?' Thomas raised his eyebrows as his sister turned to look at him, oblivious to her mood. 'How's Ellie?'

'She's okay.'

'And?' Thomas drawled.

Catherine folded her arms. 'Ellie's colleagues were a nightmare, except Faye, but the food was good. You should try it; new Italian restaurant on Steep Hill.'

'Nothing happened?' Thomas was aghast.

Catherine turned to the fridge before they could see her face. 'What were you expecting?'

'You and Ellie spent the night in the same hotel, and there's no gossip?'

'We're friends, Thomas. Sorry to disappoint you.' Catherine set their teas on the table with a thump, remembering the moment at the bottom of Steep Hill. The kiss. Her reaction, and Ellie's expression. The guilt she had experienced after she closed her hotel room door firmly in her friend's face.

Anna glanced at Thomas, obviously uncomfortable. 'We're going out soon, for a carvery.'

'But we're still eating our breakfast,' Thomas protested. Anna frowned at him, and he lowered his head to his plate again.

'You don't have to leave because I'm home. I'm going to have a bath,' Catherine said, irritated.

Lying back in the bubbles, she sighed as she heard the front door close behind them, annoyed with herself again. When Thomas had asked if he could move in for a few months while he found a job, she had been pleased to agree. Now he had Anna, and four months into their relationship, they were happy. Catherine was pleased for them, but a tiny part of her, a small voice she tried to ignore, couldn't help being a little resentful too. Admitting it wasn't easy.

Dressed again, she went back into the kitchen and found her phone. No missed calls, no texts. She scrolled through her list of contacts. How long it had been since she had spoken to some of them? Months, if not years. She could blame her job, but she knew the real reason she had lost touch with them all was her own apathy. Social media meant she kept up with new relationships, babies and bereavements, but there was no one she could phone for a chat. It was sobering, though there was one person who might answer.

–

Jonathan Knight set his elbows on the table, pressing his fingertips to his forehead. When he finally raised his head again, he had to blink a few times to bring the room into focus. He never slept well, but the late-evening rush to London and a night spent reading, browsing the Internet and staring at the ceiling in his hotel room had taken its toll. He struggled to his feet, his back aching, and went across to the counter to order another cup of coffee. As he waited for the barista to work his magic on the complicated-looking machinery, Knight heard his phone ringing. The name was a surprise. 'Catherine?'

'Hi.' Her voice was flat.

'Give me a second.' Knight smiled his thanks as the man passed over his drink. Back at the table, he took a sip before lifting the phone to his ear again. 'Okay, I'm here.'

'Are you still in London? Is there any news?'

'Not yet. Caitlin said she'd phone me. To be honest, it was a mistake to have rushed here last night; cost me a fortune in taxi and train fares. I don't even know which hospital she's in.'

There was a pause as Catherine digested this. 'Bit daft.'

He laughed. 'Jo told me the same thing.'

'How is Jo?'

'Fine. Busy. Catherine, are you all right?'

She ignored him, asking, 'Are you coming back today?'

'I'm waiting for the train now. Trying to wake myself with a few cups of coffee.'

'What time do you arrive at Retford? I'll meet you if you like.'

Knight smiled at her tone – casual, offhand. The station was about twelve miles from Catherine's house in Northolme, the nearest place to catch a direct express to London. It was unlikely she would be passing. 'Thanks, Catherine.'

—

Sleeping with her ex was always a bad idea; a terrible, potentially disastrous idea. Having turfed him out of her bed and her house, Mary Dolan had boiled the kettle, made some toast and given herself a stern talking-to. All right, it had only happened once recently. Twice now. *Shit.* She didn't know why; she'd tried to forget him years ago, but she struggled to sever him from her life. She would never be able to completely because of their daughter, but she needed to keep him further away than this. She blamed the wine. She never usually drank the stuff, apparently with good reason. It couldn't happen again. She'd be courteous if she saw him, but no more. No flirting, no giggling. He'd visited because Mary wanted to discuss how much he was going to contribute to the cost of their daughter's education now she was at university, but the two bottles of wine he had brought had disappeared far too quickly. She had no idea if they'd even reached an agreement, no doubt just as he'd planned.

As the kettle boiled, her phone pinged. She poured water onto another tea bag, sloshing it around with a grubby spoon. She needed to wash up. *Should have made him do it.* He'd done little else, except steal her spare tooth-brush. There was the sex... She couldn't remember much about last night, but it had been good when they'd been together before. Not that she'd had anything to compare it to in those days...

Slopping milk into the mug, she sat again at the kitchen table and opened the text. It was from her daughter: *Mum, please can I have £50? Sorry. Love you x*

Cheeky madam. Mary already paid an allowance into her account each month. She sipped her tea, knowing she'd send the money. After twenty years in the police force, she'd seen every mishap, accident and cruelty a body could endure, and she had no intention of her daughter becoming a victim of any of them. Walking home when you didn't have the money for a cab, sitting alone in a carriage on the last train...

She typed back: *I'll see what I can do. How are you? X* An instant reply: *Hungover. U?* Mary rolled her eyes. Big surprise. Her thumb tapped out: *Same.* She laughed as she read the response, hearing her daughter's voice in her head as clearly as if she'd been sitting at the table with her: *Disgraceful! XX*

Mary swallowed the last mouthful of tea as she logged in to her bank account on her phone and transferred the money. Even though they had separated when she was tiny, their daughter still harboured a dream of her parents getting back together. *Not going to happen.* She set the cup in the sink, half-heartedly squirting some washing-up liquid over the pile of pots languishing there, and turned to go back upstairs. A long hot bath was required.

Catherine was waiting on the platform, her long, dark hair made untidy by a gust of the wind that flew at Knight as he opened the train door. She'd lost weight since he had first come to work in Lincolnshire, and it had changed her face slightly, the cheekbones more pronounced, the shadows beneath her eyes deeper. Catherine looked exhausted, and a pang of guilt hit Knight. He had been worried about her a few months previously, voiced his concerns to their superior officer, but in the end had given in to Catherine's constant assurances she was okay. Perhaps he should have insisted she saw someone – a doctor, or a counsellor.

Perhaps he shouldn't have added to her burdens.

Knight lifted his hand in greeting as he stepped onto the platform. She hadn't seen him yet, her eyes searching the few people leaving the train. A faint smile appeared as she eventually spotted him.

'You look terrible,' she greeted him.

'Thanks a lot.' He knew better than to say she did too, or to ask how she was doing. It was better to let her talk, because he knew she would if she needed to. Theirs was a strange relationship – bonds built on the trust established soon after Knight had arrived in Northolme, when Catherine had stayed in his spare room for a few nights during an investigation. She had confided in him; more, he suspected, than she would have usually done, because of what had happened. Catherine's lover had been exposed as a killer and Catherine herself was left reeling in a maelstrom of guilt, confusion, betrayal and grief. As they climbed into the car, Knight glanced at her, noting a small tic pulsing beneath her left eye. Catherine turned her head to check over her shoulder before reversing out of the parking space and caught him watching her.

'What?' She accelerated away from the station, towards the town centre. Knight didn't know Retford at all, but Catherine had gone to school here.

'I only had a cereal bar for breakfast. How about some food?'

She glanced at the clock on the dashboard. 'We can try.'

Pulling his phone from his trouser pocket, Knight sent his girlfriend Jo a quick text. Much as he wanted to see her, he knew she would agree he should try to talk to Catherine.

They found a pub still serving meals on a side street and Catherine parked at the roadside. A smiling young waiter greeted them and led them over to a table towards the back of the room. When they had ordered, Catherine sat back in her chair, regarding Knight steadily.

'What did you hope would happen when you went to London?'

Knight blushed. 'Honestly? I've no idea. I wanted to be nearby.'

'You rushed there from Lincolnshire to see a woman who cheated on you, told you she was pregnant, but she had no idea if the baby was yours or her new boyfriend's?'

'Yeah, okay. I'm an idiot.'

'Did Caitlin even know you were there?'

'No. I'm not going to tell her, either. I suppose I was hoping...' He paused, sipping from his glass of lager. Catherine waited. Eventually, he mumbled, 'I hoped once the baby was born, I might be able to visit.'

'And see if it looked like you?'

'I don't know. Maybe. I thought I might be able to tell. I'd know if it was my son or daughter. I mean, if Caitlin even allowed me in.'

'What about the new boyfriend – what's his name again?'

'Jed.'

'Is he going to do the paternity test?'

'Caitlin will decide because she'll have to give permission for the sample to be taken from the baby.' His phone rang, and he hurriedly checked the screen. 'It's her.' He frowned. Catherine gently touched his hand. 'Answer it. It'll be fine.'

Knight lifted the handset to his ear. 'Caitlin?' He waited, listening. 'And how are you?' There was another pause. 'Okay, thanks for calling. I'll speak to you soon. Take care of yourselves.' He put the phone back in his pocket as the waiter arrived with their roast dinners.

Catherine waited until he had gone before asking, 'Well?'

'A girl. They're both fine; they're going home soon.' Knight smiled, blinking rapidly. He had been waiting for this moment for months, and now it was here, he didn't know how to react. There was relief now he knew both Caitlin and the child were well. Stronger though was the strange, confused longing. He had to know whether the baby, the little girl, was his child or not. Would he be part of her life, or would he have to forget she existed? He gazed at his plate, conscious of his eyes filling with tears, prompted by emotions he couldn't explain.

'Does she have a name?' Catherine's voice was gentle.

'Not yet.'

'I notice Caitlin didn't ask for your ideas on what to call her.' Less gentle now.

Knight pressed his lips together, took a second to steady himself. 'No, but she wouldn't. She'll decide. Was there something you wanted to talk about?'

'No, why?'

'You don't usually phone me on Sundays.'

He waited, but Catherine quickly shoved some roast beef into her mouth and chewed it. Knight watched her for a second, recognising her expression. Catherine had pulled down the shutters, closed herself off. He focused on his meal. It was hopeless to try to reach her now.

Chapter 4

The best night ever; the best he'd had since moving to Lincoln, anyway. Evan stifled a beery burp and kept walking. His mates had already gone on to the club, but Evan had wanted to get a bag of chips, soak up some of the beer before things got messy. He'd told them he'd meet them in there and staggered off alone. In his mind, hazy and confused though it was, there was a shortcut, an alley he could cut through. He shoved his hands in his trouser pockets, concentrating on putting one foot in front of the other. These cobbles were a bastard to walk on when you were pissed. He remembered his mum and dad cooing over them when they'd brought him to visit the uni, as if they'd never seen old buildings and streets before. Evan sniffed, pulling his hand free and wiping it across his nose. Plenty of cobbles in London too.

Here. The alley was narrow, littered with bin bags, pizza boxes and lumps of wood. He staggered forward, paused and unzipped his jeans. Might as well make the most of the facilities.

When he'd finished, he tidied his clothes and stumbled on, trying to remember the way to the club. Rubbing a hand across his eyes, he caught sight of a huddled form lying on the ground at the other end of the alley. What was it? Someone in a worse state than he was. Could it be a dog? It wasn't moving, at any rate. He inched forward, his mouth opening as his foggy brain caught up with what his eyes were seeing.

The body of a man, his blank eyes gazing at the stars.

Evan screamed.

Chapter 5

A sound, a horrible sound, as welcome as nails on a chalk-board. Catherine Bishop's eyes were already open, and she fumbled on the bedside table for her mobile phone, which was the source of the cacophony. She succeeded only in knocking the device to the carpet, where it lay, still shrieking. Moving slowly, she shuffled to the edge of the mattress, the balance gauge in her head tipping and telling her she was going too far. Eventually, it all seemed too complicated and she followed the phone to the floor, settling beside it. The phone was silent at last. Catherine lay there naked, her brain telling her she was cold but in a matter-of-fact fashion which indicated her personal comfort was of no consequence at all.

After a time, seemingly forever, but no more than a few minutes, she dragged her hand across the carpet to the phone. It seemed huge in her grasp, as though she had shrunk overnight, or it had grown larger. The screen was dark, forbidding. Catherine touched it gingerly with her forefinger, and it glared into life, the brash colours and confident text dazzling her. She checked the time: 7.23 a.m. She needed to move. If given the choice, which she supposed she had been, because if she didn't go to work ever again, if she lay here until she died and all her insides seeped across the carpet, through the floorboards and into the kitchen beneath, who could do a thing about it? There were people with a key to her house, it was true: her parents, Thomas, or someone in uniform could always batter the door open. Getting out of bed was a choice, a real choice, and you could either participate or you could decline the invitation and stay put. Catherine had never considered this before, and it was a comfort, a tiny glimpse of cheer. It gave her the inspiration at least to drag herself into a sitting position, her head hanging. Another image crept into her mind: her colleagues sitting in the briefing room, noticing her absence, shaking their heads, muttering to each other. She struggled to her feet, picked clean underwear from a drawer, a suit and shirt from the wardrobe and went, as if sleepwalking, through to the bathroom. She showered half-heartedly, rubbing shampoo through her hair, drying it roughly with a towel when she stumbled out of the cubicle, pulling it hard, trying to provoke a reaction in herself.

There was none.

Back in her silent bedroom, the day sat taunting her. She ignored it, wouldn't look at the sunlight streaming in where the blackout blind didn't fit, couldn't consider this day might be the one where her emotions resurfaced. It was to be fought through, endured.

She went downstairs, her limbs heavy, her head filled with grey fog and limp, wet cotton wool. Taking a glass from the cupboard, she filled it from the cold tap and drank, some of the water running over her chin and onto the front of her white shirt. She hardly noticed. She went out to the car, ignoring the tiniest voice in her head asking whether she should be driving, much less going into work.

The briefing room was stifling and smelly: stale Rich Tea biscuits, scorched coffee, the mingled, cloying sickliness of various aftershaves and perfumes. Twenty officers wedged into a space scarcely big enough for fifteen. The temperature was high, the urge to escape higher. Catherine sat at the end of the back row, nearest the door. The carpet tiles were a sea of dark blue, lurching and rippling in places. She shifted in her chair, clenching her hands into fists, biting the inside of her mouth as the snakes beneath her skin writhed and coiled. Beneath her left eye, the tic jumped and jolted. She sat straight, fighting the urge to run. Her hands shook as she attempted to focus on the massive figure of Detective Chief Inspector Keith Kendrick, currently pantomiming his way through the morning briefing. Two more minutes. Escape.

At her desk, she blinked at her computer screen, the monitor whirring and grumbling. Opening her emails, she willed her brain to focus, but the words swam and danced. The office wasn't overly noisy today, but to her it was as loud as if an orchestra sat in the corner, playing with extra gusto. DC Anna Varcoe paused on her way past Catherine's desk.

'Cup of tea, Sarge?'

Catherine raised her head. 'Sorry?'

Anna's smile dimmed a little. 'Would you like a drink?'

'Oh yes... Yes, please. Thank you.'

On the verge of saying something else, Anna hesitated, but eventually hurried away. Catherine stared at the spot on the carpet where the constable had stood, her skin lurching forward and back. After a few seconds, she caught sight of her own hands, resting on the scarred desktop, the veins more prominent now than they had been even a few weeks ago, blue and delicate. A network, carrying her blood, keeping her alive. She clenched her fist, watched them flatten and almost disappear. Opening her hand out flat again with her palm facing the ceiling, Catherine inspected her wrist. More veins. She had seen her fair share of suicides, but one swam through the mire and into her consciousness: an elderly man who had slit his wrists in his bathtub three weeks after the death of his wife. He'd done it properly too; downwards, not across. Why in the bath, Catherine wasn't sure, though she believed it often happened. Did the water help the blood to flow? Did it hurt less? It had never been explained to her, for all her contact with the dead and the suffering. Blood could travel a long way, she knew for certain; splatter on walls, spurt across ceilings, stick to surfaces and people however hard they tried to scrub it away. It could stain their skin and their lives for years.

'Here you go.' Anna set a steaming mug of tea on Catherine's desk.

'Thank you.'

As her brother's girlfriend headed for her own desk, Catherine's desk phone rang and she stared at it for a second before answering.

A female voice. 'DS Bishop?'

'Yes,' Catherine was forced to admit.

'This is Mary Dolan. Has DCI Kendrick spoken to you yet?'

She didn't know anyone called Dolan. Catherine glanced over at Kendrick's office. He was framed in the doorway, filling it, gesturing wildly. She cleared her throat.

33

'Looks as though he's about to.'

'Good. I'll talk to you soon.'

Confused, Catherine replaced the receiver and went over to Kendrick.

'Have your ears been burning?' He ushered her into his office and thudded the door closed.

'My ears?'

'You're wanted at Headquarters.'

Catherine's mouth was dry. The force's headquarters were situated a few miles north-east of the city of Lincoln itself. Why would she be summoned there? If the Superintendent wanted to speak to any of the officers based at the Northolme station, she usually drove over and surprised them, much to their delight.

'Why do they want me?'

Kendrick shuffled in his chair. 'I'm only the messenger. She wanted to know if we can spare you for a few days.'

Catherine was frowning. 'Who does? For what?'

'DCI Dolan asked if she could tell you herself.'

'I've never heard of her.'

'You won't have. She's from Nottinghamshire.'

'But...'

Kendrick made a shooing gesture with his huge hands.

'Go on. It'll be good for you.'

She stood, annoyed, almost missing the muttered words as she closed his door behind her.

'Take care of yourself, Catherine.'

—

'DS Bishop?'

DCI Dolan held out her hand with a smile. If they had met outside of work, in a bar or through friends,

34

Catherine would have found her attractive. Coppery hair, shoulder-length, with a thick fringe. Green eyes. She was a little older than Catherine, but it was difficult to guess her exact age. Fortyish? She wore a pair of dark trousers and a plain grey sweater. No rings. Black boots with heels added a couple of inches to her height. Catherine knew the tic beneath her eye was leaping again.

'Good morning, ma'am.' At least her voice was steady.

'Pleased to meet you. It's this way.' Dolan gestured with her thumb. 'And call me Mary.'

The room was small, cold, painted ice-blue which didn't make it any cosier. A square table dominated it while three black plastic chairs were stacked by the door.

Dolan lifted two from the pile with a grimace. 'Good of them to make us welcome.'

Catherine accepted a chair with what she hoped was a smile. Her face was frozen.

Mary Dolan didn't seem to notice as she settled into her own seat and threaded her fingers together, her elbows on the tabletop. 'You must be wondering what all this is about?' Dolan asked. 'There's been some confusion, I'm afraid.'

Catherine raised an eyebrow. 'Confusion in the force headquarters?'

It was a test, and Dolan knew it. She smiled. 'Hard to believe, I know.'

Relaxing a little, Catherine said, 'My DCI said I'd be needed for a few days?'

'At least. Have you heard about the body found recently?'

'An overdose, wasn't it?'

Dolan was nodding. 'Yeah, but there's more to it.'

'How do you mean?'

'A syringe was found. It was trampled by the young man who discovered the body, but we could piece it back together. No fingerprints on it.'

'None?'

'Not one. Which raises questions.' It did. The dead man's fingerprints should have been all over the syringe. 'People who knew him also say he hadn't used heroin for years. We're waiting for the post-mortem for confirmation.'

'You mean someone else injected him with the drug?'

'Yeah. It could have been a friend, someone who panicked and ran when they discovered he wasn't going to wake up. But people on the street usually look out for each other. By all accounts, the... Oh, sod it – the victim – was a loner, never had any company, didn't seem to want any.' Dolan blinked a few times. 'We're treating his death as murder at this stage.'

Whatever Catherine had expected, it hadn't been this. A murder in Lincoln was as rare as one in Northolme – virtually unheard of. 'It's a risky way to kill someone. No guarantee of it working.'

'No, it's not certain, but if the purity's high enough though, and the person you're injecting has no tolerance, it's a fairly safe bet.' Dolan sighed. 'We know who he was, but we're in the dark about everything else. That's where we're hoping you come in.'

'How do you mean?'

Dolan sat back, maintaining eye contact. 'Have you ever considered undercover work?'

Catherine stared. 'I've never had the opportunity.'

'I know. I've seen your file.'

'Oh.' Now she was blushing.

Dolan smiled. 'Your DCI had a lot of positive things to say about you. I spoke to your DI too; both assured me you were the right person for the job.'

Clenching her hands beneath the tabletop, Catherine fought to control her right knee, which was bouncing, causing her whole leg to jerk. *'It'll be good for you,'* Kendrick had said. She cleared her throat.

'You're not from Lincolnshire?'

Dolan shook her head. 'I'm in Major Crimes – EMSOU. You know how we're one big happy family these days.'

The Major Crimes branch of the East Midlands Special Operations Unit worked across Nottinghamshire, Derbyshire, Leicestershire, Lincolnshire and Northamptonshire, and was drafted in to investigate homicides and other serious offences.

'I see.' Catherine didn't know what else to say.

'Have you heard of Phoenix House?' Dolan wanted to know.

'The homeless shelter?'

'Yes. The man whose body was discovered over the weekend had spent a few nights there, and we need to do some digging.'

'Okay…'

'We're going to go through the statements we already have so you have some background knowledge. Our victim was last seen alive around nine o'clock on Saturday evening. The post-mortem isn't being done until this afternoon. I'd like you to spend some time at the shelter. Chat to people, befriend them if possible, see what they can tell you.'

'As a support worker, or a volunteer? Or...' Catherine already knew the answer.

'I'd like you to pose as a homeless person,' Dolan confirmed. Catherine squirmed, and Dolan interpreted the movement correctly. 'I know. Fooling individuals who are already vulnerable isn't my idea of fun either. But if we're to discover the truth, possibly protect them... They've closed ranks. Uniformed officers have been asking questions at the shelter, but have got nowhere. No great surprise, I suppose, but it doesn't help us.' Dolan pushed her fringe out of her eyes and checked her watch. 'Why don't we go and grab some coffee?'

As they left the room, Dolan asked, 'Have you spent much time here? I know you're based at Northolme.'

Catherine felt the familiar prickle of unease. How much did Dolan know about her? Her recent links to Headquarters were not a subject she wanted to revisit. Everyone who worked there thought her a total idiot. She knew for sure some of them did, anyway. Dolan glanced at her, and she replied, 'I've never worked here for any length of time. I've attended courses, the odd briefing...'

Dolan pushed through the door which led to the stairs and held it open for Catherine. 'We need to be discreet, not only as far as the public is concerned, but...' She glanced around. 'Do you have a partner?'

They were walking upstairs now, and it was difficult for Catherine to see Mary Dolan's face. 'No, I'm single,' she said. 'My brother's living with me at the moment, but I'll tell him I'll be away for a few days. The only thing is...' She hesitated again.

Dolan waited. As they stepped onto the landing, she touched Catherine's arm. 'I'm aware of your history. DCI

Kendrick told me.' She lifted her shoulders, shaking her head. 'You were blameless. We're going to be working together closely on this, and I wouldn't have asked you to come here if I wasn't confident you could do the job. I'm expecting my team to arrive later this afternoon, but you're going to be vital to the progress of the investigation.' She kept walking.

Catherine hurried after her. 'Thank you. Something else I should mention – my brother is seeing Anna Varcoe, who's one of our DCs back at Northolme.'

Dolan smiled, unsurprised. Perhaps Kendrick had told her more than Catherine had guessed.

'Yeah, fine. You can tell them you're staying in Lincoln for a few days – some sort of training maybe? We'll discuss it before you leave today.'

The tic was pulsing again. Catherine kept her gaze on the floor, hoping the other woman wouldn't see it. On first impressions, though, she doubted much slipped past Mary Dolan.

–

The man standing in front of him badly needed to wash his hair. Each time he moved his head, the stink of it wafted from him in stomach-churning waves. Lee swallowed, wanting to leave the queue but aware this was his only chance of a hot meal. Smelly Hair lifted a grubby hand and scratched at his greasy black curls. Lee pressed his lips together, his stomach heaving. The soup was tomato, he could see it being ladled into cups, but the only smell he was aware of drifted from the man standing in front of him. It wasn't easy to keep clean, as he'd soon discovered himself, but there were places you could go. This was one of them; they didn't offer washing facilities, but you could get some food and stash your bag safely for a while in a room off the church tacked on for some purpose which had been lost over the years. Unless they had always provided food for those in need here. Hadn't religious buildings been places of sanctuary throughout history? Except when they were being demolished and plundered. He rocked back on his heels, hands shoved in his jeans pockets.

Smelly Hair coughed, hacking and choking. Lee's tension climbed another notch, the desire to escape flashing through his mind. Standing here, begging again, this time for cheap supermarket soup, hoping for a slice of thin white bread to dunk into the cup. It was degrading. Still, no one else seemed to mind.

Smelly Hair was scratching again. The sound of the yellow, claw-like nails rasping against his scalp set Lee's teeth dancing. He imagined tiny flakes of skin floating from the man's head towards him, drifting into his nose, his mouth. Raising a hand, he covered the lower half of his face, trying not to gag. There were only two people in front of him in the queue now. *One more minute*, Lee promised himself.

The woman doling out the food was round and middle-aged. She stood behind a trestle table half-covered by a garish plastic cloth. Drops of soup marked the ladle's journey between the huge pan and the stack of polystyrene cups. He flashed his teeth at her as she held out his serving.

'Here you go, love.'

'Cheers.'

He concentrated on not spilling the soup as her gaze slid over him. There were a few more tables with wooden benches, the kind he remembered from primary school, providing the seating. He had counted twenty-two people sitting around the tables while he waited in the queue, mainly men. A couple of young women sat together, talking and laughing. He decided to avoid them for now and instead slid onto a bench opposite a surly-looking chap with a thick dark beard. As he lifted the cup to his lips, the other man shoved a plate with slices of limp bread languishing on it towards him.

'Not seen you here before,' the man said.

Great, a talker.

'New to town.' Lee mumbled it, hoping his companion would take the hint.

'What made you come to Lincoln?'

'There was a bus.'

The man laughed as he crushed his empty cup in his fist. 'Fair enough. Good luck, mate.'

Drinking another mouthful of soup, he took a piece of bread. He wasn't new to town, though it was true he'd been away a while. Still, it wouldn't hurt to cover his tracks, confuse matters. He had a job to do, after all.

–

Over at the serving table, the volunteer was still holding the soup ladle. She glanced up at the clock on the wall. There were two other women on duty today, standing chatting by the far wall. She set the ladle back in the pan with a clatter and went over to them.

'If I could interrupt you for a second – you wouldn't mind giving soup to anyone else who comes in, would you, ladies?' Her voice was calm, but she had made her point. One woman flushed while the other gave a resentful glance as she moved past them. She smiled to herself.

The vicar was in his office, tapping away on his laptop. As the door was open, she knocked and stepped inside. He turned, annoyance flashing across his face before he caught himself and smiled. Closing the computer, he looked at her.

'Can I help?'

'There's a new chap come in for soup. Maybe you could have a word?'

The vicar stood, his expression eager now. 'Of course.'

Waving a hand to indicate she should follow him out of the room, he locked the door when she was out of sight.

Couldn't be too careful with these people around.

--

Back in the small room on the ground floor, Catherine hugged her coffee cup close. Dolan was in the doorway, dragging a clanking metal easel behind her, and Catherine went to help. The room was still cold, Dolan's breath visible as she thanked Catherine. Above a scruffy white-board, Mary Dolan tacked a photograph to the wall, keeping her gaze fixed on it as she sat.

'Our victim.'

Both women were silent, absorbing the details of the image. A man's face: pale, though angry red and purple bruising discoloured his jaw. His eyes were open, a cloudy blue. Unseeing. A gaping mouth displayed a swollen tongue and bloody gap at the front where several teeth were missing. He lay on the ground, one arm thrown out to the side, the other draped over his stomach.

'Who was he?' Catherine asked. Did he look familiar? She wasn't sure. There was a tug of memory, but she couldn't place him.

Mary Dolan pursed her lips. 'John McKinley, better known as Mackie. He was a detective inspector once. He was one of us.'

Chapter 6

Ghislaine knew what he was going to say before he approached her. It happened a couple of times a week, usually in the evening, but some were more brazen than others. This one was with a gang of mates: men in their late teens and early twenties. It had bothered her more at first, but she had learnt to deal with them. She pressed her back into the rough pebbles which were set into the wall she was leaning against, and waited.

'All right, love?' He smirked. His hair was white-blonde, shaved at the sides with a ridiculous flicked fringe hovering above his eyebrows. He shoved his hands into the pockets of his jogging bottoms, pulling them even lower on his bony hips. Acne reddened his jawline, his mouth slightly open in anticipation. She said nothing. His face hardened, and he took a step forward, conscious of the mocking gazes of his friends.

'I'm talking to you, you ignorant bitch.'

She beamed at him. 'Malcolm! You're here at last!' She made her voice high-pitched, her gaze unsteady.

He glared, confused. 'Malcolm? What the fuck are you on about?'

'Have you brought the picnic?' She widened her eyes, still smiling. The other lads were laughing now, jeering. She tensed. What would he do?

Hesitating, he eyed her before spitting on the ground at her feet.

'Fuck this, lads, she's mental.'

He turned away, shaking his head in disgust, and joined his mates. One slapped him on the back, and they all moved off together.

She closed her eyes for a second, relieved. Sometimes they stood their ground, sometimes they screamed abuse. She'd been grabbed, hit and pissed on. Never, though, not once, had she allowed them to touch her skin, to violate her – pay her. She had promised herself she never would.

'Here.' A cardboard cup of coffee and a paper bag appeared beneath her nose. Jasmine squatted beside her, biting into a sausage roll. 'Shove up. Hey, what's wrong?'

Ghislaine took the bag and peered inside. 'Thanks, Jas.' She'd eaten half her own sausage roll before she mumbled, 'A bloke.'

Jasmine snorted, wiping her mouth with the back of her hand. 'Wanting to save you, lecture you or buy you? Or even all three?'

Ghislaine screwed the paper bag into a ball and pushed it into her coat pocket. 'Buy me.'

'He'd be lucky.'

'Yeah, 'cos I'm gorgeous,' Ghislaine scoffed. She rubbed her hands together, watching flakes of pastry drift towards the pavement.

Jasmine nudged her. 'I keep telling you, when we get our flat I'll do your hair, paint your nails… You'll be stunning. I'm qualified, remember.'

Ghislaine suppressed a sigh. She had only known Jasmine a few months, but she'd heard about her friend's beauty therapy diplomas more times than she could count.

She smiled, ignoring the tug of desolation in her stomach. Why shouldn't Jasmine be proud of past achievements, look forward to her future? It was a glimmer of hope. What was wrong with clinging to it?

–

'We don't know what he's been doing since leaving the force.' Dolan's eyes were still fixed on John McKinley's face.

There was a note in her voice which prompted Catherine to ask, 'Did you know him?'

Dolan sighed. 'I worked with him briefly once, a long time ago. I was still training, new and desperate to learn. He was kind, which is why I remembered him. Not everyone was.'

Dolan's involvement made more sense now Catherine knew McKinley had been a police officer.

Dolan's mobile phone beeped. 'Right, the rest of my team have arrived.'

Catherine nodded, questioning again whether she should be at work, much less embarking on an undercover investigation. Remembering the struggle she'd had earlier to motivate herself enough to even leave the house, she looked at Mary Dolan. Had the DCI not noticed her tapping foot, her trembling hands, her barely contained urge to flee the room? She doubted it.

Sure enough, Dolan met her eyes. 'Are you sure you want to do this?' Her voice was gentle. 'If not, tell me now, and I'll send someone else. I know it's not appealing – you'll be cold and uncomfortable for a few days…'

Catherine wanted to find the right words, but it was impossible. Her brain had fogged. 'I'm… I want to do it.'

'Good. We have a phone for you, and some cash. I'll be your primary contact, but my DS will be available if I'm not. You won't be able to access the shelter until tomorrow evening, but the soup kitchen will be open at lunchtime.' Dolan drummed her fingers on the tabletop, thinking aloud. 'I'd like you to go home shortly. Get the bus or train back to Lincoln tomorrow morning instead of driving, to make it look as if you're running away from something. It's a precaution, your cover story. Bring a few of changes of clothes in a bag and the money in your pocket. If anything concerns you, if you feel unsafe or threatened, we can have officers with you immediately. The presence on the streets has been increased anyway because of the robberies – you'll have heard about those?'

'A bloke stealing phones, wallets and purses, armed with a knife?'

'I'd be surprised if he tries it again now a body's been found, but you never know.'

There was a tap on the door. Dolan was out of her chair to open it and greet her team. Catherine stood too, as a man and woman entered the room. 'We'll need to scrounge another chair,' Dolan said. 'DS Bishop, meet DS Rafferty and DC Zaman. Isla and Adil, this is Catherine.'

Adil Zaman came forward first, holding out his hand with a smile. He was in his late twenties, a slim-fitting white shirt emphasising a lean, athletic build. His handshake was firm without being overbearing, and Catherine liked him immediately.

As Zaman went off to find a chair, DS Rafferty held out her hand. She was slender, her gleaming black hair pulled into an elegantly messy bun. Her eyes skimmed Catherine's face, but there was no smile.

'Pleased to meet you.' Nor was there any warmth in her tone – the words were perfunctory. They shook hands, Rafferty's cold fingers pressing against Catherine's for the briefest moment. Catherine saw the glint of an expensive-looking diamond engagement ring as Rafferty held out a battered mobile phone, a charger and a sealed brown envelope. 'These are for you.' She seemed to be addressing the wall behind Catherine's shoulder. 'DCI Dolan's number is stored under "Mary" and mine's under—'

'Isla?' Catherine took the phone, summoning a grin which Rafferty ignored.

'You also have Adil's number.' Turning to the nearest chair, Rafferty sat and rummaged through her leather shoulder bag.

Catherine lifted her chin. *What's your problem?*

Mary Dolan had been scrolling through the emails on her phone, but now she came closer to Catherine, apparently oblivious to the rudeness of her sergeant. She waved Catherine back into her chair.

'Thanks, Isla.'

Rafferty half-turned as her boss spoke, favouring Dolan with a quick quirk of her lips which could almost have been called a smile. Zaman returned with a fourth chair, which he pushed close to the table and settled into, taking his laptop from a case and and switching it on. Rafferty turned away again, but not before Catherine had glimpsed the sneer.

Dolan was speaking again. 'As I said, statements have been taken from people who were staying at Phoenix House, but they're fairly useless. Even the staff weren't particularly forthcoming. Of course, there could be

48

people out on the street who know something, but finding them is a different matter. That's where you come in, Catherine.'

'They won't trust me though,' Catherine pointed out. 'I'm a stranger.'

'But you won't be a police officer; you'll be one of them. Vulnerable, worried, scared. Wanting reassurance you won't end up dead like John McKinley. Concerned about what he was involved in, wanting to know how you can stay safe.' Dolan leant back, flashing Catherine a grin. 'There might be an Oscar in it for you.'

Isla Rafferty snorted, but quickly concealed it with a cough. Catherine's cheeks flushed as Dolan sent a frown in Rafferty's direction.

'Something to add, Isla?' the DCI asked.

'No, ma'am,' Rafferty replied.

Dolan smiled, catching Catherine's eye, causing her blush to deepen. 'We have statements from the manager of the shelter, the bloke who does counselling there, two night wardens and six of the clients, as they call the people who sleep there.' Dolan pulled her laptop towards her and opened the lid. Catherine took out her phone, ready to make some notes. Ordinarily, she would have used a tablet or notebook, but she wouldn't want to take either item to a homeless shelter. The phone would be more discreet. 'We can email you the statements too, so you'll have them for reference once you've met the residents and staff.' Dolan waved a hand. 'Come and sit around here, and we'll go through it all together.'

Catherine got to her feet, catching another glare from Rafferty. She lifted her chair, set it next to Dolan's. The DCI's perfume was subtle, but Catherine caught a note of it as Dolan shifted in her seat, leant forward and ran her finger along the data displayed on the laptop's screen. She steeled herself: a schoolgirl crush on her new boss was not going to be helpful.

Dolan bit her thumbnail as she read, her eyes fixed on the screen. Catherine swallowed. The emotions, the reactions that had been dormant during her encounter with Ellie, had sparked back into life at the most inoppportune moment. She ignored them. This assignment was going to need all her focus, all her concentration. Allowing herself to become distracted could be disastrous.

'The manager of the shelter is called Maggie Kemp,' Dolan said. 'She was keen to help, but she couldn't tell us much. According to her, John McKinley hardly slept at Phoenix House at all, except in the depths of winter.'

Catherine frowned. 'But you still want me to stay there?'

'It's a starting point,' Dolan told her. 'Most of the people there will have met John McKinley at some point. As I said, chat to them. Now, statements from the clients of Phoenix House. Four men, two women. The men were defensive, said as little as possible. Two of them are ex-army, one's been out of prison less than a month, one's more of a mystery. They all have alibis for the hours between nine p.m. on the night we believe McKinley was killed and eight thirty the next morning. The two night workers do too, I suppose. They sleep at the shelter. I'm not sure if anyone could have sneaked out at some point. They would have had to get back inside of course, unless someone let them in. It's not likely, but we should keep an open mind until you get there and find out about their procedures from the inside.'

'Okay…'

'Lee Collinson. Did two years for death by care-less driving. The ex-squaddies both admit to talking to McKinley previously, but not for a while. According to them, he was a decent bloke who would offer advice, but mostly wanted to be left alone.'

'And the fourth? The mystery man?'

'His name's Martin Cole. He's from Nottingham orig-inally, grew up in foster care and children's homes. Then he disappeared for fifteen years or thereabouts, before resurfacing here in Lincoln. We need to know where he was and what he was doing.'

'And the other two?'

'Young women. One, Jasmine Lloyd, has come to our attention a few times: loitering, possession of cannabis, a bit of drunken fighting. The other is called Ghislaine Oliver. No record. They also knew John McKinley, but not well.' Dolan exhaled, frustrated. 'No one knew him. No one saw him on the night he was killed. You may as well read the statements, Catherine. It won't take long.'

Rafferty cleared her throat. 'We should leave for the post-mortem soon, ma'am.'

'Don't call me ma'am.' Dolan's response was automatic.

'You're attending?' Catherine asked.

'Isla and I are.'

'It might be helpful for me to know the details of Mr McKinley's death before I talk to the people at the shelter though.'

Rafferty had put her phone away and was standing with her arms folded. She glanced at Dolan.

'I could phone DS Bishop in the morning and update her?' Isla Rafferty made it sound as though she'd sooner be having a root canal.

'Perfect. Go home and read the statements, Catherine. Prepare yourself. A few more points: we'll be monitoring your whereabouts through the mobile, for safety reasons. Ring us if you need to, or if you've something to report. If you're concerned, or worried, don't hesitate – phone one of us. The investigation will be run out of this room, and at least one of us will be available round the clock. I don't expect any issues or we wouldn't be asking you to do this, but we want to keep you safe. Have the phone with you at all times and keep it charged. I'm sure there'll be a facility at the shelter you can use.' Dolan glanced at her team. 'Is there anything I've forgotten?'

Zaman asked, 'Will Catherine be using her own name?'

'Yes, but they'll only use her first name when they speak to her anyway. It's standard practice in the shelter – surnames are only used in their records, they're not public knowledge. The clients prefer it, I'm told.'

Catherine collected her bag and pulled on her coat, sensing the eyes of Dolan's team on her back.

'Good luck, Catherine.' Zaman gave her another friendly smile.

'Call us anytime,' Rafferty said.

'And most importantly – stay safe. We'll be in touch.' Dolan took a step forward and rested her hand on Catherine's shoulder for a second. Catherine blinked, an emotion she couldn't explain rising in her throat as Dolan's touch sparked a current through her body. This wasn't a dangerous assignment; it was hardly an assignment at all. Their concern touched her though, penetrating the barrier she had constructed around herself.

At the door, she turned back. Zaman's eyes were already fixed on his computer, and Dolan was leaning over him, studying something he had indicated on the screen. Only Isla Rafferty noticed her still standing there. Catherine met her eyes, the other woman's animosity obvious, though Rafferty's face was blank, her gaze inscrutable. Catherine hurriedly opened the door, shaken. The prospect of having Isla Rafferty as one of her three guardian angels was not comforting.

Chapter 7

Lee wandered around the indoor market stalls, noticing little to pique his interest. Cheap jogging bottoms and sweatshirts, socks and underwear, fruit and veg. The stall he needed was by the door leading outside. The proprietor, an overweight man, his face damp with perspiration despite the chill March air, stood with a group of other stallholders, chatting and laughing. His wares were spread on the tables behind him: flimsy phone covers, chargers, SIM cards. He was also hawking a random collection of unrelated items: dog chews, designer knock-off boxer shorts and several cases of unattractive cuddly toys. A proper Del Boy.

Eventually, the stallholder broke away from his mates and sauntered over.

'Help you?'

'Having a look, thanks.'

'Take your time. It's all good stuff.'

Lee picked out a large packet of dog treats. Several of the people at the shelter had dogs. He'd love one himself but now was not the time.

'Two quid, mate. Cheers.'

He'd spent enough for a couple of hot drinks. Still, there was a point to his shopping trip.

'Do you sell mobile phones?' He hadn't meant to ask straight out. Stupid. Careless. His palms were suddenly damp, his mouth dry; he was half expecting a copper to appear and drag him away in handcuffs.

The other man narrowed his eyes. 'How do you mean?'

'Well, second-hand, or a cheap new one. I can't afford anything fancy.'

There was another pause. The stallholder's eyes had narrowed as he glanced around. 'I sometimes have a reconditioned phone or two. Not at the moment, though. Maybe you should call back another day?' He folded his meaty arms.

'Right. Right, I will.'

He almost fell over his own feet in his hurry to get away. It was progress though, a step forward. Another seed sown.

—

This was the part of the day Ghislaine hated most. More than the long, still hours of the night, with only unpleasant memories and empty longing for company. More than the queue at the soup kitchen, where she was served by smiling faces smugly doing their bit. This was the worst; wandering around town with two pounds in her pocket, aimlessly trying to fill the hours until the shelter opened, each second marking off again how pointless her existence was.

Jasmine nudged her. 'Hey. You've got that look again.'

Ghislaine wrapped her arms around her body with a shiver. 'What?'

'Fed up. Pissed off.'

Jasmine meant well, Ghislaine knew, and she tried not to snap. 'Not exactly having the time of our lives, are we?'

'Come on, Ghis.' Jasmine slid her arm around her friend. 'It's shit, I know it is, but it won't be for much longer. Our housing application's being processed. We'll have our own place by the summer.'

'You reckon?' Ghislaine knew a little of Jasmine's story; not much, but enough to concern her. Sharing a room when they were desperate was one thing, but a flat-share? Ghislaine had reservations. Still, if it got her off the streets…

'I know.' Jasmine pulled a scruffy mobile phone out of her jeans pocket and squinted at it. 'I need to go, got my appointment.'

Ghislaine laughed, shaking her head. 'Can't be late for Danny.'

'Stop, will you?' Jasmine was blushing, a rare occurrence. She gave her friend a playful push, but Ghislaine grabbed her arm, her face suddenly serious.

'Be careful, all right?'

Jasmine stared. 'Careful? What do you mean?'

With a sigh, Ghislaine let her go. 'Nothing. Take care of yourself.'

'I always do.' Jasmine tossed her hair over her shoulder.

They turned off the main shopping street, towards Phoenix House. As they neared the shelter, Ghislaine stopped.

'I'll see you later.'

'You're not coming in?'

The last few times Jasmine had met with Danny, Ghislaine had spent the hour flicking through magazines in the tiny waiting area outside the counsellor's office, keeping warm. This time, though, the flicker of unease in her stomach served as a warning. Ghislaine had ignored similar premonitions before, to her cost. She couldn't explain it, not even to herself, but she was going to obey her instincts.

'Nah, not today. I'll keep walking, might nip into the library.'

Jasmine looked for a second like she might argue, but she shrugged and turned away. Ghislaine watched her friend cross the road, Jasmine's body braced against the freezing wind, her cheap jacket offering little protection. Ghislaine tucked her chin deeper into the neckline of her sweatshirt and pulled up the hood. Phoenix House was in the centre of a row of red-brick buildings, between a tattoo parlour and a newsagent. A charity shop providing income for the shelter was housed on the ground floor, and the other two storeys provided the accommodation. The doors and window frames were painted a cheerful bright blue which always irritated Ghislaine, as did the decor inside the shelter itself. Whichever clients were around at the time had been given a few unwanted tins of paint and some brushes and left to express themselves. The end result was reminiscent of the work of a needy child, eager for parental approval. Peace symbols, rainbows, smiling faces daubed everywhere.

Painting what you want to see, how we should feel. We've imagined what gives other people hope, dragged it out of whichever pit of our minds it's been buried in for months, years, decades.

What would they have painted had they told their truth, brought their collective subconscious out for all to see, to admire? No doubt Maggie Kemp, the manager of the shelter, full of good intentions and replaced hormones, would have baulked at the sight of black wall after black wall. Ghislaine smiled to herself. *We all want to be accepted, after all, even those of us who deny it.* She forced her gaze away from the walls of Phoenix House and its siren call. It had been founded on sound principals, she acknowledged. The individuals who worked there and those who supported the shelter through gifts of time, money and food had pure motives. All the same, as she stood looking at the darkened windows, a shiver passed through her. It was a haven, a place where she was safe. And yet, she didn't want to stay here, not for much longer. Perhaps it was time to move on.

As she watched, one of the windows was illuminated by a warm, yellow light. Ghislaine turned and walked away.

Chapter 8

The CID office at Northolme Police Station was almost deserted. Knight's door stood open, and he gazed out into the main office, considering calling it a day. Anna Varcoe was the only member of the team still at work, until Catherine Bishop appeared in the doorway. Anna gave Catherine a wave, the receiver of her desk phone wedged under her chin, and Catherine mouthed, *Go home!* She strode across the scruffy carpet tiles, Knight straightening when he saw her expression.

'Aren't you having an early night?' He braced himself as Catherine marched in, grabbing the back of the chair which stood on the other side of his desk. Her fingers dug into the padded fabric as she spoke.

'You've spoken to DCI Dolan? Again, I mean.'

Knight was unperturbed. 'They wanted an officer who didn't work in Lincoln itself.'

'But they're from Nottingham – surely one of her own team would have been ideal? It's not as if I never go into the city.'

'You know Lincoln fairly well, and you're an experienced officer.' Knight glanced at the wall dividing his office from DCI Kendrick's. 'And Keith and I thought it would be… well, an opportunity for you.'

'An opportunity? Couldn't you have discussed it with me first? You must have known about this on Sunday when we met. It all seems rushed, as if they're not sure why they're bothering.'

Knight drummed his fingers on the desktop. 'Look at it this way – Mary Dolan is in charge of a Major Crimes team. Isn't she someone you would want to know your name?'

'Right, you were doing me a favour.' She slumped into the chair, still glaring at him.

'How long do you imagine Northolme will be able to justify having a team of detectives based here?' Knight hadn't wanted to spell out his worry, but it appeared he was going to have to. A few months earlier, Catherine would have realised immediately what he was hinting at, but now she seemed confused. He watched as she processed his words, took in what he meant, the tic beneath her eye visible again, her hands twisting around the arms of her chair. 'You must have considered the possibility of this place being downsized, or even closed?' Concern for her made his voice gentle. She blinked at him, bewildered, the anger dissolving.

'Of course, but…' She swallowed. 'When?'

He held up his hands. 'I've no idea, honestly. It might not happen, but it wouldn't be a huge surprise, would it?' Slowly, Catherine shook her head. Government cuts were biting hard as they were all aware, and not only in the police force. Knight stood, pulled his jacket from the back of his chair and struggled into it. 'Come on, let's go and have a drink.'

Anna was still out in the main office. Catherine rallied, flashing her a grin. 'Still here?'

60

'Not for long.' Anna glanced at the clock on the wall.

'We're going to the pub if you fancy joining us?' Knight offered.

Anna shook her head with a smile. 'Thanks, but I'm meeting Thomas.'

Outside, a cold wind whipped around the car park. Knight shivered as they approached Catherine's car.

'Tell you what, why don't you come to my place instead?' he asked. 'I bet you've not eaten?'

She shook her head, her face expressionless.

–

An hour later, Catherine sat in Knight's living room with a bowl of pasta on her lap. Knight had lit a floor lamp, its soft light already warming the room.

'I'll nip out and get some wood for the fire,' he told her. 'Jo should be here any minute.'

Catherine stared at him, her fork halfway to her mouth. 'Wait a second– you're expecting Jo?'

He laughed at her horrified expression. 'Is that a problem?'

'But I'll be interrupting—'

'You're not interrupting anything. Eat.' He wagged a finger at her as he left the room.

Catherine sighed and dug into the pasta again. Jo Webber was Knight's girlfriend, as well as the patholo-gist usually called in when any suspicious or unexplained deaths occurred on their patch. Though she liked Jo, barging in on her and Knight's cosy night in front of the log burner was the last thing Catherine wanted to do. Anyway, the topic she had wanted to discuss with him, the secret that was troubling her at night and nudging her during the day, was one that as far as she knew, Jo was unaware of.

Knight bustled back into the room with an armful of logs, and Catherine decided it was now or never. 'Can we talk about the Paul Hughes case?'

Knight squatted, opened the doors of the burner. 'Why?' He didn't look at her, focussing on the firewood.

'You know why.'

'Catherine, forget about it. The guilty men are in prison. Malc Hughes is living the quiet life in Brighton. It's over, all of it.'

They heard the front door open. Catherine closed her eyes for a second. She was innocent of any wrongdoing, she knew, and she couldn't believe Knight was in any way corrupt, but... Did she truly know him? Could she say, could she swear, that Jonathan Knight was honest? She didn't know, not now. He was kind, loyal, intelligent – but was he clean?

'It's not easy. I'm worried, Jonathan.' *I'm scared.*

Knight looked at her. 'I know, but you have to put it out of your mind. Case closed, I promise.' He slammed the wood burner's doors, brushing off his hands on his trousers as Jo Webber breezed into the room, closely followed by her boxer dog, Jess. Webber kissed Knight's cheek, turning to Catherine with a friendly smile.

'Lovely to see you, Catherine.'

Catherine forced a grin. 'You too. Without there being a dead body in the room, I mean.'

Jo's perfect features creased as she laughed, and Catherine relaxed, allowing the Hughes case to drift away. Webber's beauty and poise used to intimidate her, but as she had come to know the pathologist she realised her looks were irrelevant. Jo Webber was as susceptible to insecurity as the rest of the population. She was also the best pathologist Catherine had worked with, and anyone who could have a relationship with Jonathan Knight, socially awkward as he was, deserved some respect.

Jo settled onto the settee and tucked her legs underneath her as the dog curled on the floor at her feet, both clearly comfortable in Knight's home. He had been vague about his relationship with Jo at work, taking the teasing from his colleagues in good humour, but keeping the details private. Catherine couldn't blame him. She knew from experience what it was like to be the talk of Northolme Police Station, and it wasn't an experience she would wish on anyone.

Jo accepted a bowl of pasta from Knight, who rushed off again to open some wine.

'How are you, Catherine?'

Jo's tone was light, but Catherine reddened under her gaze. Though she was more relaxed than she had been in days, Jo was a professional, a physician. There would be no fooling her.

'I've been better,' she admitted.

'Have you seen your GP?'

'No. No, not yet.' She kept her eyes on the bowl on her lap, tears welling in her eyes, her throat tight with the effort of holding herself together.

Jo leant forward and gently touched Catherine's hand. 'Do you have someone you can talk to?'

'There's my brother. There's Ellie.' Catherine fumbled in her trouser pocket for a tissue.

'And there's me, and Jonathan. I know he's been concerned.'

'There's no need.'

'As long as you know we're here.'

'I do.' Catherine got to her feet, clutching the empty bowl. 'Honestly, Jo – thank you.'

In the kitchen, Knight was rummaging in a drawer.

'Can't find the bloody corkscrew.'

Catherine set her bowl in the sink. 'That was lovely, Jonathan.' Leaning back against the worktop, she made the decision. 'You're right, you know.' Her voice caught, the words garbled.

'Got it.' Knight held up the corkscrew. 'I'm right? How do you mean?'

'About forgetting. Moving on.'

He stared, aware she was talking about more than a previous case. Her smile wobbled, but she fought to keep it in place, ignoring the tears filling her eyes again. Knight turned to pour the wine, giving her space.

'I know why you asked me here tonight,' she told him.

'I'd made too much pasta sauce.'

She managed a laugh. 'I should be going. Early start tomorrow.'

'You'll be okay. We'll see you soon.'

'You will.'

As she passed, she threw one arm around his shoulders, pressing herself to his back for a second. She shoved her feet into her shoes and called a farewell to Jo before closing the front door behind her.

Knight took the glasses of wine into the living room where Jo was waiting, concern clear on her face. Knight handed her a glass and sat beside her. He moved closer, resting his head on her shoulder, Jo's familiar smell and the warmth of her already a comfort. Jess snored at their feet.

'Well?' Knight mumbled into Jo's hair.

She sipped her wine. 'You're right – she's struggling. She knows this goes deeper than simply having a bad day.'

'I hope we've done the right thing.'

'Her working with a different team, you mean?'

'Maybe it was a bad idea.' Knight hadn't given Jo any details, but he needed reassurance.

'After seeing her tonight, I understand why you're worried,' Jo said. 'But we can't help her until she's ready to ask us to, Jonathan.' She slid her arm around him, drawing him closer still. 'She'll be okay. She's pretty tough.'

Knight laughed. 'You think?'

Chapter 9

Jasmine's rucksack was thrown on the bed she'd been allocated. Ghislaine saw it as she was folding her clothes and called to her friend, who was brushing her teeth in the bathroom next door.

'Jas? Do you want me to shove your bag in a locker?'

Immediately, Jasmine was at the door, glaring, her toothbrush clenched in her fist like a weapon. 'No. Mind your own business.'

Ghislaine stared at her, shocked. 'All right. I only asked.'

Jasmine marched forward, abruptly bending forward until her face was level with Ghislaine's. 'Don't ever touch my stuff. Are you listening to me?'

Ghislaine took a step backwards, keenly aware of Jasmine's considerable height and weight advantage.

'Yeah, okay. Forget I said anything.'

There was a cough in the corridor and the female night support worker stuck her head around the door.

'Everything all right?'

Jasmine's snarl was gone, an easy smile taking its place. Shaken, Ghislaine sat on the chair standing between the two beds.

'Yeah, we're getting into bed,' Jasmine told her. The support worker was clearly unconvinced. She had a phone in her hand, ready to call her male colleague from the men's rooms above if necessary.

'Ghislaine?'

'Fine, thanks. Good night.'

She got to her feet and pulled back the duvet. Jasmine watched as Ghislaine got into bed and turned to face the wall. Soon, the light snapped off, and there was silence. After a while, Jasmine said, 'Ghis? I'm sorry.'

Ghislaine pulled the duvet higher, wiping the tears from her eyes in one quick movement.

'Yeah, okay.'

'I am.'

'Go to sleep, Jas.'

Later, she lay awake, loneliness coursing through her like a drug. Jasmine grunted and turned over with a deep snore. Ghislaine closed her eyes, willing sleep to come but knowing it wouldn't. She raised her head to gaze over at Jasmine. She couldn't trust her after all. The truth of it hit her hard, her face contorting as though she were in physical pain.

She was left with no one.

Chapter 10

Catherine had woken early, thrown some clothes into a holdall without stopping to think. A woman hurriedly leaving an abusive partner wouldn't have the opportunity to consider every item in her wardrobe, and why should Catherine? She left a note for Thomas in the kitchen explaining she would be away on a training course for a few days, and quietly left the house. He would have risen early and given her a lift to the train station if she had asked him, but she didn't want to have to lie to him about her whereabouts. She didn't know if Anna had spent the night with Thomas or not, but Knight and Kendrick would no doubt find a way to explain her absence in the morning briefing. It was out of her hands. There was a small tingle of relief as she realised she was taking a break from her responsibilities, her caseload, her life. From the second she had opened her eyes this morning, she had assumed her new identity. The idea was reassuring. Pressing pause on the life of Detective Sergeant Catherine Bishop of Northolme Police Station was an attractive idea.

-

It was a cold, bright morning with frost glinting on the pavements, the grass verges white and crisp. The sun had made an appearance, hovering as if undecided on whether to stay or to disappear again. Catherine huddled further into her coat as she walked, the icy air biting at her face. Her bag was heavy, and she already wished she had packed a rucksack instead. She strode through the shopping complex in Northolme's town centre, passing bleary-eyed office workers streaming towards the local council building. One or two shops were already open, and Catherine stopped at a bakery for a cup of tea and a bacon roll. Before the bowl of pasta Knight had prepared for her the previous evening, she couldn't remember the last time she had enjoyed the food she had eaten. Tried to eat. Every meal lately had the culinary appeal of stale bread and water, even the food at the Italian restaurant. She had to admit though, the bacon sandwich tasted good.

At the station, she had a short wait for the train in a draughty shelter by the platform, her hands now feeling frozen around the handle of her bag. A few other people were waiting for the train, students or people who worked in Lincoln. An elderly couple waited nearby, well wrapped in thick woollen coats, gloves and scarves. They stood close together, holding hands, and Catherine turned away with a smile. There had been relationships in her past of course, but they had dwindled away, the initial excitement replaced by a kind of inertia. All wrong. There had been someone with whom she had imagined a future, but she hadn't been who she had seemed to be. Catherine had fallen in love with an illusion, a mistake she didn't intend to repeat. Dolan was a senior officer, no doubt a straight one. The reaction Catherine had experienced meant no more than catching the eye of an attractive stranger in the street, passing them and going on with your day. What about Ellie? Should she have phoned to explain she was going away? But Ellie would want to talk about what had happened in the hotel corridor, and Catherine wasn't ready to yet. Her behaviour had been poor, and there was no excuse. Ellie deserved a proper explanation, but how could Catherine give one when she didn't understand the reason for her reluctance herself? No, best to leave it for now. Anyway, the train was approaching. Catherine stepped out onto the platform, refusing to acknowledge her own cowardice.

–

'Morning, Maggie.' Jasmine lifted her hand in a jaunty wave as she and Ghislaine swept by the older woman who stood at the admin desk, leafing through a pile of letters.

'Hello, you two. What are you doing today?' Maggie looked tired, Ghislaine noted, her stringy hair even more windswept than usual.

'Off to the job centre,' Jasmine replied.

'Excellent. Well, good luck.'

Jasmine snorted as they clumped down the stairs. '"Good luck". As soon as anyone sees "Care of Phoenix House" on our application forms, they'll chuck them straight in the bin.'

Ghislaine considered pointing out that most applications were completed online these days, but decided against it.

'You never know, Jas,' she said instead. 'Someone might give us a chance.'

'It's all right for you with your clean record and your big eyes,' Jasmine sneered as they crossed the road. She put on a high-pitched, lisping voice: '"Go on, please give me a job, I'll be ever so good".'

Ghislaine bared her teeth, but when she spoke her voice was steady. 'You're the one with the qualifications, not me.'

Jasmine tossed her hair and pouted. 'Yeah, well maybe we make a good team,' she relented. She patted her jeans pocket. 'Come on, let's get a hot chocolate. My treat.'

—

He entered the shop and stood behind them, enjoying the view. Jasmine was taller, fit and lithe with a body he'd like to explore. The other one was slim, verging on skinny, scurrying along beside her friend like a puppy eager to please. He couldn't hear what they were saying, but Jasmine was doing most of the talking. No change there. He narrowed his eyes, his gaze on Jasmine's arse. He smiled to himself. Perk of the job.

He watched Jasmine take two paper cups from the woman behind the counter, handing them to Ghislaine while she fumbled for her money.

'Wait, I'll get these.'

They both turned, surprised, as he strode towards the counter. He knew they'd seen him at the shelter, but he was new; he'd only stayed one night. He'd have to work hard to gain their trust.

Jasmine eyed him with suspicion. 'We can pay for our own.'

'I know you can. I'm being neighbourly.'

'Have you been following us?' Jasmine sipped her drink, glaring at him over the rim of the cup.

'As if. I saw you through the window, thought I'd stop and say hello.' He handed over a folded note, his last fiver, and waited for his meagre change. 'Shall we have a seat?'

Jasmine shook her head. 'We're fine standing.'

He raised his eyebrows, flashed Ghislaine a mocking grin. 'What's wrong, can't you speak for yourself?'

She said nothing, holding her cup in both hands, watching him steadily. Irritated, he shook his head and turned back to Jasmine. 'I'll talk to you. At least you've got the decency to reply.'

Jasmine thrust her chin towards him. 'Leave Ghis alone. You know nothing about her.'

'I know she's got no manners.' Instantly, he berated himself for the dig. Winding them up wasn't going to help. Ghislaine straightened her back, looking him in the eye.

'I'm sorry. Thank you for the drink.'

He nodded, confused, as she held his gaze. Grey-blue eyes, not cold, but appraising. Intelligent. He blinked, realising he'd misjudged her, having decided before she was some kind of halfwit. He'd watched her in the shelter's television room the night before, curled up in a chair and hardly speaking. He'd have to keep an eye on her after all.

'Come on, are we going to sit?' He adopted a friendlier tone.

Jasmine took a long swallow from her cup before bothering to reply. 'We're not, but don't let us stop you. What do you want?'

'You know who I am?'

'We've seen you at the shelter. Doesn't mean we're friends.'

'Do you know my name?'

Drinking the last of her hot chocolate, Jasmine scrunched the cup in her fist. 'Lee. And?'

72

He sighed. 'Look, I've heard one of the people who've stayed at Phoenix House recently is dead.'

'Yeah. It's not a secret.'

'It doesn't worry you?'

Jasmine was already turning away. 'Worry me? Why should it? Risk you take when you inject. See you.'

He stared after them, his mind working. Ghislaine. Quiet, but watchful, alert. Maybe she'd be more talkative if they were alone, if he didn't give her the opportunity to walk away from him.

He clenched his jaw. Time to plan.

-

Catherine approached the church nervously, clutching her bag close, convincing herself everyone would realise she was a police officer as soon as she stepped through the door. People could tell, couldn't they?

Having spent the morning trudging around the city centre, aimlessly examining window displays, she was ready for some hot food and a rest.

Her own mobile, the one she shouldn't have brought with her, had buzzed for a while earlier. She guessed it was Thomas, calling to ask where she was and why she hadn't told him about her 'course' before. She had ignored it, knowing she would have to find a place to ring him back in private.

Hopefully, Knight and Kendrick would have explained her absence to the team of officers at Northolme by now and Anna would be able to reassure Thomas all was well. Catherine knew she should have told him, perhaps even confided in him, told him the real reason for her sudden disappearance. She swallowed, pushing away the rush of guilt that rose in her throat. No, it was better Thomas didn't know. He had given her one concerned glance too many recently. He would have tried to dissuade her, and she might even have listened.

The crawling sensation was back, creeping along her arms and across her cheeks like a rash. She stopped, raised a hand to her face and touched her skin with her fingertips.

Hearing footsteps clattering on the tiles behind her, Catherine started. How long had she been standing there? She lifted her head as two young women strolled in and passed her, their glances curious. Could these be the residents of Phoenix House Dolan had mentioned? The taller woman stopped, and her friend followed suit.

'All right? Are you here for some food?'

Catherine let out a croak, cleared her throat and managed to reply. 'I was told there'd be soup?'

The woman pointed to a closed door, her fingernails painted a vivid purple, glittering under the meagre light.

'That way.'

The only other options were a door labelled 'Ladies' and a substantial stone archway leading to what was obviously the church itself, but Catherine appreciated their friendliness.

'Thank you.'

'No problem.' They moved off.

Still, Catherine hesitated. She could turn back, contact DCI Dolan and tell her she had made a mistake, she was not the person for this job. What had she been thinking, anyway? She was barely functioning in her own role; how could she expect to take on a new one, as well as a new persona? The face she saw in the mirror no longer felt her own. Her body wasn't reliable either, twitching and pulsing with strange, unfamiliar sensations. Why shouldn't she be someone else for a while, when the transformation had already started without her consent?

Catherine lifted her chin, remembering Isla Rafferty's sneer.

Lentil. Of all flavours, they were serving lentil. Catherine watched the beige liquid gloop off the ladle and into the cup, telling herself not to be ungrateful. She smiled as she thanked the woman who was serving and turned to look for a table, keen to sit alone if possible. Not only because she imagined the woman she was portraying would avoid company on her first visit to the soup kitchen, but because she would find it more comfortable. Her task was to chat to people and befriend them, but she also had to play her part convincingly. Interrogating people wouldn't be helpful.

The room was rectangular, a typical church hall with cream-painted walls displaying various posters and children's artwork, perhaps from Sunday School activities. The wooden flooring was scuffed in places, and the tables and benches were battered, but the place had an air of welcome. As Catherine slid onto a bench, she saw a man wearing casual trousers, a woollen sweater and a white cleric's collar enter the room. His eyes travelled over the twenty or so people who were tucking into their soup before coming to rest on Catherine. She swallowed a mouthful of bread as he approached.

'Hello there. I don't remember seeing you before? I'm Joel Rushford.'

Rushford. He had given a statement too, brief and vague, like the others. He was in his early forties, she would guess. Handsome. His voice was distinctive, quiet but with a musical quality. Was it natural, deliberate or a result of years standing before a congregation? Rushford slipped his hands into his trouser pockets, waiting.

'I heard I could get some food,' Catherine said.

He smiled, his teeth straight and white. 'Well, we offer support too, but yes. As you've discovered, there's a hot meal available every weekday, sandwiches at the weekend. And you can drop in anytime for a cup of tea and a chat.'

'A chat?'

He nodded, maintaining eye contact. 'Some people find it helps. Keep it in mind; we're here to help. Will you need a bed tonight?'

'I might.'

'Okay. There's a homeless shelter, you can try there – I'll get you a leaflet.'

Catherine went back to her soup as Rushford crossed the room, stopping to chat with a few people as he went. He soon returned, and Catherine put down her cup. Rushford now held out a white piece of paper.

'There you go. Phoenix House. Talk to Maggie. She'll help if she can.'

Slowly, Catherine took the paper. He met her eyes again with another smile as she thanked him. Catherine watched him walk away. He had been professional, courteous, helpful. And yet – had he deliberately moved his hand to be sure his fingers brushed hers as he handed her the leaflet?

Chapter 11

DC Adil Zaman blew out his cheeks in frustration. The statements taken from the people who had known John McKinley were worse than useless, as Dolan had said. Nothing concrete, nothing helpful, but a load of waffle, rambling and avoidance. He sat back in his chair. It was too low, but the mechanism controlling the height of the seat was broken. The small of his back was already aching. Zaman got to his feet, knowing he should take some painkillers before it got worse.

'Tea?' *Your Majesty*, he added, but only in his own mind. He and Isla Rafferty had worked together for over a year now, but their relationship was a formal affair. At first, he had had no idea how to address her – she was a DS after all, and therefore his superior. But Dolan didn't like being called ma'am and she was a DCI, so Rafferty could hardly insist on it, though Zaman suspected she would like to. He usually went with 'Sergeant', the more informal 'Sarge' feeling a step too far.

'It's okay, I'll make the drinks.' Rafferty smudged a hand across her eyes. 'I could use a break.'

Zaman stared. It seemed the slow trudge through pointless statements was numbing even Rafferty's brain. Her offering to make the drinks was unheard of.

'Have you found anything?' Rafferty went on, gesturing towards his computer.

'No. Even the people who work at the shelter are giving nothing away, like Mary said. McKinley hardly spent any time there, in any case.'

Rafferty twisted her engagement ring around on her finger, frowning. Zaman waited. He'd often wondered about his sergeant's fiancé – apparently someone had managed to thaw her out a little. It would take a braver man than him.

'Maybe you should go and talk to the staff again while I'm at the post-mortem, Adil. One of their clients is dead, after all – you'd think they could be a little more helpful. I'll have a word with DCI Dolan.'

As she spoke, the door opened and Dolan herself appeared, shaking drops of rain from a black umbrella.

'Chucking it down,' she muttered unnecessarily, unbuttoning her coat. She dumped it on the back of her chair, shook out her hair and set three packets of sandwiches on the table. 'Here you go; take your pick. A word with me about what?'

Rafferty stepped forward, selected the plain cheese sandwiches and put the packet by her laptop.

'I suggested it might be worth DC Zaman talking to the staff of Phoenix House again, even though DS Bishop is on her way. We've got nothing from the statements,' she said.

'Agreed. This afternoon, Adil?' Dolan smiled at him. 'We'll see you back here later on to catch up.'

'No problem.'

'Tea, Mary?' asked Rafferty.

'Thank you.' Dolan watched her leave the room. She turned to Zaman, pointing at the remaining sandwiches, eyebrows raised. 'Hope you like egg or chicken.'

He laughed. 'Either's fine with me.'

'Luckily. What did you think of DS Bishop?'

Dolan was ripping open the egg sandwiches as she spoke, but Zaman knew she would be watching him. He chose his words with care.

'She seemed eager to get started.'

What else could he say? Catherine Bishop had looked ill, unfocused and unsure. He had noticed Rafferty's reaction to her, of course – the curled lip, the dismissive tone. Rafferty had her faults, but she was good at her job. Perhaps she believed she should be the one going to Phoenix House? He concentrated on his sandwiches, hoping they tasted better than they looked.

Dolan's brow furrowed as she chewed. 'I'm hoping Catherine will soon have some feedback for us. God knows we need it.'

Sure enough, the chicken was dry. Zaman wished Rafferty would hurry up with the tea.

'I'm going to make a few phone calls, see if I can find anyone who worked with John before he left the force,' the DCI said. 'He was a decent man, a good officer. I can't understand...' Dolan shook her head, bemused. 'I'll do some digging.'

Zaman took another bite of his unappetising sandwich, his gaze straying to the photograph displayed on the wall above them. John McKinley remained a mystery.

The office inside Phoenix House was tiny, more a cupboard than a room. A shabby filing cabinet, a small desk and two white plastic garden chairs, both with bright cushions on their seats, were squeezed inside. Maggie Kemp sat at the desk, which was set against the wall, but she had turned her chair to face into the room. Catherine Bishop sat in the other chair, and though neither of the women were tall, their knees were touching.

'We can provide a bed and breakfast in the morning,' Kemp was saying. 'We also offer food at night, often pasta with sauce, or sometimes jacket potatoes. Simple and filling, you see. We rely a lot on donations, so it's whatever people have been kind enough to send in. There's tea and coffee too, and we usually have some toiletries you can buy at a discount. We do our best to provide all we can, but it's not possible to cover everything.'

'Sounds great,' Catherine mumbled.

Kemp beamed. 'There are laundry facilities you can use, with an honesty box for payment towards the electricity. You can also have a shower, and store any belongings safely here if you intend to apply for a bed for the next night. We never guarantee a place, of course, we're strictly emergency shelter only, but... Well, we'll always do our best to help.'

Kemp made eye contact with her for the first time as she made her final point, and Catherine noted the deep furrow between her eyebrows, her hair showing grey at the roots. Her hands, folded loosely in her lap, were chapped with short, unpainted nails. A woman more used to caring for others than for herself.

There was a knock on the door and Kemp glanced at it, surprised.

'Yes?' she called. The man who appeared was young, mid-twenties, Catherine guessed as she craned her neck to look around at him. He had messy blonde hair and blue eyes. With an apologetic smile, he said, 'I'm sorry to disturb you, Maggie, but another policeman is wanting to speak to you. He's insistent.'

Catherine stiffened. Was she going to be recognised before she'd even been offered a bed? It would be the shortest undercover posting in history. Maggie reached out to her, noting the action even if she was unaware of the true reason for it.

'Now don't you worry. Thank you, Danny.' There was a tiny edge to her voice, as if he should have known better than to mention the police in front of a client. 'It's an ongoing matter, nothing for you to be concerned about, Catherine. We'll see you between eight and ten thirty tonight.' Maggie was getting to her feet. 'I'm sorry to have to cut our meeting short, but I'm sure we've covered everything essential.' She spread her hands as if attempting to waft Catherine out of the door. 'Leave your bag in one of the lockers, if you like,' Kemp called as Catherine left her office.

In the corridor, Adil Zaman stood waiting. Catherine kept her face blank as she approached him, and although Zaman smiled politely, he gave no sign he knew who she was. She hurried past, into an area she presumed was communal. There were a few sofas, slightly battered but in decent condition. A dining table with playing cards and board games stacked on it was by the window, and in the corner stood a TV and DVD player on a cabinet and several chairs. A bookcase, a coffee table and two desks comprised the rest of the furniture. Catherine stopped for a second, glancing around. Magnolia walls and a navy-blue carpet, half home, half office. A well of panic rose inside her, an urge to run, to get away from the place and the people. Although the room was empty, she imagined she could sense the despair of those who would be here later, the clock on the wall marking the passing of another night of games they didn't want to play and films they didn't want to watch. Like prison, only they were free to leave at any time. But to go where?

–

'I'm not sure I can add anything to what I told the uniformed officer the other day.' Maggie Kemp took off her glasses and rubbed the bridge of her nose. 'I was busy with a client.' Her tone held a note of reproach. Zaman smiled a little as he opened his notebook, deciding that perhaps the blunt approach was best.

'I appreciate you've already spoken to one of my colleagues, Mrs Kemp, but a man who has stayed at your shelter within the last few months is dead.'

She raised her head. 'Which I'm aware of.'

'I can now tell you we believe Mr McKinley's death wasn't accidental, which means speaking to you all again, I'm afraid.' Zaman wasn't going to go into detail, but perhaps the mention of murder might encourage a little more honesty.

'You mean Mackie was deliberately killed? You're telling me he was murdered?' Zaman nodded, and she stared at him, stricken. 'But no one's mentioned murder before; we never even considered...' Kemp pulled a crumpled tissue out of her pocket and dabbed at her eyes. 'It was bad enough believing he'd gone back to taking drugs.'

'Would you have been surprised if he had?'

Kemp sniffed. 'I never spoke to him about his drug use. We have a mental health worker, Danny Marshall – he's excellent – and he recommended counselling, but Mackie didn't agree.'

'Wasn't he willing to take advice?'

'He struggled to accept help. He'd had a difficult time. I mean, all of the people who come through our door have.'

'I understand.'

'Mackie only spent a few nights with us, if it was freezing or snowing. He said he preferred the streets. Some people do, can't bear being inside, even for a few hours. Mackie was different, though. Reserved – an intro-vert. I once said to my husband…' She stopped and shook her head. 'It's silly.'

'Not at all,' Zaman reassured her. 'Anything you noticed – impressions, observations – we want to know about them.'

'It's… Well, Mackie seemed to me to be punishing himself. Staying out in all weathers, barely eating, keeping himself isolated. A martyr.'

There was a silence. 'Did he ever explain his behaviour?'

'No. As I said, we rarely saw him. Perhaps Joel Rush-ford could help – he's the vicar at St Mary's. They run a soup kitchen most of our clients visit. I know Mackie went there regularly. Even he had to eat sometimes.' Her smile was sad, wistful. She blinked a few times. 'As I said, some people can't accept our help, however much we want to give it. It's one of the most difficult parts of what we do, for me at least.'

'A martyr? Interesting.' Mary Dolan rested her chin on her hand. 'And could Rushford tell us anything more today than he did before?'

'He wasn't at the church. I'm going back tomorrow.'

'Okay. We've still nothing from the CCTV, no witnesses to speak of, no motive. I've been looking at McKinley's personnel file, his arrest records. He left the force after ten years' service,' Dolan told them.

'Why?' Zaman asked.

'No real reason's given. More poking around to do there, I'd say. We need more from the people who knew him more recently.'

Rafferty coughed. 'But no one at Phoenix House can tell us anything.'

'Not us, no, but hopefully they'll talk to Catherine if they believe she's one of their own.'

Isla Rafferty looked at the tabletop with a frown. She wasn't counting on it.

–

Catherine was walking into the driving rain, huddled into her coat, reluctantly passing the railway station. What she wanted to do was get onto a train, go home, climb into bed and pull the covers over her head. For the past few hours, since most of the shops had closed, she had been wandering aimlessly, each minute seeming like ten. The shelter would be open by now, and she should make her way there. Her feet ached, her clothes were damp and her task was daunting. How did people survive like this, day after day, week after week?

The doors of the church where she had eaten her soup were open, and she could hear people talking inside as she walked by. She slowed, hesitating, with no way of knowing whether a service was going on, or if food was being served again. Hunger tightened her stomach, but she wasn't sure if she could eat. She had left her usual purse at home, bringing only a small wallet which had none of her debit or credit cards inside. Too tempting. Being without her warrant card made her vulnerable too, but if she was to pull this off, even for one night, it was necessary. She intended to survive on as little cash as possible, having not even checked how much was in the envelope Rafferty had given her. More than John McKinley would have had, for sure.

Her new phone was ringing, the unfamiliar ringtone taking a few seconds to register with Catherine. When she finally answered the call, Isla Rafferty's voice was cold.

'The post-mortem didn't give us any new information unfortunately, as we expected. The pathologist did say she believes McKinley couldn't have tied the tourniquet we found on his arm himself. It was on his right arm. McKinley was right-handed, according to people who knew him and the pathologist's findings – muscle development or however they work these things out. If he injected himself, why do it in his right arm, using his left hand? It's not as though he had to find a different site to inject because of infection or damaged veins – there was no other evidence of drug use at all. We're still waiting for the toxicology reports, of course. John McKinley weighed less than nine stone when he died.' Rafferty paused for a second, as if giving Catherine time to visualise McKinley's too-thin frame. 'He had many old injuries, bruising and cuts which were still healing, as well as the newer wounds we could see on his face.'

'He'd been attacked before?' Catherine hunched her shoulders, pausing beneath the shelter of one of the trees growing outside the church. A car hissed past, its wheels flinging cold, dirty water in Catherine's direction. She took a quick step backwards.

'Evidently. It's not unknown for rough sleepers to meet with violence.' Rafferty sounded bored, and Catherine couldn't help herself.

'Is it? I hadn't realised.'

Rafferty hesitated. 'I'm sorry. You're aware, of course.'

'I've heard rumours.' Catherine closed her eyes, leaning back against the tree trunk as the rain stung her face.

'Where are you, DS Bishop?'

'Where am I? I'm getting soaked. What difference does it make?'

'We would have expected you to be at the shelter by now. Instead, you're... by the railway station?'

Catherine straightened, glancing around as if Rafferty might be lurking behind the tree. 'Wait a second. You're watching me?'

'It's a safety precaution.'

'Keeping track, you mean.' Catherine was furious, and didn't attempt to hide the fact. 'I'm on my way to the shelter now.'

'Excellent.' Rafferty left another silence. 'John McKinley's feet were a mess. Blisters, sores, infected toenails...'

'Sounds awful, but I'm not sure why it's relevant?'

'Might be a good idea for you to get out of the rain. I'll speak to you soon.' Her voice was brisk; it was an instruction, not a show of concern. Shoving the phone into her pocket, Catherine trudged off again. Bloody Rafferty, sticking her nose in, watching like an exasperated parent waiting for their child to skive off school. Sitting there smugly, warm and dry, wanting, waiting for Catherine to fuck up. Well, she wouldn't. Catherine wiped the rain from her face as she promised herself she would complete this assignment, however long, whatever it took. There was no way she would give Rafferty the satisfaction of knowing she had been right, that Catherine was a risk, and she would fail.

No way.

As she walked she heard her own phone, the one she probably shouldn't have brought with her, ring. By the time she had wrestled it out of her pocket, it was silent. She swiped the screen into life. Missed call: Thomas. She tapped the green icon to ring her brother back.

'Catherine. Where are you?' His voice was strange: brittle and restrained.

'Thomas, what's wrong?'

'It's Anna. She's been stabbed.'

Chapter 12

Wrapping her hands around the mug of coffee, Ghislaine closed her eyes as the warmth seeped into her frozen fingers. The TV blared in the corner, all the misery and conflict of the world condensed into a half-hour news bulletin. Ghislaine ignored it. She only had to glance around the room if she wanted a window into the suffering of others. There were four blokes playing cards at a white-painted dining table while two dogs, one brindle, one black, slept at their feet. Her eyes passed over the men quickly, assessing them. The man who'd followed them, Lee, was here again tonight. He looked up from his hand of cards as she appraised him, and she glanced away, blushing.

'Where's Jasmine tonight?'

The question came from one of the night support workers, sitting at the desk set against the wall behind her. Ghislaine turned her head as Carl Baker smiled at her. He was a big man, wild ginger curls covering his head, hands resting on his huge belly.

'She should be around.'

'I'm allocating beds.'

'I'll ring her.' Ghislaine sighed. When had she become Jasmine's babysitter?

Carl rummaged through the piles of paper littering the desk and unearthed a cordless phone, which he held out to her.

'Here. Save your credit.'

'Cheers, Carl.' She tapped in Jasmine's number and waited. 'Voicemail.'

Carl frowned. 'Well, she knows the rules.'

The door of the shelter opened at eight in the evening and was locked at half past ten, meaning Jasmine had ninety minutes to secure a bed for the night. Ghislaine sank back onto the settee, its dodgy springs creaking beneath her. Where the hell was Jas? Her appointment with Danny had finished hours ago. Sometimes she would go to a pub, or back to the squat she used to live in, but she was trying to stay away from her old friends. Ghislaine sipped her coffee, worry knotting her stomach.

'It's up to her, Ghis.' Carl's voice was soft, sympathetic. 'We're all doing our best to help her, but the rest is her choice.'

'Yeah, I know.'

Ghislaine blinked away the scars on Jasmine's arms, the muttered protests, the muted yelps that plagued her dreams. She'd been woken several times by the misery of Jasmine's unconscious.

She stood, cradling her drink, and went over to the small bookcase which stood by the door leading to the women's bedrooms. Running a finger along the spines of the battered paperbacks, she selected an Agatha Christie mystery she remembered reading before. There was comfort in stepping into another world, the characters like distant relatives; vaguely familiar but indistinct.

She had read two chapters when the downstairs buzzer sounded. Carl's face lit up.

'This'll be her.'

He heaved himself out of his chair. It seemed to breathe a sigh of relief, the back straightening, the wheels clicking. Ghislaine kept her eyes on the lines of text as she heard footsteps clattering on the stairs.

'Did you hear the sirens?' Jasmine launched herself across the room, coming to a stop in front of Ghislaine. Carl followed more sedately before lowering himself back into his chair with a groan. Ghislaine studied her friend's face, taking in Jasmine's excited expression and flushed cheeks.

'What sirens? Where have you been?'

Jasmine flopped on the sofa, dropped her rucksack at her feet and crossed long, slim legs in front of her. The card players were watching with interest, and Jasmine flicked her hair, shooting a quick glance in their direction.

'Ambulance and police cars, loads of them.'

Ghislaine closed the book, but kept her thumb inside to mark her page.

'What's happened?' she asked.

The four men had stopped their game, turning in their chairs to hear the news.

'A stabbing, about half an hour ago.' Jasmine's eyes glinted. 'In the crowd, they were saying the victim was a copper. He stabbed her in the back, blood everywhere. They're saying she'll die.'

Ghislaine could smell alcohol on Jasmine's breath. Had Carl noticed too?

One of the men snorted. 'A copper? What sort of idiot would knife a copper?'

'They don't know, do they? He got away.' Jasmine's voice held a note of satisfaction. Ghislaine shuddered, unconsciously turning away from her friend. The new man, Lee, met her eyes again, his face unreadable.

–

The car park was deserted, visiting hours long gone and the dreamlike, neon-lit night fast approaching. Catherine leapt out of the taxi and slammed the door, throwing one of the notes Rafferty had given her towards the driver. The rain was still falling, gusts of wind driving it into her face. She ducked her head and ran for the hospital's main entrance.

Thomas was hunched on a blue plastic chair, his arms wrapped around his body. Dressed in a damp shirt and jeans, his hair was soaked and he was shivering. A drinks machine lit a corner where a man slumped, looking dazed. Beside him, a woman was staring at the wall, her eyes vacant. Catherine ran towards her brother, pulling off her coat. Thomas staggered to his feet, allowing her to gather him into her arms. Catherine held him tight.

'How is she?'

Thomas shook his head. 'I don't… She's in surgery. I don't know any more.'

Catherine guided him back into the chair, draping her coat around his shoulders. He managed a tremulous smile, and she took his hand.

'What happened?'

'We'd parked the car, were walking to the restaurant – the Italian place you mentioned? This bloke appeared – I don't even know where he came from. He grabbed Anna, pulled her away from me, said if I left my phone and wallet on the ground, he wouldn't hurt her. He had a knife, held it in front of her face. I was terrified, threw my stuff down as fast as I could. Anna was watching me, smiling like I was doing exactly the right thing. He swung his arm back… The look on his face, like he was deciding where to aim. I saw the blade glinting, slamming into her back. I heard it, Catherine, heard the knife tear into her…'

His hand flew to his mouth as he retched, his shoulders heaving. Appalled, Catherine rubbed his back, her mind blank as she tried to find words of comfort. After a time, Thomas swallowed his sobs.

'Sorry,' he whispered.

Catherine shook her head. 'Don't tell me if it's too difficult.' She knew he would have to repeat his story soon enough.

Thomas scrubbed at his eyes. 'It's okay, I want to tell you. Anna made this noise. I can't describe it, like nothing I've heard before, gasping and choking. She fell forward. I ran to her, but I couldn't get to her in time. Her face hit the pavement, and she was quiet. I saw the blood…'

His face was pale, his eyes wide with horror. Catherine squeezed his hand.

'What about the attacker?'

Thomas shook his head. 'I don't know where he went. He didn't pick up the wallet or phone though; he must have panicked and ran. I didn't know what to do. Anna was gasping, there was blood every time she breathed… I took off my jacket, put it under her head, screamed for help. I grabbed my phone back, called an ambulance. A man and a woman came rushing over. He took the phone from me, and I stayed with Anna. The woman was on her knees, talking to Anna, said she knew first aid. I don't know what she did. The blood...'

Thomas was staring at their hands, still joined. Catherine saw traces of vivid red staining the skin around his fingernails as he pulled away from her.

'Thomas...'

He leapt to his feet, scrubbing his hands together in a frenzy, as if trying to fling them away from his body. Catherine caught hold of him.

'They gave me some wipes in the ambulance. I thought I'd cleaned it all away...'

'Stop,' Catherine told him. Then, with authority: 'Thomas. Stop.'

The people in the corner were staring now, open-mouthed. Catherine glared at them and led Thomas away. In some nearby toilets, she washed his hands gently, as if he were a child. He still shivered, despite her coat. When his hands were clean and dry, they went back to the waiting area, where she fed coins into the drinks machine and got them both a cup of tea. She tipped three sachets of sugar into one and stirred it well before handing it to her brother.

'Were there police officers at the scene?' she asked him.

He shook his head. 'Not when we got into the ambulance, but they were on their way. I asked for both on the phone. There was an officer there wanting to talk to me, but he didn't stay long. The people who came to help us said they'd wait for the police.' He frowned, his mouth working. 'I never even thanked them.'

'We'll find them. They'll be giving statements,' Catherine reassured him. 'Drink your tea.'

Thomas took a mouthful, screwing up his face at the sweetness of it. 'I phoned Anna's parents; they're on their way. I didn't know what to say. I've only met them twice.'

'Did the paramedics tell you anything?'

His mouth trembled. 'Not as such. I was panicking, especially about the blood she was losing, but they stay calm, don't they? Amazing.'

'Thomas!' A middle-aged couple hurried towards them, worry creasing their faces. Thomas stood, tears soaking his cheeks again, disappearing as they enveloped him in a three-way hug. Thomas explained what little he knew, Anna's parents staring at him, faces pale. As they huddled together, Catherine drew away. She felt like an intruder. Anna was her colleague, her friend, but Thomas was family, someone who loved her. She looked at her brother again – his tear-stained face, Anna's mother's arm around his shoulder – and walked away, around the corner and into a darkened corridor. The lights came on above her, triggered by her movement, as she pulled out her phone. It was late, and she was being selfish. She made the call anyway. It rang for a while before she answered.

'I was asleep, Catherine.' Her voice was bleary.

'I know, I… I'm sorry. I wanted to say I'm sorry.'

There was a pause. Ellie spoke again, her voice softer now. 'No, I'm the one who should apologise. When I kissed you, I thought… Well, it obviously wasn't what you wanted.'

Catherine shook her head, helpless, fumbling for the words to describe the mess of her mind. When she and Ellie had first met, they had quickly become friends, which was all Catherine had expected. There was no attraction, at least not at first. Slowly, gradually, she

94

had begun to notice the dimple that creased Ellie's left cheek when she smiled, the hints of gold and red in her dark-blonde hair. Each time they met, she had found her gaze had lingered on Ellie's face, her lips... There had been a shift in their friendship, a charge in the glances they exchanged. Unconsciously, they sat closer together, touched each other more often. Catherine hadn't expected it, hadn't realised what was happening. And now? Now she had spoilt it.

'Catherine, I shouldn't have done it. It won't happen again.' Ellie's voice was quiet, her hurt evident.

'Ellie, I... It's not you.' Catherine closed her eyes.

Ellie's laugh was harsh. '"It's not you, it's me"? Are we at that stage already?'

'Of course not. I'm trying to explain.'

'What is there to explain? We're friends, I hoped for more. I kissed you, you ran away, you've avoided getting in touch. It seems pretty clear to me. We should say good night now, and pretend it never happened.'

'I'm away for work; it happened at the last minute. I wasn't avoiding you.' It sounded pathetic, even to her own ears.

'Away? Where?'

'Lincoln.' Catherine winced.

'Lincoln? Not Australia, not the moon. Lincoln.'

'I know. It happened quickly. I can't talk about it.'

'But you can use it as an excuse to not get in touch? Good night, Catherine.'

'Ellie, wait. I'm at the hospital.'

Breaking the news about Anna would now seem like manipulation, as if Catherine were trying to use the situation to garner some sympathy. It was a risk she had to take, because Ellie would want to know. She had met Anna, and liked her. Keeping the news from her wasn't fair.

'The hospital? What do you mean? Are you okay?'

Catherine told her as much as she knew. Ellie was shocked, expressing her disbelief, asking about Thomas and Anna's parents. 'Do you want me to come over?'

Catherine was touched, knowing how difficult it must have been for Ellie to make the offer after her rejection. It would have hurt, and she wished she had behaved differently. Ellie was right – she had invited the kiss, had wanted it, right until the second it happened. Catherine swallowed, ashamed.

'It's okay, you're in bed,' she said. 'I'll have to phone DI Knight, if someone hasn't already, and the rest of the team. Thank you though.' She felt tears in her eyes, wanting Ellie to be there, to pull her close, tell her Anna would be fine.

'Are you sure? I don't mind, honestly.'

'It'd be great to see you, but you need your rest. I'm okay, honestly.'

When they had said goodbye, Catherine selected Knight's number. He answered immediately, said he was on his way.

Then there was nothing to do but wait for news.

Chapter 13

At Phoenix House, people were drifting off to bed. Ghislaine was still reading her Agatha Christie book, keeping half an eye on Jasmine, who was chatting with the newcomer, Lee, in a corner. Her rucksack, the one she'd made such a fuss about Ghislaine touching, was on her shoulder. Jasmine was laughing as she leant towards Lee and touched his arm. Ghislaine glanced at the clock and decided she'd had enough. She went across to them.

'I'm off to bed, Jas.'

Lee looked at her with a smile. 'Yeah, it's getting late.'

'Lightweights,' Jasmine mocked.

'Early start tomorrow,' Lee told her, getting to his feet.

'Oh yeah?'

He grinned, tapping his nose. 'Got a meeting.'

'Oh right. Conference call with the Japanese office, is it?' Jasmine snorted.

'Bit closer to home than Japan. What can I say? I'm a busy man.'

He disappeared, heading for the men's bedrooms.

'Twat.' Jasmine smiled as she followed Ghislaine into their own room. 'Good-looking twat, but a twat all the same. I would though, wouldn't you?'

Ghislaine sat on her bed. 'Thought you didn't like him?'

'I don't have to like him.' Jasmine pulled off her sweat-shirt, tugged at her socks. 'What do you reckon to the copper being knifed?'

'How do you mean?'

'Reckon they'll catch him?'

'How do I know?'

Jasmine grinned as she unbuttoned her jeans. 'Couldn't find their arses with both hands. Anyway, they won't know where to look.'

In her underwear, she strutted towards the bathroom, leaving Ghislaine, unease prickling her skin, staring after her.

–

With the sides of the plastic chair digging into her thighs, her eyes scratchy and sore, and the sickening worry for Anna dominating her thoughts, Catherine was unlikely to get much rest. Unable to sit still, Thomas was pacing the small waiting area, running his hands through his hair and cracking his knuckles. Anna's parents sat close together. Mr Varcoe wiped his eyes every few seconds with a handkerchief while his wife reassured him in a voice little more than a whisper. An hour before, a nurse had informed them their daughter was still in surgery, but they had heard nothing since. Thomas finally sat on the chair beside Anna's mother, his eyes red, his voice choked.

'I'm sorry. I wish it were me in there instead of Anna.'

'Stop.' She was firm. 'This isn't your fault, Thomas.'

Her eyes were exactly like her daughter's, and Catherine had to look away, tears blurring her vision again.

Four heads snapped up as they heard footsteps approaching, but it was Jonathan Knight walking towards them, his face pale, his lips tight. As he reached Anna's parents, he held out his hand and introduced himself, offering condolences. They greeted him blankly, their eyes straying past him, towards the door the nurse had emerged from. Knight shook Thomas's hand and patted his shoulder.

'Are you okay?' Knight asked as he sat beside Catherine. She shook her head, her lips pressed together. Knight slid his arm around her trembling shoulders.

'I should be at the shelter. They lock the doors at ten thirty; it's too late now.'

Her voice was shaking too. Knight held her tighter.

'One night won't matter. I'm sure DCI Dolan will understand. Why don't you phone her?'

Catherine grimaced. 'Should I?'

'She needs to know.'

She got to her feet, knowing he was right. Around the corner, Catherine listened to the phone ring, half hoping Dolan wouldn't answer. At least she could leave a voicemail and say she'd tried.

'DS Bishop?'

It was Isla Rafferty.

'Oh, I...' Catherine's voice disappeared.

'We're still in the incident room,' Rafferty told her. 'The DCI's gone to the loo. Is there a problem?'

Rafferty's tone implied she knew there was, and she had been expecting it. Catherine explained.

'I see. I'll tell DCI Dolan. I'm sure she'll understand. We'll speak again tomorrow.'

'Thank you.' Catherine kept her tone detached, professional, to match Rafferty's, though she was surprised. There was another of Rafferty's seemingly trademark silences, long enough for Catherine to move the handset away from her ear and glance at the screen to see if she'd lost the connection. At last, Rafferty said, 'I hope she's okay.'

'Me too. But thank you.'

Rafferty cleared her throat. 'Though I'm not sure what you hope to achieve by—'

Without hesitation, Catherine cut Rafferty off midsentence, turned off the phone and shoved it in her pocket. She'd no doubt be in trouble for doing so, but she didn't care. Let Dolan complain; let Rafferty roll her eyes and sneer. It didn't matter. John McKinley was dead, and as much as Catherine wanted to find the person who had killed him, Anna Varcoe was still alive. The only people who mattered tonight were Anna, her parents and Thomas.

As she made her way back to retake her seat in the waiting area, a man appeared, dressed in dark blue scrubs, rubbing his eyes with one hand. Catherine's heart rate quickened. His expression, his posture – none of it boded well.

'Good evening. You're Anna Varcoe's family?' he asked.

'Yes,' Mrs Varcoe replied. Thomas opened his mouth to explain, but she took hold of his arm, wordlessly telling him he was family now too. He was quiet, his eyes fixed on the doctor's face. Knight glanced at Catherine with the faintest of smiles. Her hands were knotted together in her lap, dreading the medic's next words.

The doctor cleared his throat. 'I'm one of the team who's been caring for Anna. Mr and Mrs Varcoe, if you'd like to follow me?'

Mr Varcoe shook his head. 'Tell us, Doctor, please, all of us. How is she? How's Anna?'

'I'm afraid her condition has deteriorated.'

Chapter 14

Conversation hummed through the room, outrage and disbelief simmering. Mary Dolan had arrived at Lincolnshire Police's headquarters early, summoned from her hotel room by a phone call from the Chief Constable himself. She stood at the front of the briefing room as the scrum of assembled officers found themselves seats. DS Rafferty and DC Zaman sat in the front row, both looking tired. Though she was used to working with a variety of officers on different investigations, she was glad they were with her. Zaman caught her eye and smiled, while Rafferty stared straight ahead, her face blank, a notebook open on her lap.

Runnning her hands through her hair, hoping she didn't look as knackered as she felt, Dolan cleared her throat. Instantly, there was silence. Scanning their faces, she saw what she had expected – every officer in the room leaning forward, eager to hear what she had to say. There was always a buzz in the air on a new investigation, but this time, it was heightened.

'Good morning. You all know why you're here. Last night, a police officer, one of your colleagues, was attacked and left for dead.' Dolan paused as a formal photograph of Anna, proud in her uniform, was displayed on the smartboard behind her. 'Detective Constable Anna

Varcoe. Twenty-six years old, stabbed during an attempted robbery.' She fixed the assembled officers with a hard stare. 'DC Varcoe was off duty, out for the evening with her boyfriend. She's a popular, dedicated officer who's now fighting for her life. I know you'll want to find the person who did this as much as I do.'

At the back of the room, the door opened. Dolan watched as Catherine Bishop slipped inside, taking a seat in the back row. In her casual coat and jeans, her hair wild and her eyes red, Catherine drew a few glances. Dolan made eye contact, but Catherine's gaze slipped away.

'We don't have much to go on at the moment. No witnesses, except Thomas Bishop, Anna's boyfriend. We need to speak to him again today, and we're going to be looking at CCTV footage to see if anything suspicious has been recorded.'

A hand was waving on the third row.

'Do we believe whoever's been robbing people at knifepoint is the same person who stabbed DC Varcoe?' The hand belonged to a man with a shaved head and dark eyes.

'According to the intial statement we had from Thomas Bishop, yes. I think we have to assume he is, at least until we know more.'

'What about him, the boyfriend?' He leant forward, tugging at his tie with a grimace. He wore a pale-blue shirt, the collar too tight, his neck reddening above it. 'Are we sure he's as innocent as he's making out?'

Dolan glanced at Catherine Bishop. She was huddled into her jacket, her face impassive. Though she'd asked Catherine to come to the station, she hadn't expected her to be present at this briefing. There was no way she would be allowed to work on the case, not when the victim was one of her closest colleagues, especially not with the family connection, as Catherine would know. Dolan could only assume she had decided to sit in anyway. She wasn't going to ask Catherine what the hell she was playing at, not here, not publically. Not yet. She turned back to the officer who had been questioning her about Thomas Bishop, fixing him with a scowl.

'What's your name?' she demanded.

He grinned, enjoying himself, pleased to have got a reaction. 'Melis, ma'am. DS Giles Melis.'

Dolan inclined her head, mentally telling herself to stay calm. She needed every officer in the room on her side, and tearing one of their colleagues to shreds in front of them on the first morning of the investigation wasn't going to help. She forced a smile.

'As I said, DS Melis, we need to talk to him again,' she said. 'We've no reason to believe he's lying to us, but of course we can't take his word for it either, especially as we can't talk to DC Varcoe yet.'

'Any idea when she'll be well enough to give a statement?' Melis again. Could no one else in the room speak?

'No. No idea. Any other questions?' *From someone else,* her tone implied. Melis sat back, arms folded, apparently satisfied. There was a silence. Dolan waited for a few seconds.

'As you'll appreciate, there's a lot of interest in this case, both from the public and from the media.' She took a few paces to her left, frowning, gathering her thoughts. There would be no need to rally these officers – the person who had stabbed one of their 'family' had already given them all the motivation they would need to track him down.

'It's unlikely DC Varcoe was deliberately targeted because she's a police officer, but we need to keep the possibility in mind,' Dolan continued. 'Whoever did this has already threatened and robbed three other couples. Last night, he almost killed Anna Varcoe. She's still critically ill, nowhere near out of the woods yet. Let's find him, and quickly.' She waved a hand towards Isla Rafferty, who was studying her notebook. 'Most of you don't know DS Rafferty: she's there on the front row. Talk to her or DS Barnard; they'll tell you what you're doing today. See you all back here at six o'clock.'

There was shuffling and muttering as chairs were pushed back. Dolan watched as Rafferty got to her feet and made her way over to a corner. Though she knew she had to pass on the actions that Dolan had agreed to the detective constables and unformed officers, Rafferty's expression was stern as she frowned over her notepad. It was no surprise when most of the officers in the room made for Barnard, who stood in the centre of room, relaxed and ready to exchange a few words, give out instructions. He was familiar to them, of course, but it wasn't the only reason. Barnard was approachable, radiating calmness and capability, while Rafferty built an invisible wall around herself and ducked behind it. Dolan hid a smile as Adil Zaman glanced at the crowd gathering around Barnard, but dragged himself towards Rafferty, the first person to even look at her. Dolan shook her head and strode over, jerking a thumb towards Rafferty's corner.

'Come on, let's be sensible. Half of you, over there please. DS Rafferty doesn't bite.'

'Are you sure?' someone muttered, and there were a few amused snorts.

Dolan set her jaw. 'Come on, move it. Or do I have to divide you myself, as if you're at primary school?'

Reluctantly, they went. Rafferty raised her head, flashing Dolan a look which wasn't easy to interpret. Gratitude? Defiance? Shame? Possibly all three. Dolan turned away, masking her irritation. Rafferty was a mystery; a capable, thorough officer with the people skills of a stone. She was excellent in the interview room, but not good at a hospital bedside. Yet Dolan believed in her, trusted her, without truly understanding why. Zaman was an open book: pleasant, likeable, transparent. Easy to work with, keen to learn. Rafferty was prickly, warning people off with a snarl, like a bad-tempered dog. Dolan looked at Rafferty again, who was reading quietly from her notebook while the crowd around her nudged each other, smirking. Perhaps she should talk to her. Was Rafferty unhappy? Perhaps she'd be better suited to another team, another boss? Dolan knew she wasn't the most patient of people, but she baulked at the idea of transferring Rafferty out of her team. Rafferty was a DS and managing people was part of her job, as she would have known when she was promoted. What was her problem?

Catherine was aware of the interest of the officers passing her, on their way to talk to witnesses or join the fingertip search of the area where Anna had been attacked. She knew she must look awful, conscious she was in need of a meal, a shower and a change of clothes. Leaning against the wall, she watched them pass, detached, as though there were a pane of glass between them and herself. The first day of an investigation was always vital, and extremely busy – statements to be taken before witnesses forgot what they had seen, briefings, media updates. Yet for Catherine herself, there was no urgency. She could see the purpose on the faces of the officers in the room, the determination to find the person who had attacked them all, in a sense. Dolan looked tense, tightly coiled. And Catherine, who knew Anna, who worked with her, chatted with her, laughed with her – Catherine could do nothing. She knew what Dolan would say: *Get back out onto the street, dig around, make yourself useful. You already have your assignement. Why are you here?* It was what she would point out, in Dolan's position.

Catherine watched as Dolan stalked across the room, waving a hand at Isla Rafferty. A thin stream of officers drifted towards Rafferty's corner. Dolan was clearly used to people doing as she told them – a leader. Dolan's face was grim, her mouth an angry line. Today she wore a charcoal suit, her hands on her hips, shoulders hunched, her green eyes narrowed. Catherine pushed herself away from the wall. Time to piss her off a little more.

'Ma'am?'

Dolan turned, still scowling. 'Catherine. I didn't expect to see you here.'

As predicted. 'I wanted to know what was going on.'

'And so you decided to sit in?' Dolan was controlling her temper, but Catherine knew she was on thin ground.

'I'm sorry,' she said. 'Anna's my friend.'

Dolan sighed, her expression softening. 'I know. Look, let's go and talk.'

They went to the small, cold room where they had discussed Catherine's assignment. On the wall, the battered face of John McKinley was still displayed.

Though Catherine knew it was her imagination, as she crossed the room she saw a note of reproach in his swollen, unseeing eyes. She had done nothing to discover who had killed him, and here she was, hanging around Headquarters instead of being out on the street. She dragged out a chair and sat at Rafferty's desk while Dolan remained on her feet, staring at the photograph of McKinley. With a sigh, she turned away, frowning at Catherine as she took her mobile phone from her jacket pocket. She examined the screen, now hiding a smile. It was unfair, Catherine knew, but she felt a spike of resentment as she watched Dolan tap out a reply. Her expression suggested the message was not work related, and Catherine's annoyance grew. Anna was lying in hospital, hooked up to machines and equipment, hanging onto life by her fingernails, and the DCI in charge of finding the person who had attacked her was busy sending soppy texts.

Shoving the phone into her handbag, Dolan cleared her throat. 'My daughter,' she said, her tone clipped. 'She's at university.'

Catherine was surprised Mary Dolan was old enough to have a child in higher education, though she was careful not to show it. Dolan ran a hand across her eyes, her mouth. She stood for a moment before dropping heavily into the chair beside Catherine's. The perfume again; the charge of electricity shooting along Catherine's spine. The warmth in her belly.

Dolan laid her hands on the tabletop, palms down, and as she did so the cuffs of her black shirt pulled back, revealing scars across Dolan's wrists, white against her tanned skin. Not on the back, where a person intent on suicide might make determined incisions, but on the front. Catherine stared at them, concerned, her mind grasping at possibilities, none of them pleasant. With swift movements, the DCI tugged her sleeves back into place. There was a pause. Catherine waited for Dolan to explain the old injuries, but when she spoke again, it was about her daughter.

'I gave birth the month before my eighteenth birthday. It was a surprise, a shock. A disaster at the time. Getting pregnant halfway through my A levels wasn't part of the plan.' Pushing her chair back, Dolan balanced on two legs. 'I wanted to do a degree – biology.' She snorted. 'Some biology student I was. Obviously missed the lesson on contraception.'

Catherine was silent as she considered this. Her attraction to Dolan had to be controlled. Dolan was her superior officer, and was making a point of telling Catherine about her daughter. Was it a hint, perhaps a warning?

Dolan rocked on the chair a few more times and allowed its legs to thud onto the carpet. 'My parents were gutted, but in the end, they helped. More than her dad did, anyway. I lived at home, studied at the local university. After graduation, I joined the force.'

'Can't have been easy.' Catherine knew she should speak, though she wasn't certain why Dolan was telling her this.

Dolan waved the comment away. 'I know you want to go out and find the person who stabbed Anna. I understand. What *you* need to understand is, it isn't going to happen. You're too close to her. Your boss is on his way over though.'

Catherine stared. 'DI Knight? Why?'

'Superintendent Stringer suggested it. Things a bit slack back at your station in Northolme, are they?'

'No.' But Catherine remembered what Knight had said: '*How long do you think Northolme will be able to justify having a team of detectives based here?*' Perhaps the end of their station was coming sooner than they had guessed. Dolan half-turned in her chair.

'The Super no doubt has her reasons,' she said.

A blush rose in Catherine's cheeks as she considered it. Why would Jane Stringer want Knight here in Lincoln? For a moment, she considered telling Mary Dolan everything: her worries, her fears, her concerns about Knight. Dolan looked again at the picture of John McKinley on the wall. 'He's your priority, Catherine. Someone killed him – find them. He was a police officer, the same as Anna is.'

Catherine bridled. 'I know.'

There was a silence, long enough for Catherine to regret her tone. Making an enemy of Dolan as well as Rafferty would not be a good idea.

'You asked if I knew John McKinley,' Dolan said. 'I didn't tell you everything.'

'You said you worked with him briefly.'

'And I did. It was a missing child case, a four-year-old. The parents were desperate, or seemed to be.'

'They knew more than they let on?'

'They'd killed her.' Dolan's voice was flat. 'The dad had, anyway. His wife was too terrified of him to tell the truth, at least at first. John McKinley managed to get her to open up. He was kind to her. You can imagine, he was one of very few people who were. Not that it helped her, in the end.' Dolan swallowed, then spread her hands.

'What I'm trying to say is, we'll find who stabbed Anna. Someone must know who did it, seen him running away, whatever. John McKinley deserves our attention too, and we're no further on with finding who killed him. I know it's hard when your family are involved. The murder, the four-year-old – my daughter was the same age. I used to go home at night, watch her sleep, ask myself why I was getting involved in such shitty cases when I could have been at home with her.'

'My ex was a teacher. She used to sit at the dining table at night, marking essays while I was in the shower, trying to wash the smell of blood and death away.'

'Never goes though, does it?' Dolan's laugh was forced. 'We carry it around, forever proabably. Might be the reason why most of us are single. Listen, Catherine. I need you back on the street, back at the shelter. Give it a couple of days.'

'Okay. You can't imagine my brother was involved?' The memory of Thomas in the hospital, the blood on his hands. The anguish on his face, in his voice.

Dolan shook her head. 'Because of what Melis said? Ignore him. He wanted a reaction.'

'But he didn't know who I was; he couldn't have done. I've never seen him before.'

'Doesn't matter. He was letting me know he was there, being provocative. He must have known what he was saying was bollocks.' Dolan stood, rubbed the small of her back. 'I'll ring you later today, or Isla will. How are you finding DS Rafferty, by the way?'

Catherine hesitated, and Dolan pounced. 'Knew it. She's pissed you off. Isla can be difficult. Stay patient, though. You want her on your side.'

Catherine wanted to ask why she should be expected to make the effort, when it seemed Rafferty would be making none. Still, Dolan had said she would only be needed for a few days, and soon she would wave Rafferty goodbye. It was some comfort as she stepped outside and discovered it was raining again.

Chapter 15

Jasmine shook back her hair and watched Joel Rushford's eyes scan the room until he found her. He might be a vicar, but he was a man like any other. She lifted her chin and licked her lips, meeting his gaze, knowing he would be the first to look away. He was smooth, confident, especially here, in the confines of his church. But Jasmine knew how vulnerable he was. He had secrets; everyone did. The trick was finding them out – one of Jasmine's talents. There were others, though not to be dwelled on in church.

Jasmine shuffled forward, nearing the front of the queue. Soup again. Fucking soup. Crappy bread and a smear of margarine. She wasn't ungrateful – they fed you for next to nothing after all, but Jesus. Would it kill them to make sandwiches more than once a week? She nudged Ghislaine.

'What do you reckon would happen if we asked for a steak?'

Ghislaine shook her head. 'You might get oxtail soup if you're lucky. I'm nipping to the loo.'

Jasmine turned, annoyed Ghislaine had waited until now, with only three people in front of them. 'Fuck's sake...'

Ghislaine had gone, the door swinging closed behind her.

The corridor was cold, the outside door standing ajar, allowing a draught to chill the air. Ghislaine pulled her satchel higher onto her shoulder as she hurried towards the toilets. The dull ache low in her stomach and the date told their own story. How she was supposed to buy tampons and sanitary towels with only two pounds in her purse was another. She pushed open the door to the Ladies and stepped inside, her nose immediately assaulted by the huge bowl of lavender scented potpourri one of the good ladies of the church had left on the windowsill. She set her bag by the sinks and turned towards the cubicles. As she was sliding the lock into place, she heard footsteps. The cubicle door was pushed hard from the outside. Ghislaine stepped back, shocked, her hands in front of her face to protect herself. A face appeared in the gap between the side of the cubicle and the door, a male face. Lee, the new man at the shelter, the one who had bought her and Jasmine's drinks at the cafe the previous day. The one who had made her uneasy each time she had met him. He grinned at her, pulling the door open fully, rocking back on his heels as if him being there in the women's toilets, forcing his way into her cubicle, was perfectly fine.

'What are you doing?' Ghislaine managed to say.

'Wanted a quiet chat.'

He was still smirking. Ghislaine's initial terror was rapidly giving way to fury, and she took a step towards him. Her hands went to her hips, chin jutting.

'A chat? You barge in here...'

He held up both hands in a gesture which was meant to be placatory, but only served to infuriate her more.

'Can't you read?' She jabbed a finger towards the door. 'This is the Ladies.'

'Yeah, I know.' He lifted his shoulders, trying for a charming smile. It left Ghislaine cold. 'I wanted to talk to you without your mate listening in.'

Fighting to control her breathing, not wanting him to see how rattled she was, Ghislaine braced her hands against the sides of the cubicle doorway. She wished, as she had on many occasions during her time living on the streets, that she had had some self-defence training, but two steps forward and her boot in his groin was a fairly straightforward move. As if reading her mind, he shifted his body, angling it away from her.

'Well, I don't want to talk to you.' Ghislaine's voice was quiet but emphatic. 'There are loads of people in the church hall, some in the corridor. Get out of here now, or I'll scream the place down.'

He tilted his head, obviously finding her amusing. 'Scream? You reckon?'

Three paces and his hand was at her throat, his face close enough for her to smell coffee on his breath. Terror hurtled through her, her mind careering out of control. He wasn't hurting her, not yet, but the threat was there, the implication being he could if he wanted to. She shrank in his grasp, powerless as a mouse with a cat's paw curled around it, planning her next move. Stamp on his toes, boot his shin or wait it out? He could hurt her, she knew. Kill her even. There were people around, it was true, but he could slip away unnoticed. And who would miss her? Jasmine would notice her absence, but if she was talking, flirting, she would be a while. Her body might be found quickly, but he could jump on a train, catch a bus, lose himself in the warren of streets.

He brought his face even closer, his breath warm against her ear. She wriggled as he spoke. 'Now, all I want to do is talk. Don't scream, don't make a sound, and I'll let you go. Do you understand?'

She glared, hating him. Because he was taller, stronger, he assumed she would have to do what he said, that he could manipulate her in any way he chose and she would be compliant. At last she nodded, pressing her lips together. He let her go and turned away, wiped his hands on his jeans. Noticing the movement, she sneered.

'What's wrong, you think I'm dirty? I had a shower this morning.'

He frowned, shaking his head. A flicker of emotion passed over his face, quickly enough for Ghislaine to believe she was mistaken.

Shame.

'I'm sorry,' he told her. 'I shouldn't have...'

She raised her hand to her throat, soothing the skin his touch had burned.

'No, you shouldn't.'

He was quiet, watching her. The skin wasn't tender – his movement had been quick, not painful, but like most of the men she had met before, he believed he could take anything he wanted from her without consent.

'I want to talk to you about John McKinley,' he said.

'He's dead.'

He was still blocking her path, and Ghislaine took a step to the side, desperate to get out. He mirrored the movement.

'You must have talked to him?'

116

She shook her head. 'No. Well, once or twice. We said hello, no more. Now let me out.'

'Not until you've answered my questions.'

'Why should I? Anyway, I've told you, I never spoke to him.'

He stepped closer, forcing her to move back against the wall, trapping her there. 'I said I don't want to hurt you.'

'So let me leave.'

She whipped a hand towards him, not even sure what she was aiming for. He grabbed her wrist, kept hold of it.

'Listen. Someone killed John McKinley, and I want to know who.'

She struggled, trying to wrestle her arm away, but he kept hold. 'What are you talking about? He died of an overdose.'

'Yeah, he may have done, but who gave it to him?'

'You're making no sense. Why should I listen to someone who tried to strangle me?'

'I needed you to listen.' His voice was low, dangerous.

'And you thought this was the best way to get my attention?'

'I've learnt… Well, I've been living somewhere rough. Things kicked off ten times a day.'

'And? You grab someone by the throat, and expect them not to mind? Tell them you've had a hard time and ask them to forgive you?'

Prison. He was talking about prison, she guessed. Like she'd never met anyone who had been in prison before. How long had he been on the street? There were loads of ex-cons, ex-forces too. People who could look after themselves, people who fought dirty, those who had learnt the hard way how to survive. He was nothing special.

He ignored her, his voice animated now. 'The police are keeping it quiet. What does it matter if a homeless person overdoses? Got what he deserved; you mess with drugs and overdoses happen. Bloke on the streets, no one to care, why should they waste time and money finding out who killed him?'

His mouth twisted as he finally let her arm drop. Ghislaine glanced over his shoulder. Could she push past him? Was it worth the risk?

'You seem to know plenty about it. More than me. Like I said, I can't help you,' she told him, desperation evident in her voice. 'Anyway, why do you care?'

'I don't. But someone needs punishing for it, and the police don't give a shit. It could be any one of us, you know. Cremated on the cheap, investigation closed. No one giving a toss if we're alive or dead.'

He glanced over his shoulder as Ghislaine stiffened at the sound of footsteps approaching. He hurried into a cubicle and slammed the door behind him. Ghislaine saw her face in the mirror, pale even to her own eyes. Here was her chance to get away from him. She grabbed her bag, still on the floor by the sinks where she'd left it. She would skip the soup, text Jasmine some excuse and find another toilet.

Perhaps a doorway would be better than the shelter tonight?

–

Catherine paused, certain she had heard a man's voice. Since the Gents was nowhere in sight, he must be in the women's toilets. Why? His tone had been curt, possibly threatening. Several possibilities crossed her mind, none of them pleasant. As a police officer, her instinct was to march in and and see what was happening. In her current guise, however, she should turn and walk away.

As she dithered, a young woman emerged from the toilets. She was clearly holding back tears, her cheeks red. Catherine made her decision.

'Are you okay?'

She took a step back, and Catherine recognised her. She was one of the women she had seen here yesterday, who had passed her as she summoned the courage to go further into the church. Not the taller woman, the shorter one who hadn't spoken.

'I'm fine.' She flicked a glance over her shoulder.

Catherine wasn't convinced. 'Did something happen in there?'

'I was talking to someone.' She heaved her bag onto her shoulder, clearly ready to make a run for it. Catherine stepped closer.

'I heard a man's voice, sounded like he was threatening you. Are you sure you're all right?'

'You heard a voice? Maybe you should see a doctor. Listen, I need to go.'

'Did he hurt you?'

She glared. 'Who are you, my mum? It's none of your business.'

'I'm not old enough to be your mum.'

'Funny. Plus, my mum wouldn't give a shit. Leave me alone, all right?'

Catherine raised her hands. 'Fine. I only wanted to help.'

'Help?' Her voice was pure scorn.

Groaning inwardly, Catherine realised she had gone too far. She should have walked back into the soup kitchen, pretended she hadn't heard a thing.

'I'm sorry. You're right, it's nothing to do with me.'

The other woman studied her face, frowning. 'You were here yesterday.'

'Yeah.'

'Didn't they tell you to come to Phoenix House for the night?'

'They did, but...' *Watch what you say*, Catherine told herself. 'I didn't fancy it in the end. Found a doorway near the cathedral.'

Blue-grey eyes assessed her. 'Must have been cold with no sleeping bag.'

Shit. Catherine smiled. 'Yeah, I was freezing. It was my first night on the street. I'm not exactly an expert.'

'So I see.' She gave another glance towards the toilet door. 'I could show you a few safe places to sleep if you don't want to come to the shelter. It's not for everyone. Some nights I don't go there myself. It depends who's around.'

Catherine couldn't believe her luck. 'It's kind of you. Thanks.'

She shrugged. 'No problem. I know how shit it is when you're new. Cold, miserable and fucking scary.'

'Tell me about it. I'm Catherine, by the way.'

They were walking now, towards the church's outside door.

'My name's Ghislaine. Do you want to get us some soup? I'll wait outside.'

Catherine nodded, and hurried through. Ghislaine Oliver, one of the women Dolan had told her about. Would her new friend wait? Only one way to find out.

–

Outside the church, Ghislaine shrank against the wall, hoping Lee would stay inside until she had disappeared. She would never usually have talked to a stranger as freely as she had to Catherine, but there was an air of sadness and defeat about her she recognised. Homeless people were no different to the wider population, Ghislaine knew – every person and their story were unique. Some might believe people were on the street because of their own actions, because of addiction, laziness or crime. It wasn't true, not for most of them. She had seen addicts, of course she had, but she had also seen people with mental health problems, people who had been kicked out of their family home, people who had lost their jobs and simply couldn't afford their rent any longer. Those who left foster care or children's homes, with nowhere to go but the streets. And those like her, whose family homes weren't safe. Ghislaine pushed the thought away, because with it came the memories and she refused to give them space in her head. She might carry them with her, polluting her past and tainting her future, but she had taken back control of her life. She smiled, remembering. He had been respected, especially in his work, but his true nature had been hidden from the public gaze. To those who were vulnerable though, he was a monster. He had terrorised her, colouring her view of herself and the world around her. She had punished him, in the end. He would not ruin her life.

Most importantly, he would never hurt another child.

Chapter 16

The table was strewn with spilled salt and smears of tomato ketchup, but it was in a quiet corner. Catherine set the tray of food on it. The small cups of soup hadn't been particularly filling, and she had offered to buy Ghislaine a meal in McDonald's. She was wary of appearing too generous or, worse, overfamiliar, but Ghislaine had smiled.

'Cheers. I've not had a burger in months.'

She had disappeared into the toilets as soon as they entered the restaurant, leaving Catherine to order. When Ghislaine crossed to the table, eyes on the floor, Catherine studied her. She looked so young with her pale skin and wide eyes. She was skinny, her jeans and sweatshirt hanging loose. Her shoes were battered canvas pumps, fine for the coming months, but Catherine hoped she would be able to find sturdier footwear before another winter set in. She doubted it. Ghislaine sat, and Catherine passed her food across.

'You didn't need to do this, you know,' Ghislaine said, grabbing a handful of fries. 'You should save your money.' She opened the cardboard carton and lifted her burger, sinking her teeth into it with a sigh.

'It's fine. It's not mine anyway,' Catherine replied without thinking. Ghislaine stopped chewing, and Catherine quickly back-pedalled. 'I took it from the bastard I used to live with.' She focused on her food, ignoring the pang of conscience that followed the lie.

Ghislaine ate for a while before saying, 'You're here because of your bloke?'

'Yeah. I'd had enough.'

'Must have been bad if you'd sooner be on the street.'

Catherine swallowed. 'It was.'

Unperturbed, Ghislaine kept chewing. They ate the rest of the meal in silence. When she'd finished, Ghislaine sat back and picked up her milkshake. 'So what did your boyfriend do? Knock you around?'

'Sometimes.'

'Left your face alone though.'

'Don't they always?'

'My mum's boyfriend didn't.'

There was a silence. Catherine considered sending Rafferty a text, asking her to find the man Ghislaine had mentioned. See if there was anything they could arrest him for. She knew she should bring the conversation around to John McKinley, but she wanted Ghislaine to trust her first. She had to confide in her, even if the details were far from truthful.

'Where are good places to sleep in Lincoln?' Catherine asked.

'Around the college. Bit of privacy, and shelter. There's an art gallery, more out of the way. Around there's okay too, there's a sort of pavilion thing. You're taking risks sleeping alone anywhere though.'

'Because I'm a woman?'

'Yeah. Some of the things I've seen, stories I've heard – assault, rape...' Ghislaine shuddered. 'You don't want to know. You'll see, though. Some knobhead will find you, give you a line, not want to take no for an answer.'

'Has it happened to you?'

Ghislaie laughed. 'I stay close to other people, though sometimes they're the problem.'

'Safety in numbers.'

'Yeah.'

'What about the man in the toilets?'

Taking another long drink of her milkshake, Ghislaine sat back in her chair. She took her time before finally replying.

'Lee. He's stayed at the shelter a few times. He was asking about someone I knew.'

'Knew?'

'He told me the best places to sleep when I got here, the same ones I'm telling you about now. Mackie. Nice bloke. Looked out for people.'

Catherine lifted her own drink, sipping at it slowly while she decided what to say. 'What happened to him?'

'People come and go. Some are offered housing, some go home, some move on to another city. Some die. Mackie was one of them.'

'That's awful.'

'Yeah. I heard Mackie died of an overdose. I've seen it a few times – people drift off and never wake up. Mackie though, he never seemed like a user, not when I knew him. I hadn't seen him for a while; he stayed out all weathers. But to be killed...'

Catherine looked at her sharply as Ghislaine covered her mouth.

Ten minutes later, Catherine left the restaurant and headed for the hill. She needed to speak to Dolan, Rafferty as a last resort, but first there was a visit she needed to make.

Chapter 17

Catherine was told Anna's bed was in the far corner of the intensive care unit. She crossed the ward, conscious of the sound of her footsteps as she passed the other beds, most of which were occupied. Relatives or friends sat quietly, while nurses and doctors flitted around like worker bees.

Though the ICU was quieter than Catherine had expected, there was a sense in the cool air that time here stood still. Each patient, each relative, had paused. Waiting for news, hoping for a change in condition. Death whispered from the walls, a quiet, almost comforting presence. The unit seemed to Catherine like another world. A tiny pocket, where a movement, an alarm, a tiny, imperceptable shift, could be the difference. The living and the dead clung close together here. A place where people held their breath, and hoped.

She tried to keep her eyes on Thomas as she walked. He sat in a chair by Anna's bed, his head bowed. Passing the beds, however, it was impossible not to absorb details of the people she saw in the second she was part of their world. A young man, his eyes sore and swollen, a tattered tissue hanging from his hand, looked dazed as a woman clutched at his arm. They stood by a bed where another man lay, vivid red and purple bruising discolouring his face, his head bandaged. A multitude of mysterious tubes breathed and drained while monitors sang out messages.

An elderly woman was hunched in a chair, her twisted finger marking her place on a page of prose. She sat next to a bed where a man, his eyes closed, his chest bare, lay silent as she read to him, her voice calm but her hand trembling.

Anna wore a pale-blue hospital gown. She lay on her back, her face turned towards Thomas, her eyes closed. From the other side of the bed, plastic tubes, supported by a metal arm, snaked over the bed. One led to the mask over Anna's mouth and nose, another disappeared under the thin white blanket covering her lower body. Several bags of fluid hung from a stand positioned at the head of the bed, next to a bank of monitors. Creeping forward, Catherine tried to remember Anna was still there, under all the equipment, but it wasn't easy. She remembered Anna as she'd last seen her – at her desk in their office, phone in her hand, as Catherine had seen her hundreds of times before.

'She's worse.' Thomas' voice was quiet, colourless, as if all the hope had been washed out of him. Catherine stood beside him, squeezing his shoulder as nausea rolled around her gut.

'Worse?'

'An infection. I don't know how, it's spotless in here, and we're always using the hand scrub, keeping ourselves clean. We've been careful. They're doing what they can, I know, but it's the last thing she needs. They're talking about moving her to an isolation room.'

Catherine swallowed. She leant forward, gently touching Anna's hand where it lay on the blanket, averting her eyes from the cannula.

'How long have you been here?' she asked her brother. 'Have you had any sleep? Food?'

Thomas sat straighter. 'How long? I'm not sure. Pretty much all the time. The nurses send you out sometimes so they can do what they need to.' He blinked rapidly, lifting his hand to stroke Anna's cheek. 'This is shit, Catherine. Anna doesn't deserve this. It could kill her, you know.'

Catherine stepped closer and wrapped an arm around his trembling shoulders. 'Shush, Thomas.'

'She can't hear us.' He fumbled a tissue from his pocket and scrubbed at his eyes.

'You never know. Listen to me – she'll be okay.'

'So I keep telling her parents. We all say it to each other, but I'm not sure of any of us believe it.'

He threw himself back in the chair, the legs squealing against the floor. A nurse glanced their way with a frown.

'Come on, Thomas, this is isn't like you. Where are Mr and Mrs Varcoe?'

'Gone for some food. They've been here most of the night. Mum and Dad have been in too. You're only meant to have two visitors to a bed, so we took it in turns.'

'Shouldn't you go home, have a shower, get some rest?'

Thomas sniffed, taking in her appearance. 'Shouldn't you?'

Catherine ignored him. 'Go. I'll stay with Anna.'

'What about your training course?' He raised tired eyes, rasping a hand across his stubble.

'It's fine. Go on, Thomas.'

Should she be persuading him to leave the hospital when she knew Dolan was sending officers to speak to him again? But he was obviously exhausted. Thomas heaved himself to his feet.

'All right. Will you tell Anna's parents I'll be back this evening?'

He leant forward to stroke Anna's hair. As he passed Catherine, he kissed her cheek. Tears welled in Catherine's eyes as she watched him lurch towards the door. Her brother, usually happy-go-lucky, now grey and drawn. She reached again for Anna's hand.

Chapter 18

'What did you tell her?' Jasmine asked.

'I mentioned a few safe places to sleep.'

'Not the squat?'

'The squat? The one where you lived? I don't even know where it is.'

Jasmine smiled, satisfied. 'Lee was looking for you at the soup kitchen.'

Ghislaine stiffened. Noticing the movement, Jasmine grinned.

'About time you had a boyfriend.'

'Give up, Jas.'

'What happened?'

Ghislaine blushed. 'Nothing.'

'Come on, Ghis, tell me. What have you been doing?' Jasmine's eyes widened. 'They say it's always the quiet ones. Can't let you out of my sight, can I?'

They were in a pub; not the seedy, grubby one Jasmine usually favoured, but one of the chain bars in the city centre. Half a lager each meant they could sit at a table in the corner, out of the way, and enjoy the warmth for an hour. Ghislaine always worried how long they'd be tolerated. Jasmine wouldn't have given it a thought, would relish a slanging match with the bar staff if they were challenged.

'We only talked.'

'Oh? I had a "talk" with our sweet and innocent vicar earlier,' Jasmine leered.

'He hurt me, all right?' Ghislaine mumbled. She hadn't wanted to confide in Jasmine, but her friend was relentless if she suspected information was being kept from her. She ignored the comment about Jasmine and the vicar. Jasmine had been boasting about her fling with him for weeks, but Ghislaine only half believed it. Jasmine wasn't known for her truthfulness, and was never one to let facts get in the way of a good story. Joel Rushford was attractive, Ghislaine had to admit, and Jasmine had her sights set on him. Whether he reciprocated her feelings was another matter.

'Hurt you?' Immediately, Jasmine shoved back her chair. 'The fucker. I'll kill him.'

Ghislaine sighed. 'Not what I meant, Jas.'

Jasmine's assumption that the violence had been sexual told Ghislaine more about her life than any amount of night terrors ever would. Jasmine believed she was the one who protected Ghislaine, but it wasn't true. Beneath the brash exterior, the loud clothes and make-up, the persona, hid the real Jasmine: a tiny, terrified girl whose childhood had been obliterated by the abuse she had endured. Ghislaine didn't know the details, but she recognised a survivor when she saw one. She should; she was one herself.

'So what did you mean?' Reluctantly, Jasmine lowered herself back onto her chair and swigged from her glass.

Ghislaine told her about the altercation at the church, while Jasmine listened, frowning.

'He says Mackie was killed? Murdered?'

'Yeah.'

'Fuck.' Jasmine wouldn't look at Ghislaine now, her eyes darting from side to side. Ghislaine watched, disconcerted.

'Where did you go after the soup kitchen?' she asked.

Jasmine bristled. 'Why?'

'No reason.'

'The squat, if you must know. Saw a few old mates.'

'Right.'

'Had a chat. Had a drink. Didn't do any smack.'

'I didn't—'

'I'm not stupid, Ghis. It's poison.'

'Come on, Jas. I know you're not…'

'Turned my back on my old life months ago.' Jasmine was becoming increasingly agitated, shifting in her seat, rubbing her arms. Ghislaine watched, dismayed.

'Listen, I'm going to head off,' Jasmine told her. 'You can have the rest of my drink. I'll see you later.'

Ghislaine wanted to say more, offer an apology, but Jasmine was gone. Taking a long swallow of her lager, Ghislaine came to a decision.

She slipped out of her chair and hurried to the pub's main door, dodging a crowd of students clustering around the pool table. Jasmine was still in sight, her rucksack on one shoulder, moving quickly. Ghislaine left the pub and followed her.

Chapter 19

'We're still looking for the knife,' Mary Dolan said. Standing in front of a large whiteboard with Anna Varcoe's name scrawled in capital letters at the top, she was explaining their progress to DI Jonathan Knight. It wouldn't take long. DCI Dolan looked tired, and she was going to be under increasing pressure to obtain results, a conviction. He'd had to push his way through a scrum of journalists as he approached Lincolnshire Police's Headquarters, many of whom had seen Knight as fair game. Despite his protests, he'd been photographed, even filmed, as he crossed the car park. He had to admit, looking at the statements and evidence which had been collected, that there wasn't much to go on. Appeals were being made in the media for any witnesses to the assault on Anna to come forward but so far, aside from the ones who gave first aid, no one had.

'It's hard to believe in a city centre there were no other witnesses at all,' Knight said.

'Which is why one of the officers here suggested Thomas Bishop may know more than he's letting on.'

Knight raised his eyebrows. 'Thomas?'

'Of course, you'll know him.' Dolan didn't look impressed.

'Not well, though I'd be surprised if he were involved.' Thomas had seemed to Knight to be a nice bloke – decent, if a little immature.

'Everyone's always surprised when someone they know is involved,' Dolan snapped. She ran her hands through her hair. 'Sorry. Uncalled for. It's bloody frustrating. Whoever stabbed Anna must have had blood on his hands, his clothes. There were people around, drinking, out for meals, whatever. But we have nothing.'

'It's early days.' Knight turned away from the whiteboard, frowning.

'Tell the press and the Superintendent that.' Dolan grimaced.

'Have you heard from Catherine today?'

'Catherine Bishop? I've seen her. She arrived here this morning, wanting to work on Anna's case.'

'Doesn't surprise me.'

'I told her we need her to carry on at Phoenix House, regardless of what's happened.'

'And she agreed?'

Dolan gave him a stern look. 'She didn't have much choice.'

There was a knock on the door, and DS Rafferty came in. Dolan introduced her, and Rafferty managed a curt nod in Knight's direction as he smiled at her.

'Ma'am, DS Bishop's here,' Rafferty said.

'Again? Speak of the devil.' Dolan moved to a chair and sat with a weary sigh. 'Thanks, Isla. You'd better bring her in.'

Rafferty opened the door wide, and Catherine appeared. Knight was immediately struck by her unkempt appearance. It was less than twenty-four hours since their last meeting, but Catherine already looked thinner and paler than she had the previous night. Her hair badly needed a wash, and her clothes were grubby. Glancing from Dolan to Knight, Catherine seemed apprehensive.

'What are you doing back here, DS Bishop?' Dolan asked.

'I have some information.'

'Is there a problem with your phone?' Rafferty sniped. Catherine narrowed her eyes. Knight was silent, resenting Rafferty's tone but knowing this was not his argument.

'I've been told John McKinley was a friend to people he met on the street. He advised them, looked out for them,' Catherine said.

'That's all?' Rafferty was incredulous.

'Thank you, Isla.' Dolan rocked back on her chair, folding her arms. 'Anything else, Catherine? As I told you a few hours ago, we need you on the street.'

Catherine lifted her chin. 'I've also been told Lee Collinson believes Mackie was murdered. How did he know?'

There was a silence. Rafferty went over to a computer and tapped a few keys.

'John McKinley left the force years before Lee Collinson was arrested. Collinson has only recently arrived at Phoenix House, and says in his statement he never met McKinley.'

'I doubt there's a motive there.' Dolan's lips tightened. 'Anyway, if he injected McKinley, why would he draw attention to himself? We need to find out how he knew the truth about McKinley's death.'

Catherine shook her head. 'I couldn't push, not without raising suspicion.'

'Even the press hasn't ferreted the truth out yet,' Dolan said.

Rafferty inspected her fingernails. 'It doesn't matter to them.'

'We can't bring him in,' Knight said.

'No, we can't. It would be obvious where the information had come from. It's up to you, Catherine. Talk to him. Try to find out what he knows.' Dolan stood. 'I know you've not had much time, but we don't have any real suspects, which needs to change.'

Knight saw Catherine clench her jaw, angered by the dismissal. He could sympathise. Working with new people was never easy, and Catherine's assignment made the situation more complicated. The animosity between Catherine and the other DS, Rafferty, was also clear.

'I'll be off.' Catherine turned on her heel.

'Keep in touch.' Dolan was already back at the whiteboard, while Rafferty was still at the computer. Neither of them saw Knight walk out behind Catherine.

He followed her into the corridor outside, where she span around to face him, furious.

'Thanks for volunteering me for this, by the way.'

'What's the problem with DS Rafferty?'

'Apart from her being a complete bitch?' Catherine spat. 'Sorry. I don't know. She obviously has a problem with me, but I'm not sure what it is.' She stepped over to one of the doors leading off the corridor, knocked on it and barged inside when there was no reply. Knight followed her.

'What are you doing here?' Catherine asked.

'Supporting DCI Dolan.'

'Why?'

'Because she's SIO on Anna's case now, as well as working with you to find out who killed John McKinley.'

'But you know Anna. Isn't there a conflict of interest?' Knight shrugged, and Catherine shook her head. 'I still don't see why they came here to investigate the death of a homeless person.'

'He was an ex-copper,' Knight reminded her.

'Yeah, years ago. It doesn't make sense.'

'Where are you going now?'

'Now? I was hoping to have a shower in the staff bathrooms, but my bag's still at the shelter. Maybe there'll be some soap and shampoo I can nick. I'll have to find somewhere to sleep as well.'

Knight frowned. 'Isn't the idea you sleep at Phoenix House?'

'McKinley hardly ever did. Why should I?'

'Dolan expects you to.'

Catherine gave a humourless smile. 'I will, when I'm ready. She'll have to trust me.'

Knight gazed at her, worried. Her brave face wasn't fooling him. He could see the tic beneath her eye dancing again.

'You know, you don't have to do this, Catherine,' he told her.

'What do you mean?'

'You can go home, back to Northolme.'

She snorted. 'And prove Rafferty right? She already treats me as though I'm incapable. No, I'm staying.'

Knight knew when he was beaten. 'Remember, you can call me any time.'

'And you'll come and rescue me?' Catherine's hands were on her hips. 'I'm okay, Jonathan. Find the person who stabbed Anna.' She rubbed a hand over her eyes. 'I need to go.'

She stumbled through the door. Reluctantly, Knight let her leave. As he made his way back to the incident room, Dolan and Rafferty appeared, walking towards him.

'Thomas Bishop has arrived for his interview,' Dolan said. 'Thought you might like to observe?'

Chapter 20

This was a part of the city Ghislaine didn't know at all. Rows of streets running parallel to each other, lined with cars. Red-brick terraces, some with a small front yard, some with doors opening directly onto the pavement. Others still with narrow passageways separating the houses at street level, though they were joined on the floor above. Satellite dishes, boarded windows, yellowing nets, smart wooden blinds. A place of contradictions, well-maintained houses propping up their more down-at-heel neighbours. Some had been rendered, one painted a particularly ill-advised shade of mustard. Several displayed 'To Let' signs, some with boards advertising single rooms to rent. For students, Ghislaine presumed, though in this part of town, less salubrious uses for the rooms were possible.

She had kept her distance from Jasmine, aware her friend would be furious if she knew Ghislaine was following. It had been easy in the city centre to stay behind Jasmine as she sauntered along, using people as camouflage, or ducking into shops when necessary. Out here though, it was much trickier. Fortunately, Jasmine hadn't looked back. Her pace had increased in the last few minutes, some of the swagger gone as she hurried towards her destination. Her shoulders were hunched, as if her stomach hurt. Ghislaine sighed, fearing her suspicions were right.

Jasmine turned into a gateway about halfway along the street. Ghislaine feigned interest in a newsagent's window and counted slowly to twenty to give Jasmine time to get inside. Her mouth was dry, her heart rate noticeably increasing. She didn't want to go nearer – in truth, she didn't dare. Whoever Jasmine was visiting, they were unlikely to be enthusiastic about a friend tagging along, and Jasmine wouldn't be either.

But she had to know. If Jasmine was taking drugs again, there would be no bed for her at Phoenix House. Part of the agreement was you were clean. No drugs, no alcohol, no criminal activity.

No second chances.

And without Phoenix House, without the security of knowing she had a safe bed at night, what would Jasmine do? Slip further back into her old habits, Ghislaine was sure. Drugs, theft, prostitution.

Now determined, Ghislaine crossed the road, surreptitiously glancing at the house Jasmine had gone into. It didn't look like a squat. Yes, the paintwork was peeling, the garden thick with overgrown with weeds, but there were curtains in the windows, and a car parked outside. An older model, but clean and well maintained. Ghislaine kept walking, studying the property as covertly as possible. At the far end of the street, she stopped again. Above her head, a faded black and white sign informed her this was 'Merry Road'. But who lived here? Remembering Jasmine's salacious comments about the men she knew, Ghislaine considered them. Danny Marshall, the counsellor at Phoenix House, was a possibility. Ghislaine wasn't sure how much he was paid, but she doubted it was a lot. Would Danny be stupid enough to sleep with Jasmine? Possibly. There was Joel Rushford, the vicar, but he wouldn't live on a street like this. His home would be in a village, or on a leafy side street. He was far too conscious of his reputation and image to live on a street full of run-down terraces. Unless, of course, he was renting this place. Ghislaine immediately dismissed the idea. Rushford was slimy, but he wasn't an idiot. Jasmine was a temptation, nothing more. This visit wasn't about Phoenix House. She knew why Jasmine had come here.

A figure was approaching on a BMX, wearing baggy tracksuit bottoms and a hooded sweatshirt, his face impossible to distinguish. Ghislaine stood back to allow him to pass her. A rucksack, like the one Jasmine guarded so fiercely, was slung over his shoulders. He manoeuvred the bike into the same gateway Jasmine had disappeared into. Ghislaine walked back towards the house. It was a risk, but what was the point in following Jasmine all this way if she didn't get some answers?

The BMX was thrown carelessly on the square of grass in the tiny front garden. Ghislaine glanced at the door as she hurried by – number twenty-four. She was tempted to knock on the door to see who answered, but with Jasmine inside, the risk was too high.

She would come back, get some answers. Decide whether to confront her friend.

Chapter 21

Knight and Dolan watched on the monitors as Thomas Bishop was escorted in. A small space, with magnolia walls, scruffy carpet tiles and no window. As interview rooms went, it wasn't too grim, but it wasn't welcoming either. Thomas might not be a suspect, but he was being treated like one. He looked exhausted.

Thomas glanced around him, obviously wary, as DC Zaman and DS Rafferty followed him into the room. Knight was sympathetic. He understood they needed to speak to Thomas again, but he believed it to be a waste of time. Thomas had already given a statement, garbled and confused though it had been. It was unlikely there would be any more to add. In Knight's experience, witnesses' memories didn't improve over time.

When everyone was seated, Rafferty asked Thomas how Anna was.

'She hasn't responded to the antibiotics they've given her,' he told them. The admission obviously pained him, and he rubbed his eyes. 'The stab wound, the surgery they had to do to repair the internal damage, the blood transfusions – all they did to save her, and it's an infection that could kill her now.'

'Her condition's critical?' Zaman asked.

Thomas gave a weary nod. 'They've told us she's dangerously ill. The infection is affecting her whole body – kidneys, her blood pressure. It... It's so unfair, you know? Anna's a wonderful person, great at her job, loves helping people. Now she's lying there dying because some prick wanted my mobile.' He covered his face with his hands, sobs choking him. Rafferty and Zaman exchanged a glance. Knight swallowed, blinking back the tears filling his own eyes. Anna Varcoe was one of his officers, and Thomas was right, she didn't deserve this. No one did.

'Mr Bishop?' Rafferty waited. 'Thomas?' Sitting forward, she touched his hand. He stared at her, his face red and wet with tears. 'We understand you want to get back to the hospital, back to Anna. But we need to catch whoever did this to her, and until we're able to interview Anna, you're the only person who saw what happened.'

Rafferty's voice was reassuring, compassionate. After hearing how she had spoken to Catherine Bishop, Knight was surprised to see her empathising with Catherine's brother.

Thomas wiped his eyes with his palms. 'I want to help. Anything I can do, tell me. I know my first statement was useless.'

'Thank you.' Rafferty asked him to recount the events of the stabbing. He tried, his voice halting, the words as painful now as they had been the first time he had told his story. His account of what happened, the man appearing and demanding his mobile phone and wallet, tallied with the statement he had given earlier, as Knight had known it would.

'The man who stabbed Anna,' Adil Zaman said. 'Can you describe him again please, Mr Bishop?'

Thomas lay his hands flat on the table separating him from the two police officers. He narrowed his eyes, dredging up memories he would sooner forget. 'He was tall, slim. White.' He sighed, frustrated with himself. 'To be honest, I can't remember any more. As soon as I saw the knife, my attention was focused on it, especially as he had hold of Anna.'

'It's understandable, and a common reaction,' Rafferty told him. 'When you say "tall", can you be more specific?'

'Well over six feet. Loads taller than Anna, and me too.'

Zaman stood. 'I'm five foot eleven, Mr Bishop. Was the man you saw taller than me?'

Thomas opened his mouth, frowning. 'Can I stand too?' he asked Rafferty. 'He seemed massive, but...'

He stood beside Zaman. 'Weird. I would have sworn he was loads taller than me, but he can't have been. I'm only five foot seven– a proper short-arse.' He managed a shaky grin. 'He was more like five ten or eleven then. More your height. I'm sorry.'

'It's fine. It often happens,' Rafferty reassured him. 'It's difficult to be accurate, especially when there's a weapon involved. Your attention tends to focus on it – the threat. It's to be expected.'

Thomas sat. 'Doesn't help much if I can't describe him though.'

'Try this. Close your eyes,' Rafferty suggested. 'I know this isn't going to be easy, but picture yourself on the street with Anna. You parked the car...'

'Anna did; she was driving.' Thomas looked sceptical.

'Give it a go, Mr Bishop. Please?'

In the observation room, beside Knight, Dolan shifted in her chair. 'Isla's good at this sort of thing. She should be, she's been on enough bloody training courses.'

Knight was willing to be convinced as Thomas Bishop sat back in his chair, closing his eyes. When he relaxed, Knight recognised the resemblance to his sister, Catherine.

'Now, Anna parked the car — where?' Rafferty asked.

'The top of Steep Hill. A car park by the castle wall.'

'Okay. Try to imagine yourself back there, walking to the restaurant.'

Thomas paused. 'It was colder than we'd expected. I decided to go back to the car for our jackets.'

'Did Anna go with you?'

'No, she waited. We put our coats on, Anna took my hand, we kept walking. I asked about her day. Anna knew a shortcut — a narrow street, cobbled. I don't know the city too well.' He hesitated, pressing his lips together.

'I know this is difficult, Thomas. You're doing fine,' Rafferty told him.

'We were laughing about something. I heard footsteps behind us, but I didn't take any notice until I heard his voice.'

Rafferty tensed. Next to her, Zaman sat motionless. 'What did he say, Thomas?'

'He said, "Excuse me." We stopped, turned around. I presumed he was going to ask the time, maybe see if we had a light, but he grabbed Anna's arm, pulled her towards him. The knife was already in his other hand.'

'Which hand?'

'The right. He held Anna with his left.'

'Okay.'

'He said, "Your phone and wallet – leave them on the ground and walk away. Then I'll let her go." I put my stuff down, but I couldn't leave Anna.'

'What happened next?'

'I stood staring. Anna was still. He kept waving the knife, and I could see he wasn't going to let Anna go if I didn't, but he lifted the knife, and… He stabbed her.' Thomas raised his hands to his mouth.

'Could you see his face? Can you tell us what he looked like?'

Thomas shifted in the chair, his eyes still closed. 'I had the impression he was young, because of the way he moved. I remember his eyes… Brown, or hazel. I couldn't see anything else. He wore a dark coat with a hood, a scarf over his mouth and chin. Blue jeans, I remember. Black leather gloves. And boots, black boots. Muddy.' He paused, took a shaky breath. Rafferty stayed silent, and Knight knew she wouldn't want to interrupt. Thomas was remembering details absent from his first statement. 'When I saw the knife, I knew he wasn't messing around. A thin blade, but long.' He shuddered.

'Thomas, I want to talk about the attacker's voice again.' Rafferty's voice was hardly more than a whisper. 'Did you notice an accent?'

'His voice was muffled, because of the scarf. I didn't notice an accent.'

'Try to imagine yourself back there. Is there anything else you can tell us?'

Thomas opened his eyes. 'I keep going over it in my head, trying to remember some detail to help you, but there's nothing.'

'Are you sure it was a man?' Zaman asked. Rafferty turned her head, shooting him the briefest look of surprise.

'Well, yeah. His clothes, his voice… It was a man, I'm positive.' Thomas seemed bemused.

Zaman smiled at him. 'I wanted to check.'

'All right. Thomas, I'd like you to close your eyes again, go through the whole incident once more, please. Focus on putting yourself back there.'

'Again? I know you want to find the bastard who did this, but I'm sure I've told you all I remember.' Thomas glanced at the clock on the wall. 'I need to get back to the hospital.'

'One more time. Please?' Rafferty folded her arms.

'All right.'

Thomas sat back in the chair, his hands now loose in his lap. His eyes closed again, and his breathing slowed. The interview room was silent. Knight waited, aware of Dolan shuffling beside him. Knight had counted to forty-five before Thomas said, 'There's nothing. I'm sorry.'

Rafferty sighed. 'Okay. Thank you, Mr Bishop.'

Knight turned to Dolan. 'Can I have a word with Thomas before he goes? I want to ask about Anna.'

'Follow me.'

Rafferty and Zaman were leaving the room as Dolan and Knight turned the corner. Knight hurried into the room and dropped into the chair Rafferty had vacated. Thomas stared at him.

'Jonathan, what are you doing here?'

'I'm helping out. You've given us valuable information. The description could be vital and if we get an image of the suspect's face too…'

'I've already said I'll do an e-fit. I want him found. It won't help Anna, I know, but...'

'How is she? You mentioned an infection?'

'You were listening?'

'Watching too,' Knight admitted.

Thomas snorted. 'So I'm a suspect.'

'No, not at all. But until we can talk to Anna, you're the only witness we have.'

'She's still unconscious. They said,' he blinked a few times, 'they said lots of people don't survive this type of infection, around half of those who develop it. Fifty per cent. I know Anna's young and fit, but it doesn't seem to matter. Machines are doing everything for her. All we can do is hold her hand and wait.' Thomas gazed at Knight, his eyes so like his sister's it was unnerving. They were darker, but the shape was the same, as was the pleading expression Knight had seen in Catherine's eyes more than once. Thomas was reaching out to him, as a friend, as Anna's boss, someone who worked with her every day, knew her, cared about her. Knight coughed.

'I'm sure the doctors and nurses are doing all they can...' Even to his own ears, it sounded pathetic. They would be; it was their job. It wouldn't be a comfort to the man sitting in front of him.

'They are. They're amazing.' Thomas pushed back his chair and got to his feet. 'Knight followed him to the door and out of the room. 'Where do I go to get this e-fit thing done? It'll help, won't it?'

Knight wished he knew what else to say. A crumb of comfort, some hope. His mind was a blank. Thomas was clearly already grieving, resigning himself to the fact Anna would not recover. And all Knight could do was nod his head and not say a word.

–

Dolan, Knight, Rafferty and Zaman regrouped in a quiet corner of the incident room. Around them, the place buzzed with activity. Uniformed officers, plain-clothes detectives and civilian support staff, all determined to hunt down the man responsible for critically injuring one of their own. On the smartboard on the far wall, the face of Anna Varcoe was still displayed, smiling at them. Knight noticed more than one officer glance at it, turning back to their task with their jaw set. He couldn't bring himself to meet Anna's eye.

Rafferty sipped from a bottle of water. 'At least we have a description now.'

'We also need the e-fit,' Dolan reminded them. 'It shouldn't take too long. We need to release it to the press.'

'Is Thomas no longer a suspect?' Knight asked.

Dolan pursed her lips. 'He never was, not in my eyes. We've all seen liars in the interview room, good actors, but watching him today, I'm certain he's genuine. His story stands up, and it's vague enough to be the truth. If he'd have remembered every detail, especially in his first statement, I'd be more inclined to be suspicious.'

'Agreed,' Knight said.

'We need to focus on finding this man. Get his face in the papers, on social media, everywhere. He must be shitting it to know the woman he knifed was a copper.' Dolan bared her teeth. 'Will be when he's all over the news, anyway.'

Knight turned to the window, parting the vertical blinds. As he'd expected, the gaggle of journalists continued to wait. Dolan came over to see what he was looking at.

'They're still out there,' Knight said. 'TV cameras too.'

Dolan peered out at them. 'There are some at the hospital too, apparently.'

'Good to know an attack on a police officer is still worthy of all this attention,' said Rafferty.

'I've a press conference in an hour.' Dolan didn't sound thrilled at the prospect. 'Me, Detective Superintendent Stringer and Chief Constable Southern.' She turned away. 'Can't wait.' She called across to a uniformed sergeant. 'Any joy from the fingertip search?'

The man shook his head. 'No, ma'am, not as far as I know.'

'Thank you.' Dolan smiled.

Rafferty shuffled her feet. 'Time for the briefing, ma'am… Mary.'

Officers were already leaving the room as Dolan scrolled through emails on her phone.

'Let's get on with it.'

—

At the front of the room, Dolan was growing increasingly frustrated as officers reported back on their day's work. Every line of enquiry was drawing a blank. Phone calls they had received from potential witnesses had been followed up, but no useful information had come to light. The time-consuming, morale-sapping task of trawling through CCTV footage had proved similarly fruitless. The knife used to stab Anna was still missing. No one had seen her assailant. His escape, whether on foot or in a vehicle, had not been noticed.

'At least not by anyone we've spoken to yet.' Dolan told the assembled officers about the description provided by Thomas Bishop. DS Melis, her friend from the morning briefing, now sitting in the front row, greeted the news with a scornful laugh.

'He's remembering this now? How convenient. And he's described half of Lincolnshire.'

'Mr Bishop is completing an e-fit. We'll need it circulating as widely as possible.' Dolan refused to acknowledge Melis. Seeing this, he waved his arm in the air. Dolan narrowed her eyes. 'Yes?'

'I'm still not convinced he didn't stab his girlfriend himself. The robberies committed in the city recently would be the perfect way to camouflage it,' Melis said.

'Thomas Bishop isn't a suspect,' Dolan told him. 'He has no motive, and the statements of the people who helped him and Anna Varcoe immediately after she was stabbed corroborate what he told us. The knife wasn't found on him, and he had no time to dispose of it. We know because of the 999 call he made. If he'd delayed at all, Anna Varcoe would've been dead before the paramedics arrived. Even if he sprinted off to chuck the knife somewhere out of sight, we would have found it. Anyway, the people who helped them were on the scene quickly. Mr Bishop travelled in the ambulance with DC Varcoe and was interviewed by one of our officers soon after. He had no opportunity to dispose of a knife.'

'Thomas Bishop had blood on his clothes though,' one of the detective constables pointed out.

Dolan acknowledged the point. 'Consistent with his story, according to the first impressions of our friends in forensics. Let's wait for full reports from them and focus on our other lines of investigation.'

'Such as?' Melis folded his arms.

'Finding the knife. Our man knew where to wait for Anna and Thomas Bishop. We know where the attack took place – let's go back to the shops, the businesses around there. When we have our e-fit, show it to everyone you can find. Our suspect must know the city well, and he'll have spent some time in the street where Anna was stabbed. Maybe having lunch, a cup of coffee. Someone must have seen him.'

Melis groaned. 'Ma'am, with respect...'

'Respect? You're showing respect by challenging me, DS Melis?' Dolan rounded on him. 'This investigation is close to twenty-four hours old, and we don't have a lead yet, apart from a basic description of our suspect. We've checked with the statements of the other people this man has robbed. Their descriptions of him were even vaguer than the one Thomas Bishop gave us, but certain points tally.'

'True, but Bishop could have read about it in the newspaper. The descriptions were released to the press, weren't they? It's easy enough to remember them – dark clothes, hood over his face, blah blah blah.' Melis spread his hands. 'I believe we should keep an open mind.'

Dolan stalked over to where Melis sat, glowering at him. 'I watched Thomas Bishop being interviewed today. He's not our man. If we fixate on trying to prove he is, this investigation will go nowhere.'

'You mean you're afraid of making a mistake?' Melis taunted. 'Another mistake, should I say?'

Dolan hesitated, her expression not changing. 'If you have something to say, DS Melis, let's hear it.' Her hands were on her hips.

'The Emily Brennan case. Four years old, dead after "falling" in the bath. Her father killed her – you didn't arrest him.'

'Yes, we did.'

'Yeah, eventually. Once he'd terrified his wife into keeping her mouth shut by kicking ten tonnes of shit out of her.'

'We—'

Melis hadn't finished. 'She told you eventually, admitted the truth in her hospital bed.' He blinked. 'And then she died from her injuries.'

There was silence. The officers sitting either side of Melis sat frozen, while Melis himself bowed his head, as if he were in church. Dolan was still, her eyes glazed, watching a scene unfold that no one else could see. A tiny broken body. A man, his eyes swollen from crying, led away in handcuffs. And a woman, quietly cremated, the only mourners a neighbour and three police officers.

Case closed.

At the end of the front row, Isla Rafferty got to her feet. She went to Dolan, spoke quietly to her. Dolan took a deep breath, let it out slowly. She lifted her head, staring at Melis.

'The case you're referring to is not relevant to this one.'

'I disagree. I...'

'Detective Sergeant Melis, do you want to continue as part of this investigation?'

Melis was unshaken. 'Yes, ma'am.'

'Then wind your neck in.' She gave him one final glare and turned away.

Chapter 22

Catherine Bishop huddled in a quiet corner of the pub with a cup of the cheapest coffee on the menu. She had managed to take a shower while she had been at Headquarters, but wouldn't be able to change her clothes until she arrived at the shelter. Hopefully, she would be able to grab another shower before bed. It was seven thirty in the evening; time for her to make her way to Phoenix House to spend her first night there. She wasn't looking forward to it. She was less apprehensive after speaking to Ghislaine, but her task seemed overwhelming. Ghislaine had confided more than she had hoped for, but not everyone would be so forthcoming. She knew she would be expected to share a bedroom with the other women. Not a prospect she found appealing. As far as she was aware, she didn't talk in her sleep, but how could be sure? She was afraid of saying the wrong thing, exposing herself as a fraud. The knowledge she was deceiving people, as she had said to Dolan when they had first discussed the assignment, also troubled her. Agreeing to this assignment had been a mistake. The sensation of snakes twisting and coiling beneath her skin was back, the dry mouth, the sense of dread. Sitting there, unsure whether she would have a job to go back to at Northolme Police Station, uncertain of the future of her relationship with Ellie, she felt totally alone.

And there was Anna.

She took another sip of coffee, knowing she should phone Thomas to ask how she was. Catherine had to admit, though she would never have said as much to her brother, Anna had looked even worse than she had expected her to when she had visited her earlier. Catherine was no stranger to the victims of violent crime, but the sight of Anna lying there attached to the machines and monitors had frightened her. How could someone be reliant on so much equipment, and still be alive? But Anna was fighting. Whether she could continue to was an issue Catherine didn't want to consider.

'DS Bishop?'

Lost in her worries, Catherine had failed to notice Isla Rafferty enter the pub and approach her table. Rafferty stopped and cleared her throat.

'Is there a problem? Is it Anna?' Catherine was half out of her chair.

'No, no, don't worry. DCI Dolan asked me to find you.' Rafferty glanced into Catherine's coffee cup. 'Can I get you a refill?'

'Yes, please. Americano.' Surprised, Catherine held out the mug. Maybe Rafferty would spit in it on her way back to the table. Slipping the phone they'd given her out of her bag, she checked the battery. Rafferty had no doubt used it to discover where Catherine was. The battery was full, and there was a decent signal – no reason for Rafferty to be here in person. There had been no clues in her face. She appeared tired and drawn, but Catherine was sure she did herself. It was a police officer's default look, especially in the middle of a major investigation. Rafferty managed a smile for the barman as he set two mugs on a tray and added two packets of crisps to it. As Catherine watched, Rafferty rubbed her hands over her face, the diamond in her engagement ring catching the light for a second.

'I thought you might be hungry,' Rafferty said, depositing the tray on the table.

Surprised, Catherine took one of the bags of ready salted as Rafferty sat down. 'Thank you.'

Rafferty nodded. Catherine tore open the other pack and Rafferty took the other bag and tucked in. Catherine waited for her to explain why she was there, but Rafferty just kept chewing, her eyes not meeting Catherine's. As the silence grew awkward, Catherine said, 'Doesn't your fiancé mind you working late most nights?'

Rafferty gave a quick shake of her head. 'He's used to it.'

'Sounds more understanding than my last partner.' Catherine blew on her coffee. 'What does he do?'

'He's a paramedic.'

'Really? I bet you hardly see each other.'

Rafferty gave the small twitch of her lips Catherine recognised as her version of a smile. 'We manage.'

'How long have you been together?'

'Four years.' Rafferty put down her drink. 'Listen, DS Bishop, I don't mean to be rude, but Mary wanted me to give you some instructions.'

Catherine laughed. 'Okay, I'll stop chatting.'

Rafferty actually blushed. 'Sorry. Not what I meant. Anyway, the DCI wants you to ask around when you get to Phoenix House, see if anyone there knows any more about the stabbing of Anna Varcoe. There must have been people around when it happened, witnesses, even if they haven't come forward. The homeless people in the city spend more time out on the streets than anyone. DCI Dolan reckons it's worth a try.'

'I'm to ask about the attack on Anna, as well as sneakily try to find out who killed John McKinley?'

'Yes. I'll be honest, we're struggling to make any progress in either case.' Rafferty folded her crisp packet, dropped it onto the table. 'It's frustrating.'

'At least you haven't arrested my brother yet.' Catherine watched Rafferty's face.

She avoided Catherine's gaze, keeping her eyes fixed on her drink. 'Some people have suggested it.'

Catherine's laugh was scornful. 'Thomas faints when he has an injection. I can't imagine him stabbing his girl-friend.'

'Neither can I. I spoke to him earlier.'

'DI Knight told me,' Catherine admitted. Knight had phoned, though perhaps he shouldn't have done. Catherine was past caring. 'He said you managed to get a description from Thomas.' He'd also told her Rafferty had rescued Dolan when she was in danger of losing control of a briefing.

'And an e-fit. Though one bloke wearing a hoody looks much like another.' Rafferty shook her head. 'Not your brother's fault. In those circumstances, as soon as he saw the knife, his attention would have been fixed on it.'

'Especially when the attacker also had hold of Anna.'

There was a silence as both women considered what had happened next. Glancing at her watch, Rafferty said, 'I should go.' She got to her feet.

'Me too. Off to Phoenix House.' Catherine made sure her reluctance wasn't obvious in her voice. Why had Rafferty come here? At Dolan's request, she'd admitted as much. But to pass on a one-sentence message that could have been communicated by phone, even by text?

'Hopefully you'll get us some answers.' Rafferty didn't sound convinced.

Catherine smiled. 'No pressure. Are you going home now?'

'No, to a hotel; Mary too. Adil's going back to Nottingham. He and his wife have a new baby.'

'He'll be keen to get home to them.'

'He's already gone. Mary was going to come to see you herself, but she had a press conference.'

'Lovely.' Catherine wrinkled her nose as they walked towards the exit doors. The pub was busier now, and Catherine saw Rafferty drawing admiring glances from a group of men clustered around the bar. One of them grinned as they passed and said, 'Leaving already, love? Shame. I was going to buy you a drink.'

Rafferty ignored him and pushed open the door. In the street outside, it was drizzling. Rafferty frowned, fastening her jacket.

'At least we have the e-fit to show people now,' she said. 'It would have been more difficult if Thomas hadn't remembered what he did.'

'DI Knight said that was down to your interviewing technique,' Catherine told her with a smile.

'Your brother was calmer than when the initial statement was taken, and it helped him recall the detail.'

Rafferty dismissed the compliment, leaving Catherine to wonder why she had bothered to mention it. Rafferty hadn't been as prickly tonight, though she hadn't thawed completely. Did she have an issue with Catherine's sexuality? If so, she wouldn't be the first. No doubt she knew about it; everyone else at Headquarters did.

They parted soon after, Rafferty heading for her hotel by the side of the Brayford Pool, and Catherine making for Steep Hill. It was now after eight o'clock. Time to secure herself a bed.

As she walked she took out her phone to call her brother, but it went to voicemail. She thumbed a quick text instead, asking about Anna. If Thomas was in the ICU, he'd have switched his phone off. She hoped he had gone home to get some rest after his interview with Rafferty and Zaman, but there was no guarantee. She glanced at the sky, thousands of stars vivid against the darkness. A cold, clear night.

She hoped Anna would survive it.

Chapter 23

With a smile of thanks, Catherine took the bowl and set it on her lap. Pasta shells with a tomato and herb sauce. She dug her fork into the bowl, trying not to worry about the cleanliness of the utensils or the man who had prepared the food, now watching her with anxious eyes. He was missing several teeth, and his clothes, though clean, were old. His corduroy trousers were worn through in places, and his bottle-green sweater was unravelling at the elbows. His hands, despite the yellowy, overlong nails, were clean, and Catherine chastised herself for her snottiness.

'I hope I didn't burn the sauce,' he worried.

Carl Baker, one of the support workers, laughed, patting his shoulder as he passed. 'It's fine,' he said. 'You've done a great job.'

The room was quiet while the residents of Phoenix House ate their evening meal, but when it was finished, the noise swelled. A crime drama blared from the TV, while the men played cards. Catherine sat back with a cup of tea. Who she should approach first? Ghislaine had given her a quick smile and said hello, but had otherwise ignored her and hidden away behind a magazine. Trying to avoid Lee Collinson, Catherine guessed. The other woman, Jasmine Lloyd, had been focusing on her phone, but now she turned to Catherine with a smile.

'What's your story?'

Catherine launched into the fictional account of her life she had agreed with Dolan. Jasmine listened, picking at her fingernails. When Catherine had finished, she tossed her hair.

'Men. Bastards, the lot of them.'

Carl Baker laughed. 'Say what you think, Jasmine. Don't hold back.'

'True though. How many of the women who've stayed here have had their lives ruined by some bloke or other? Their dad, their stepdad, some mucky little shite their mum's brought home?'

'Maybe women with kids should know better than to bring strangers into the house,' one of the men playing cards at the table said as he turned.

Jasmine spluttered, outraged. 'Yeah, blame the fucking...'

'Jasmine,' Carl admonished.

'Blame the victim. Always the bloody same.' Jasmine slammed her mug onto the coffee table. Carl raised his eyebrows, but didn't speak. 'You reckon women should stay at home once they've had kids, never leave the house, Lee?'

Lee shrugged. 'Not what I said. Kids are vulnerable, they need protecting.'

'They're not the only ones,' Jasmine told him. 'Why else would we all come here?'

'The streets aren't safe,' the man who had cooked said. 'I've had the shit kicked out of me – sorry, Carl – more times than I can remember.'

Catherine sipped her tea, guilt ambushing her again. She was lying to them all by being here. It was fine for

163

Dolan to ask her to go and integrate herself at Phoenix House, but the reality wasn't as easy. People who had spent any time on the street quickly learnt self-preservation. Cultivating their trust was going to take time, a luxury Catherine didn't have.

'I've been lucky,' she said. 'The worst beatings I've had were before I came onto the streets.'

Jasmine laughed, and even Ghislaine looked amused.

'It's what, your second night of being homeless?' Jasmine hooted. 'Plenty of time for you to get a kicking or two, to have a gang of blokes chase you, feel you up or worse. You might decide you're better off going back to your bloke.'

Catherine scowled, as much out of shame as anger. 'No way.'

Still laughing, Jasmine heaved herself off the sofa and sauntered over to the men.

'Don't take any notice of Jas.' Ghislaine kept her voice low. 'She's all talk. Don't let her get to you.'

'No problem, but thanks.' Catherine didn't want to push Ghislaine away, but there was no point in allowing herself to be drawn into a conversation with someone she'd already spoken to, heartless as it may sound. She wandered over to the bookcase, pretended to study the spines of the books stored there, hoping she at least looked casual.

One of the men asked, 'Do you want us to deal you in?'

'What are you playing?'

He smiled. 'Doesn't matter when there's no money involved.'

'You know the rules, Joe,' Carl called across from his desk. 'No gambling, no drinking, no drugs.'

'No fraternising between the sexes. Jasmine takes no notice though.'

'Oi!' Jasmine thumped his arm. 'Wouldn't touch any of you lot with a bargepole.'

'What about the vicar?' Joe continued to tease her. 'Or Danny Marshall?'

The fourth man chimed in. 'Or the plumber who was here the other week? Or the bloke who drives the furniture delivery van?'

Jasmine was laughing, obviously enjoying the attention. 'Cheeky bastards. Give us some cards.' She dragged a chair over to the table.

Joe ran his hand across the top of his head. 'It'll have to be pontoon. We won't have enough cards for anything else if we're all playing.'

Lee Collinson said, 'I used to play pontoon a lot when...' He stopped, embarrassed.

'When what?' Jasmine asked.

'Never mind,' he muttered.

Silently, Catherine finished the sentence for him: *When I was inside.*

'Mackie liked a game of pontoon sometimes, didn't he, lads?' Carl Baker said. 'Won't have another game with him, poor bloke.'

Catherine collected her two playing cards. Now she had to be careful. Ghislaine had told her who Mackie was, of course, but the others wouldn't expect her to have heard of him. She studied her cards, listening.

'Can't believe he's dead,' Jasmine said. 'I know he wasn't here a lot, and he didn't say much when he was, but he'd always give you the time of day.'

'More than some people do,' Joe agreed. 'Remember the young lad who nicked all of the takings out of the shop till? What was his name? Miserable little shit he was, never spoke unless it was to ask for money.'

'Yeah, well, we all know what his problem was,' the man who had cooked said. 'And that particular problem costs a *lot*.'

'Where do you reckon he went?' Jasmine asked.

'I bet he's dead, same as Mackie. Overdose,' said Joe.

'Mackie was murdered,' Lee suddenly chimed in. Every head in the room turned towards him.

'Come on, Lee,' Joe scoffed. 'He'd been on heroin before, got clean, went back to it and forgot he wouldn't be able to tolerate as much as he used to. End of story.'

Lee shook his head, his expression darkening. Quietly, Carl heaved himself out of his chair and crossed the room to stand by in case of trouble. Lee dropped his playing cards onto the table.

'I'm telling you, Mackie was deliberately killed.'

Jasmine wasn't impressed. 'How do you know? You've only been here five minutes.'

'Shows what you know.' Lee licked his lips. 'I've known him for years.'

'Yeah? Bullshit,' said Jasmine.

'Believe what you want.' Lee pushed back his chair and stalked away. 'I'm off to bed.'

Carl stepped forward. 'Same one you had last night, Lee.'

'Thanks.'

As the door closed behind Lee, Jasmine laughed. 'He'd say anything to get some attention. Are we playing cards or not?'

Catherine looked towards Ghislaine, who had lowered the magazine. As soon as she could, Catherine would send Rafferty a text. Lee must have lied when giving his statement. If he was telling the truth now, why hadn't the fact that he had known John McKinley already been discovered?

—

The mattress was lumpy, and Catherine didn't want to consider how many people had slept between the sheets before her. The duvet cover and pillowcase, both covered with garish pink stripes, were more suited to a child's bedroom than an adult's. Still, it was warm and clean, which was all she needed. She rolled onto her side, propped herself on her elbow and plumped the pillow. It was thin and smelt vaguely musty, but again, was fit for purpose. There were four beds in the room, two with chipped wooden frames, which had been allocated to Jasmine and Ghislaine. The other was a divan similar to Catherine's. Jasmine, undoing her jeans, pointed at the spare bed as Catherine settled back under the duvet.

'Be grateful Carl didn't give you that one,' she said. Ghislaine frowned at her, but continued to fold her clothes.

'Why?' Warily, Catherine took the bait.

'A woman died in it a few months ago. Older woman; Sue was her name. Me and Ghis were in here, snoring away, never guessed she was dead. She must have been quiet about it.'

Jasmine stepped out of the jeans and lifted her top over her head. Catherine averted her eyes.

'Bloody hell. What did she die of?' she asked. Another death, this time inside Phoenix House.

Jasmine gave a ghoulish grin. 'They never told us officially. Maggie Kemp said it was a heart attack, but surely we'd have heard her gasping and groaning? Always seemed strange to me. Bit of a shock, wasn't it, Ghis, finding a dead body? Though it'd happened to you before.'

Ghislaine climbed into bed. 'Yeah, poor woman.' She turned on her side, facing the wall. Jasmine was rummaging in the front pocket of her rucksack, eventually unearthing a toothbrush and tube of toothpaste. 'They said the funeral directors took the sheets she died in, but knowing Maggie Kemp, she'll have grabbed them before they took the body away. Doesn't like to waste anything, our Maggie.'

'Can't be easy running this place, though,' Catherine said. 'Doubt they get any funding from the council.'

'They get donations, and there's the charity shop. They must pay the bills. And they can afford to employ people – Maggie and Danny, the support workers who keep their eye on us. God knows what they think we're going to do.' Jasmine rolled her eyes.

'What about the lad they were talking about earlier – the one who emptied the till?' Catherine asked.

'Jake? No mystery – he walked into the charity shop downstairs, took all the money, went to his dealer, shoved the lot in his arm, did a runner. Plenty of trains and buses out of here. I bet he's done the same in every town and city in the country.' There was admiration in Jasmine's voice.

Catherine watched as she shivered. 'Freezing tonight. I'm going to brush my teeth.'

As Jasmine left the room, Ghislaine sat up. 'Did she take her rucksack?' she whispered.

Catherine was bemused. 'Yeah, she did. Why?'

Slumping back beneath her duvet, Ghislaine sighed. 'Doesn't matter.'

Confused, Catherine closed her eyes. She didn't expect to sleep, not in a narrow single bed with much-washed covers and two other women snoring a few feet away. Her second day on her assignment was almost over, and what had she learnt? A woman had died at Phoenix House, and it hadn't been publicised. No surprise. The shelter's manager, Maggie Kemp, and the board wouldn't want any adverse publicity. Their goal was providing a safe bed for the night, helping the people who slept under their roof find their feet again. However innocent the woman's death had been, it might still discourage people from seeking out refuge.

Lee Collinson claimed to have known John McKinley. Why would he announce it? It was clear the other residents of Phoenix House still believed Mackie's death was an accidental overdose. Catherine heard Jasmine return to the room, the light clicked off and there was darkness. A few creaks as Jasmine got into bed, some shuffling. Silence. What if Mary Dolan was wrong? The pathologist, Dr Jo Webber, had agreed it was unlikely Mackie had tied the tourniquet found on his arm himself, but surely she could be wrong too? Believing something to be true didn't always mean it was. The whole case seemed like a mirage; a hazy, intangible picture. There were too many uncertainties. Catherine couldn't shake the feeling she was wasting her time, or being kept out of the way.

Or, she was missing something.

Chapter 24

He opened a blank document and saved it in the folder labelled 'CLIENTS'. Why he bothered keeping records, he wasn't sure – most of what he heard was bullshit. Still, it was what he was paid for. It was a pittance, admittedly, but he was making a difference.

He'd completed a degree in business studies, started having counselling when his mum was diagnosed with cancer and the family fell apart. A few months after Danny's mum died, his dad killed himself. Hung himself in the garage, was still swinging when Danny's younger brother came in from school and discovered him. More grief. More guilt. More counselling. In the end, Danny decided he may as well do the courses, get the diplomas. Most of the advice given by the earnest do-gooders he and his brother saw was common sense anyway.

Danny went to make himself a coffee before his newest client arrived. He'd seen her already, taken in the slow movements, the tic beneath her eye. He sighed as he dropped the teaspoon he'd used into the sink. He'd ask about drugs, she would lie. There would be some waffling about past traumas, childhood abuse or neglect. Some of it was genuine, Danny knew, and those were the people with whom he truly connected. Those who were slowly destroying themselves with drugs and drink, or often both

– well, he did what he could. They had to want to change; it had to come from within them. And most of the time, it was too difficult. The mountain was too high.

Back in his office, he checked his appointments for the rest of the day. He worked part-time at Phoenix House and did a few hours of counselling at three local secondary schools. He enjoyed working with young people, especially those who still had some hope, plans for their future. Those who had a future at all. Some of those most in need of his skills, such as they were, Danny knew he would never talk to. Some avoided school altogether, some turned up every now and again, but none would come and knock on his office door and ask for his help. The Phoenix House clients of the future, he expected. No doubt the wrong attitude, and he would never have said it to anyone else, but it was the truth. Those who couldn't afford further education, or hadn't the desire or capability for it, what future was there for them? Most of the places where they could have found jobs had long gone. The factories, the foundries, the steelworks. Now, it was shops or call centres. The dole queue. Or… Danny sipped his coffee. He knew of plenty of other opportunities the city afforded. His brother had taken them a long time ago, after the deaths of their parents. Straight off the rails – how predictable. Danny found himself sneering as though Steven were sitting in front of him, although he hadn't seen his brother for several years. He'd still be in prison, jailed for sticking a broken bottle into some bloke's face during a drunken fight. Danny had visited at first, until he'd realised he and Steven were miles apart, and always would be. His brother was the one person he had given up on.

Steven, and himself.

There was an appointment with Jasmine later to look forward to. Danny didn't fool himself that Jasmine had turned a corner, but she was making progress. It was all he could hope for, all he could offer. She was bright, and she made him laugh. She told him in each appointment, no more drugs. Every time he smiled and encouraged her, not believing it for a minute. Addiction would claim her in the end. Jasmine was broken, and it was far beyond his meagre skills to offer her any kind of salvation. Maybe that's what Joel Rushford at the church was doing. He was providing more than spiritual guidance, Danny was certain. Well, fine. In the end, Jasmine would always come back to him. They understood each other.

He drank his last mouthful of coffee and checked his watch. She was late. They always were. To say they had nowhere to go, nothing to do, the clients of Phoenix House were poor timekeepers.

Eventually, there was a knock on the door, and Danny Marshall forced a smile of welcome.

–

Part of the charade was joining in with Phoenix House's counselling programme. Catherine was dreading it, but it would give her a chance to speak to Danny Marshall. After hearing the jibes the previous evening about the relationship between him and Jasmine, Catherine knew she would have to keep her appointment with him. If he was having a relationship with Jasmine, or even the odd sexual encounter, who knew what other rules he might be breaking? Dolan was sure John McKinley's death was linked to Phoenix House, but Catherine didn't see any reason why it should be. He had spent little time there after all. She had sent a text to Dolan and Rafferty soon after waking in the small bedroom in the shelter. Jasmine and Ghislaine had still been asleep, and Catherine had crept out of bed, gone to have a shower. She had stowed her bag in one of the lockers in the corridor overnight, but Jasmine, she was amused to see, had her rucksack under the duvet with her, the top of the bag visible on the pillow. Catherine knew she should make a note of it, tell Dolan and Rafferty. There might be a simple reason for Jasmine's caution, but there could be other explanations too.

—

Marshall was nervous, Catherine noted. It was clear in the quick movements, the number of times he touched his face and hair as he welcomed her inside the tiny office.

'How was your first night here?'

'Fine. I got some sleep.'

'I hope Jasmine and Ghislaine made you welcome?'

His fatherly tone irritated Catherine. He was younger than her, but clearly felt she was there to be patronised.

'They did, especially Jasmine.' She stared into his eyes, watched him blush.

'She's a... friendly girl.'

Catherine raised an eyebrow. 'I've heard.'

Marshall coughed, his cheeks on fire. Catherine smirked. She was going to enjoy her role this morning.

'Now, ah, Catherine. I'm here to discuss any issues, any problems you might have. Any addictions, health problems. To talk about your plans. Now you're here at Phoenix House, we'd like to offer any help we can give you to get you back on your feet.'

'On my feet and out of your shelter, you mean?'

Danny opened his mouth, closed it again. 'We want to help,' he said eventually.

Catherine wriggled in her chair, making herself comfortable. 'Okay, well, here's what I need.' She counted them off on her fingers. 'A house, detached, with a pool. Cars – one sports, one practical. A few million in the bank. A cook, a butler and a cleaner. Several dogs, and someone to walk them. What do you reckon?'

He shook his head. 'If you're going to be offensive...'

'Offensive? What, you'll throw me out?'

'I can have your access to Phoenix House revoked, yes.'

'Good for you. All right, what can you get me?'

'Do you have a drug habit?'

'No.'

He smirked, believing himself in control again. 'Okay. Mental health issues?'

'No.' *Maybe.*

'If you don't tell me the truth I can't help you.' He watched her face. Catherine fervently wished for her warrant card. She wanted to tell him exactly who she was and what she was doing here, ask him some questions he wouldn't be able to smarm his way out of answering. When she didn't respond, he turned to his laptop, tapping on the keys.

'Have we finished? Am I dismissed?' Catherine asked.

'You can leave at any time. I can't help if you won't let me.'

'Fine. I'd like to talk about my life, why I...' She swallowed. 'Okay, I need help.'

Danny Marshall turned in his chair with a sympathetic smile. 'People don't end up working here by accident, you know. We've all been through trauma: me, Maggie, Carl... If you want to help others, you should understand them first. I'm not here to judge.'

'I know. There's a real mix of people here. It must be difficult for you.'

A bit of flattery never hurt anyone.

'Some are easier than others. If people are resistant to help, yes, it's difficult – impossible in some cases. I know Maggie would agree – it's the most heartbreaking part of our job. Watching someone you know you could help walking away.'

'Especially if they're addicts.'

'Drugs destroy lives.' Danny shrugged.

'Like the bloke from here who overdosed and died.' Catherine held her breath.

'Mackie? Yes, what happened was sad, but he was offered help. Both Maggie and I did our best. Maggie's husband even came in to talk to him. He used to be a police officer too, you see, and hoped he could... Well, maybe help to ease Mackie's burden. Anyway.' Danny caught himself. 'We're here to talk about you, Catherine.'

She smiled. The appointment hadn't been a waste of time after all.

Chapter 25

Mary Dolan had a headache. A horrible, pounding, sickening headache. She sat at her desk in the corner of the incident room with her forehead propped on her hand as Detective Superintendent Stringer entered the room.

'She's coming this way,' Jonathan Knight murmured.

'Wonderful.' Dolan groaned. 'Look at her face. Has someone shat in her shoes?' She straightened as Stringer reached them. 'Good morning, ma'am.'

Jane Stringer's smile was taut and fleeting. 'Has any information come in overnight?' she demanded. 'Witnesses? You'll have seen the newspapers, I presume? The attack on DC Varcoe is still front-page news, even in the national papers.'

'I have, ma'am,' Dolan said. 'We're also trending on Twitter, and being ripped to pieces on Facebook.'

Stringer's nostrils flared. 'And have we made any progress?'

'No more than we had last night.' Dolan was trying not to let her irritation show, but it was difficult. What did Stringer expect? It was less than fifteen hours since their press conference. The e-fit of the man they were searching for wouldn't have been seen by many people until this morning.

'The Assistant Chief Constable would appreciate an update.'

'I'm sure he would, ma'am, but I've nothing to tell him.'

'Go and see him anyway,' Stringer advised. 'Otherwise, I'm sure he'll be paying you a visit.'

Dolan glared at her. 'Some time to do my job would be appreciated.'

'Delegate, Chief Inspector.' Stringer turned on her heel and stalked away. Dolan watched her go, furious. Knight held out his mobile.

'DS Bishop. She rang me when she didn't get an answer from you. She'd like a word.'

–

The Assistant Chief Constable, Edward Clement, had the long, woebegone face of a miserable donkey. It was no surprise his nickname throughout the force was 'Eeyore'. Dolan knocked on his door, not looking forward to the meeting.

'Enter.'

She strode into his office and stood to attention. Clement made her wait, tapping at his computer keyboard before asking her to sit.

'An update please, DCI Dolan. Any news?'

Dolan crossed her legs. 'No, sir. Not yet. We're still following leads that came in overnight after the e-fit was released. Officers are back on the streets, knocking on doors and talking to shopkeepers and passers-by in the city centre.'

Clement let out a long sigh. 'I know it's a difficult investigation. An attack on a police officer always is.'

'I don't believe DC Varcoe being police is relevant though.'

'Perhaps not.' Clement took a white handkerchief from his jacket pocket and blew his nose, loudly and at length. Dolan waited, trying not to let her distaste show on her face. 'If she dies…'

Dolan sat straighter. 'Sir…'

'If she dies, it will be a total disaster.'

'Yes, sir. It will.' Dolan was thinking of Anna's family, her friends, but she doubted Clement was.

'We need to find this man, Chief Inspector. Today.'

'Today. I see.'

'Tomorrow at the latest,' Clement relented. 'Otherwise, you'll be replaced as SIO.'

'Thank you for the warning.'

'What about the homeless chap, what was his name?' Clement waved a hand, as if the movement would jog his memory.

'McKinley. John McKinley. Ongoing, sir. DS Bishop's doing a fine job.'

'Bishop?' Clement sniffed. 'Christ. Be wary of her. She could have caused us a great deal of embarrassment a while back. See it doesn't happen again.'

Dolan bit back a scream. 'Yes, sir.'

'Are we wasting time with the McKinley case?' Clement mused. 'Using resources there that could be better channelled in another direction?'

'Wasting time? A man's dead.'

Clement thinned his lips. 'I know you and the pathologist believe he was murdered, but it's pretty tenuous stuff, don't you think? Might be time to wind the investigation down. Reapportion resources.'

Dolan was silent, knowing if she spoke again, she wouldn't be able to control her fury. Clement met her eyes, a slight smile hovering around his mouth as if he knew what she was thinking. 'I'll speak to the Chief Constable about it, and let you know. Dismissed, Chief Inspector.'

'But…'

'Dismissed.'

Chapter 26

Rafferty had managed to find a spare desk in the incident room. With Zaman and Dolan also crowding around it, there wasn't much space.

'Find out everything you can about Maggie Kemp's husband, Pat,' Dolan told her officers. 'I want to know when he left the force, and why.'

'Mrs Kemp should have told me her husband used to be police.' Zaman sounded aggrieved.

'We should have realised.' Dolan ran her hands through her hair. 'We also need to find out more about this "Jake" character – his surname, when he stayed at Phoenix House, any past convictions. Ask Maggie Kemp about him too. We need to speak to Joel Rushford again, and Danny Marshall.'

Zaman and Rafferty exchanged a glance. 'Wouldn't we be compromising DS Bishop's position if we speak to them again now though?' Zaman asked.

Dolan threw up her hands. 'Did you speak to Rushford yesterday?' she demanded of Zaman. 'You said you were going back to see him.'

'I did. He could only spare five minutes, and was utterly useless.'

'Ask him about Jasmine Lloyd – be blunt. Catherine said some of the people at the shelter last night were teasing Jasmine about her relationship with him. Find out if there's any truth in it.'

Rafferty interjected, 'And what about Marshall?'

'The same. Make everyone aware the investigation into John McKinley's death is a murder enquiry – rattle a few cages. Lee Collinson – speak to him too.'

'What about DS Bishop?' Rafferty asked.

'What about her? You're worried if we're heavy-handed it'll be obvious who's been telling tales?'

'Yes.'

'Speak to Rushford first, or even one of the soup kitchen volunteers. One of them must like gossiping. Engineer the conversation, get them to tell you about Rushford and Jasmine. It seems to be common knowledge at the shelter, though it might not be on Rushford's own territory. Look.' Dolan lowered her voice. 'It's a risk, I know it is. If I was worried there was any danger to Catherine, I wouldn't ask you to take this approach.' She told them about her meeting with ACC Clement, and his threats. 'We need to solve this quickly, otherwise the person who killed John McKinley will get away with murder.'

'If it was murder,' Rafferty murmured.

Dolan stared. 'Are you serious, Isla? You don't believe we've a case? What about the wiped-clean syringe, Dr Webber's evidence about McKinley not being able to tie the tourniquet himself?'

'I know, ma'am. I agree it's suspicious. But I can also see how the ACC could think we're wasting our time.'

'You think John McKinley isn't worth it, you mean? You think we should ignore the fact that someone ended his life?'

'No, of course not. I... I can't see us making progress. I'm not even sure what questions we need to ask. I've never investigated a crime this vague. There's nothing concrete.' Rafferty looked miserable. 'Four days since the body was found, and we're no nearer to knowing the truth about what happened.'

Dolan was nodding. 'I know we've not made much progress, and it's frustrating. I also have faith in the pair of you. The answers are out there, and we'll find them. Go and speak to Rushford and Marshall, Maggie Kemp and her husband. I'll have a look at Pat Kemp's records. Ask Maggie Kemp about the mysterious Jake, too.'

–

Catherine leant over the bed, gently touching her finger-tips to Anna's cheek. Her skin was hot and waxy. Thomas stood at the other side of the bed, watching the monitors. He still wore the clothes he'd had on yesterday, Catherine noticed. He'd evidently come straight back to the hospital after his interview and had been here ever since.

'You've not been home,' Catherine said.

He turned, his face drawn, his hair greasy. 'No. I don't want to leave her, except when your colleagues force me to, of course.'

There was nothing Catherine could say, and she stayed silent.

Thomas shook his head. 'I keep thinking, if I stay, if I keep watching, she'll be okay. If I'm here, nothing will change. I know it's stupid. Her parents are here, the nurses, the doctors, and they're all much more use than I am.' He turned away again, his shoulders shaking.

'Thomas, go home. Have a shower, get some sleep. Put on some clean clothes, come back later. You'll be in hospital yourself if you're not careful.' Catherine walked around the bed and took his arm. 'Go on, go now. Please, Thomas. I'm worried about you.'

His mouth twisted. 'Okay. Okay, I'll go.' He bent to kiss Anna's cheek. 'I'll see you later, sweetheart.'

Catherine watched him leave. She sat again, holding Anna's hand. 'He's an idiot. He loves you though.'

A nurse appeared. He smiled at Catherine as he turned to the monitors.

'How is she?' Catherine asked. The nurse took a clipboard from the foot of Anna's bed.

'She's not responded as well as we'd have liked to the antibiotics, I'm afraid. You'd have to speak to her doctor. Are you family?'

Catherine explained her relationship to Anna. The nurse was sympathetic, but didn't say any more. As he moved away, Catherine saw Anna's parents hurrying back into the ward, and got to her feet. Anna's mother leant over her daughter and stroked her hair.

'Don't tell me you've persuaded Thomas to go home?' she asked. 'We've been on at him all morning, but he wouldn't listen.'

'It wasn't easy.' There was an awkward pause. Catherine glanced at Anna. 'Well, I should be going.'

'They say she's worse,' Anna's father said abruptly.

Catherine's throat tightened. 'Thomas said. I'm sorry.'

'Every time I look at her I expect her to have gone,' Mr Varcoe whispered. 'If we leave the ward, I'm waiting for the phone to ring. We can't eat, don't sleep. And when the doctor comes around he frowns and shakes his head, says we need to wait and see, but nothing changes. There's no improvement. Have you caught him yet?'

Mrs Varcoe put her hand on her husband's arm. 'Shh, love. Remember where you are.'

He gave a harsh laugh. 'I'm not likely to forget. I take it you don't know who hurt her?'

'Not yet. I'm sorry,' Catherine admitted helplessly. Mr Varcoe said no more, but shot her a look filled with contempt. Catherine backed away. 'See you soon, Anna.'

It felt like a lie.

Chapter 27

'I don't like this.' Adil Zaman hadn't been sure whether to voice his concerns to Rafferty or not, since Dolan had sent them here. He would never disobey an order, but he wished Dolan had thought better of it. 'If we go in there asking questions, someone's going to guess DS Bishop isn't who she's pretending to be.'

'If we're careful, it'll be okay,' Rafferty told him. 'What else can we do?' They were in Zaman's car, hunting for a place to park. Glancing over her shoulder, Rafferty caught sight of the baby seat. 'How's your daughter?'

Zaman glanced at her, surprised. Rafferty rarely mentioned his home life. It was unnerving. 'She's doing well. She smiled at me when I got home last night.' Zaman beamed. Though Rafferty was clueless when it came to children, especially babies, this was obviously a milestone.

'Good. Great, Adil.' She looked again at the baby seat, now rolling around in the footwell. 'Isn't it supposed to be attached?'

Zaman laughed. Rafferty was bemused, not having meant to have made a joke, but pleased all the same.

'Do you want kids, you and your fiancé?' Zaman asked, spotting a car park at last and turning into it. Rafferty leant forward and pointed to a free space.

'One day. Not yet.' The lie came easily. She didn't, not at all. Bringing a child into the mess of her life wouldn't be fair, but she didn't want to admit it, especially to a colleague.

–

There was room for three chairs in the tiny office of Phoenix House, but it was a squeeze. Adil Zaman rested his cup of coffee on his knee before fumbling with his tablet computer. Maggie Kemp squeezed past him and sat, setting her own drink on her desk.

'I'm surprised to see you again, DC Zaman,' Kemp said.

Zaman smiled. 'We have some new lines of enquiry to pursue.'

Maggie Kemp gave him a hard look. Rafferty was surprised at the flash of steel – she'd not met Mrs Kemp before but from her statements had expected someone meek and reserved. The few minutes since Maggie Kemp had answered the door to them had done nothing to dissuade her from her initial impression. However, Rafferty realised Maggie Kemp would need to have some backbone to deal with clients, staff, the local council, government departments, police and anyone else her job brought her into contact with. It had been naïve to expect her to be a pushover.

Kemp smoothed the navy corduroy skirt she wore across her thighs. 'How can I help you?'

Rafferty glanced around them. 'How good is your security, Mrs Kemp?'

'Security? What do you mean?'

'If one of the people staying here got cold feet in the night, wanted to disappear, would they be able to get out?' Rafferty asked.

'Get out? They're not prisoners, Sergeant.'

'No. We have several people whose alibis for the night John McKinley died hinge on the fact that they were here at Phoenix House for twelve hours. If they're able to easily slip in and out of the place, we need to know.'

Maggie Kemp shook her head. 'The outside door's locked at all times. I have a key, as do two of our night workers, Carl and Teresa.'

'Do you need the key to open the lock from the inside?'

Kemp lowered her eyes. 'No. There are two bolts, but you don't need a key to turn the latch.'

'Which means, in effect, the alibis are useless?' said Rafferty.

'If someone left during the night, they'd be missed in the morning. The bolts would still be unfastened too if they didn't come back in. One of the night support workers is awake and in the common room all night, completing paperwork or reading. They take it in turns, staying awake every other night. If someone wanted to creep out, they'd have to get past them. There's no other way to the front door.'

'But presumably they have to use the loo at some point? They might even nod off for a while?' Zaman asked.

Kemp pressed her lips together. 'I hope not. You'd have to ask them.'

'I take it there are no CCTV cameras inside the shelter?' asked Rafferty.

'No, just in the shop. We want it to be as relaxing as possible in here. I know it's not luxurious, but we do our best.'

There was a silence. Rafferty flicked a glance at Zaman, who sat forward.

'Why didn't you tell us your husband was once a police officer, Mrs Kemp?' Zaman met her gaze as he asked the question, his tone making it more of a demand. Kemp blinked, her eyes confused behind the thick lenses of her glasses.

'Pat? What's Pat to do with anything?'

Zaman spread his hands. 'He's on the board of Phoenix House, isn't he? And he spoke to John McKinley shortly before his death?'

Kemp looked down her nose at the two police officers. 'He talked to Mackie, yes. It was a few weeks before Mackie died though. It's irrelevant, in any case. Pat spent less than five minutes in here with him. Mackie didn't want to listen.'

'What did your husband say to Mr McKinley?' Rafferty asked.

Kemp lifted her shoulders, let them fall. 'I wasn't at their meeting. You'd have to ask Pat.'

'I find it hard to believe you didn't discuss it.'

'Nevertheless, it's the truth. As I've said, you'd have to ask my husband.'

'We intend to.'

Rafferty backed up the statement with a hard look of her own. Maggie Kemp was unmoved, sitting with her hands folded in her lap, totally relaxed. Zaman held out the tablet.

'Do you recognise this man, Mrs Kemp?'

Kemp leant forward, squinting at the e-fit Thomas Bishop had provided.

'Who is he?' she asked.

'We're hoping you can tell us.' Rafferty was stern.

'It could be anyone. You're asking me to recognise a pair of eyes, DC Zaman. I'm afraid I can't.'

'Have another look,' Zaman urged. 'Is it someone who's stayed at Phoenix House?'

She took the tablet from him, studied it for a few seconds.

'I'm sorry, I don't know. I'd love to say yes, I recognise him, especially if it helps you catch the person who killed Mackie. I presume this man is a suspect?'

Zaman took back the computer, ignoring the question. 'Mrs Kemp, do you remember a man called Jake staying at the shelter?'

The reaction was immediate. Maggie Kemp scowled. 'Jake Pringle? Yes, I do. He stole from us.'

'Money, wasn't it?'

'A couple of hundred pounds, plus the petty cash tin. Food and toiletries. It wasn't what he took, it was the fact he did it at all.' Kemp removed her glasses and rubbed her eyes.

'Could he be the man in the e-fit?'

'I doubt it. As I've said, I'd need a better image to be sure.'

'You sound hurt by Jake's actions.'

'I consider myself a good judge of character, but Jake had me fooled. He had us all fooled.'

'All?'

Kemp put her glasses back on. 'Myself, Danny Marshall, the two night support workers – we all hoped

Jake had put his past behind him. He'd been caught shoplifting in the past, but he'd kicked his drug habit, had a job in a pub kitchen… We were helping him with a housing application. I understand it's difficult, but Jake seemed to have done all the hard work.'

'Do you know where he went?' Rafferty wanted to know, taking the lead again.

'No, Sergeant. If I had, I'd have informed the police.'

'Would you?'

Kemp lowered her eyes. 'Perhaps not.'

'Could he still be in Lincoln?' Rafferty asked.

'I doubt it. One of our residents would have seen him.'

'Not necessarily; not if he was no longer on the streets.'

'Again, I doubt he's found housing. He'd have no deposit, no references. I'd be surprised.'

'But you said he'd found a job in a pub?' Zaman pointed out. 'Some places let staff live in.'

'But if he was stealing from us, Constable, I expect he was stealing from them too. Petty cash, tips, things he could sell – who knows?'

Kemp sounded philosophical, but Rafferty could see the truth in her eyes again. Jake Pringle's betrayal had hurt.

'Do you know which pub it was?'

Kemp named a place on the outskirts of town. 'Danny helped him get the job; he's mates with the manager there. He's never mentioned Jake since he snatched our takings and ran.'

'What happened? Is it true he grabbed the cash from the till?'

'Yes, Sergeant. He waited until one of our volunteers had the till open to serve a customer, then he raced in, barged her out of the way, took the money and sprinted for the door. He already had the petty cash tin. It was found in a car park nearby, smashed open. There's no doubt it was Jake. I saw the CCTV footage myself.'

'Do you still have it?' Zaman asked the question before Rafferty could.

Kemp raised her eyebrows. 'No, it's recorded over after twenty-four hours.'

'But the footage was evidence of a crime, Mrs Kemp.' Rafferty's frustration was evident in her voice.

She snorted. 'We're not technical here, DS Rafferty. By the time a police officer eventually arrived, the footage was gone.'

'But surely…'

Maggie Kemp held up her hand. 'I know. I was furious too when I found out, but it's not something I had any involvement in. We can't afford a better system. It's a shame we need CCTV in a charity shop at all, and we decided the money a more sophisticated system would have cost would have been better used buying food or paying our bills.'

Rafferty made a note, not happy. She looked at Maggie Kemp, noting the other woman's calm. Dolan had told them to rattle a few cages. Perhaps it was time to try.

'Why did your husband leave the police force, Mrs Kemp?' she asked.

Kemp opened her mouth, closed it again. Zaman's phone was ringing, and he excused himself to answer outside the office.

'Mrs Kemp?' Rafferty prodded.

Kemp sighed. 'You'd have to talk to Pat to understand. He'd joined the force to help people, but he felt constrained.'

'Lucky he's not on the force now,' Rafferty told her. 'More budget cuts than you can imagine.'

'I'm sure, DS Rafferty. We're not rolling in money here at Phoenix House either, as you know. The main issue Pat had was the recidivism he saw. Arresting the same people repeatedly, seeing them go to prison, eventually come out and carry on offending because they knew no better, or hadn't had the right opportunities.'

'He gave up a career, a pension, because of a few old lags?' Rafferty was deliberately provocative. Maggie Kemp lifted her chin.

'And attitudes like yours, Sergeant.'

Rafferty sneered. 'Commendable. Noble, you might say. What does your husband do now?'

'When he left the police, Pat went to work for a gardener and tree surgeon. He has his own business now.'

'Mighty oaks from little acorns grow?' Rafferty got to her feet. 'I'm sure being on the board of Phoenix House helps satisfy your husband's need to nurture as well. We'll be back to talk to the night support workers. Thank you for your time.'

Maggie Kemp sat back, her expression unchanged.

In the corridor, Zaman was still on the phone. Rafferty approached him, raising her eyebrows. Zaman held her gaze.

'Okay, Mary. Thank you. Yes, ma'am, we'll see you later.' He put the phone away. 'The DCI says Pat Kemp left the force a month after John McKinley. No disciplinary, no scandal. He resigned, like McKinley did.'

Rafferty blinked a few times as she took in the new information. 'Let's go and find him.'

Maggie Kemp had given them her husband's mobile number without resistance. As Zaman drove, Rafferty ascertained where Kemp was working: a house in a village south-east of the city.

'He didn't sound overjoyed to hear from us,' Rafferty commented, flicking through her notes.

'His wife knows McKinley was murdered. She must have told him.'

'No doubt. Maggie Kemp stated she was at home with her husband the night John McKinley was killed. They ate together, watched some TV, she had a long bath while he walked the dog, they were both in bed and asleep by eleven. Let's see if Mr Kemp's memory is as good as his wife's.'

Pat Kemp was pushing a petrol lawnmower across an already immaculate front lawn when Rafferty and Zaman arrived at the address he had given them. Spotting their car, Kemp paused and watched Zaman park it at the side of the road, behind his own pickup truck. He turned off the mower as they approached.

'Morning, officers.'

'Thank you for seeing us, Mr Kemp.' Rafferty rubbed her hands together. 'It's a cold day to be outside working.'

'Keeps me out of mischief. Tea? The owners of the place are at work, but they've put a kettle in the shed so I can make myself a drink.'

They followed him around to the back of the property, where he ushered them into a large, surprisingly comfortable wooden shed. On a plastic garden table stood a kettle, four blue mugs, a box of tea bags, a large bottle of water and a radio. Four matching chairs with thick cushions provided the rest of the furniture. Kemp waved them towards the seats and filled the kettle.

'Have to bring my own milk, but it's more than most people bother to provide,' he said, pulling out a chair for himself and settling in it. 'Now, what can I help you with?'

'Hasn't your wife called you?' Rafferty asked.

Kemp frowned. 'Maggie? No, why should she? I wouldn't have heard, in any case, with the mower going. It was only because I'd stopped to empty the grass box I heard my phone when you rang. A bit of luck.' His expression suggested he'd sooner have missed the call.

Rafferty smiled. 'It was, Mr Kemp. Why did you leave the police?'

The kettle was wheezing away as it came to the boil, and Kemp cupped his hand around his ear. Both Rafferty and Zaman had seen his eyes widen at Rafferty's question, however quickly he had tried to hide the involuntary response.

'I'm sorry?' Rafferty reached out a hand, turning off the kettle. Kemp's mouth opened and he frowned. 'Hang on, I was making tea.'

'You can when you've answered my question.' Rafferty's voice was ice. Kemp blew out his cheeks, ran a hand over the back of his head, leaving his hair sticking out at an angle.

'This is a waste of all of our time,' he told them. 'You can find out why I left yourselves.' Kemp heaved himself to his feet.

'Please sit, Mr Kemp.' Rafferty leant forward and touched his arm. 'We want to talk to you about John McKinley.'

Kemp looked at her, tears in his eyes. 'I know,' he said softly. Kemp wrapped his hands around his mug of tea, staring out into the garden. 'He never had much luck – John, I mean. When I first met him, he loved the job. Loved it. I did too, but in the end… It grinds you down eventually, doesn't it? You two know what I'm talking about, especially if you're in CID or whatever they're calling it these days. Murders, suicides, RTAs – all the blood, the gore and the… the *emotion*. Dealing with fear, grief and anger – most of it directed at you – when all you want to do is help. It made me hate my job. It isn't a job, anyway, as you'll know. It's a way of life. There's all the crap within the force itself. Career coppers, walking over anyone in their way to grab onto the next rung of the ladder. Taking the credit for someone else's work. Abuses of trust, abuses of power.' He stopped suddenly, as if remembering he wasn't alone. 'Sorry. You know all this.'

Rafferty and Zaman were silent, wanting Kemp to keep talking.

'Anyway, I handed in my resignation. Disillusioned, I suppose. At least now, working outside, getting my hands dirty, I'm my own boss, my own man, not stuck taking orders from people I have no respect for.'

Rafferty shifted in her chair. 'Did John McKinley have the same view? We know he left the force a month before you did.'

Kemp drank more tea, set his cup on the table and wiped the back of his hand across his mouth. 'I didn't know John well. I saw him around the station sometimes.'

'Yet you came to talk to him at Phoenix House? You wanted to help him?' Zaman pressed.

Kemp tipped back his head, studying the wooden roof. 'Yeah, I did,' he said eventually. 'I remembered him, smart in his uniform, with a wife, a family. He had a future. When he arrived at Phoenix House, it was a shock. He was clean then, but he admitted he'd used drugs in the past. He was drinking though – drinking a lot. I hoped – stupidly, as it turned out, but I hoped I might be able to talk to him, help him. Maybe even offer him some work. He wasn't interested. Told me I was too late, I should have done something sooner. He walked out in the end.'

'What did he mean, you should have done something sooner?'

Kemp said, 'He'd already been on the streets in Lincoln for a while, but he hardly ever came to Phoenix House. I didn't know how he was living. I presumed he meant before he'd got himself into such a state.'

'Mr Kemp, where were you last Saturday night?' Rafferty asked.

'Saturday?'

Rafferty's voice was firm. 'Yes, sir.'

'Maggie and I got home about five thirty. We'd been out to do the weekly shop. I can give you the names of the places we went to, if you need them. We had dinner – Maggie had made a pie the day before and we finished it.' Kemp frowned, concentrating. Rafferty watched his face. 'We put the TV on, I read the paper. Maggie had a bath, I took Archie out. I had a shower when I got in – it had rained and we were soaked. We went to bed.'

'Have you ever used drugs yourself, Mr Kemp?' Zaman asked.

Kemp glared at him. 'I beg your pardon?'

'It's a reasonable question.'

'Because whoever it was who injected Mackie had to have known what they were doing, you mean?' Kemp shook his head. 'No. No, I've never used drugs. Not now, not ever.'

'Thank you, Mr Kemp.' Rafferty stood. 'We'll leave you to your work.'

'Wait a minute. Have you spoken to Mackie's ex-wife?'

Rafferty didn't need to check. 'No. They were divorced a long time ago.'

'They were,' Kemp said, his mouth twisting. 'But if anyone knew about using drugs, Dawn McKinley did.'

Back in the car, Rafferty tried to call Dolan, but only reached her voicemail.

'The soup kitchen first, then Danny Marshall,' she told Zaman. He started the engine.

'No solid answers from Pat Kemp. He had no idea who the bloke in our e-fit is either,' he commented.

'He gave us another lead though. Dawn McKinley – someone else to question, at any rate.' Rafferty stared through the car window as Zaman executed a three-point turn. 'He looked like he was going to cry at one point.'

'When he was making the tea? I know.'

Drumming her fingers on her thigh, Rafferty frowned. 'Which seems an extreme reaction to being asked to speak about the death of someone he claims he hardly knew.'

Chapter 28

In St Benedict's Square, in Lincoln's city centre, Catherine Bishop sat on a wooden bench, her bag at her feet. Situated off the main shopping thoroughfare, the square held a church of the same name, now no longer in use as a place of worship. Catherine had walked past it more times than she could remember, and though she had paused at the war memorial which stood outside the church building before, it was a place she had hardly noticed. In this part of the city, familiar chain shops and throngs of people meant you could be anywhere. There was nothing of the individuality that made the uphill area of the city special. Catherine tucked her chin further inside her fleece. Though the sun was bright, a cold wind meant sitting still for any length of time wasn't advisable. It would soon be time to return to the soup kitchen, though Catherine had no great desire to go there again. Perhaps she would buy some chips instead. She wouldn't be missed, and if Dolan and Rafferty wanted to complain, let them.

Catherine drew her feet onto the seat of the bench and wrapped her arms around her knees, ignoring the disapproving glances of a passing elderly couple. Resting her forehead on her arms, she closed her eyes, oblivious to the stares of those around her. The sense of despair that had been haunting her for weeks was threatening to engulf her. She wished again she had never agreed to the assignment. She needed help; she could admit it now. Mentally, she was struggling. These feelings, this ache, wasn't going to leave her without some persuasion. Jo Webber had noticed, as had Danny Marshall. And Knight, and Kendrick. Who else? Who else had seen it clearly, when she herself was blind to her own struggles? Perhaps Ellie had sensed it without understanding why Catherine had pushed her away. With tears in her eyes, tears she couldn't explain, Catherine got to her feet as though she were sleepwalking. Her limbs were heavy, her mind and body begging her to stop, to rest. To give in, submit. She stood for a moment, the ground appearing to lurch beneath her feet.

'Are you all right?'

Catherine blinked, recognising the voice. Blindly, she turned her head as a hand gripped her elbow.

'Come on, let me buy you a coffee.'

Like a child, Catherine allowed Jonathan Knight to lead her away.

Chapter 29

'This needs to stop, now. She can't carry on, look at her.'
Knight was pacing in front of Mary Dolan, who sat in the
small office which served as the makeshift incident room
for the McKinley investigation. By the door, Catherine
Bishop slumped in a chair, her face blank, eyes on her
shoes. 'She's ill. She needs to see a doctor.' Knight came
to an abrupt halt. 'Mary, please.'

Dolan pushed back her chair. 'DS Bishop?' She moved
over to Catherine, crouched in front of her. 'Catherine,
look at me.' Slowly, Catherine raised her chin, fixing her
gaze on Dolan. Tears were falling again, but Catherine
seemed not to notice them. She was silent, weeping noise-
lessly. Dolan took out a tissue, wrapped Catherine's hand
around it. 'Time you went home, Catherine.' Her voice
was gentle. Catherine blinked a few times, tried to speak.

'No, I... I haven't finished.'

Dolan stood, her knees cracking. 'Yes, you have.'

Catherine was defiant now. 'No. I'm okay. Please.'

'Catherine, Jo wants to talk to you,' Knight said. 'She'll
go to your GP with you too, if you like. You can have
some leave, get some help.'

'No.' Catherine turned, glaring at Knight as the tears
continued to fall. 'The investigation isn't over. We don't
know who killed Mackie, and until we do, I'm staying

201

here.' She scrubbed her hands across her eyes, frustrated. 'Can't stop bloody crying...'

Dolan and Knight exchanged a glance. Dolan raised her eyebrows and slipped out of the door. Knight stepped closer to Catherine, took her by the shoulders.

'Listen to me. You're obviously ill, and as your commanding officer...'

Catherine snorted. 'As my what? You wanted me to come here, to do this. Now you've changed your mind? What happened to it being "good for me"?'

'I didn't know you were ill.'

'I'm fine. Let me get on with my job.'

She tried to twist away, but Knight held on. 'Catherine, listen. Go home, go on sick leave and get better.'

Catherine turned on him. 'What's wrong, Jonathan? Do you want me out of the way?'

'What?' Knight was horrified. 'I'm worried about you – have you looked in a mirror recently? You're ill, Catherine.'

'A mirror? No, you don't get many on the street, funnily enough. It's difficult to worry about your appearance when you don't know where you're going to sleep.'

'You're not homeless.'

'No, but the poor bastards I've been spending time with are. I'm talking to them, lying to them, knowing I'll soon be safe in my own bed, my own house, and they'll still be out there. No, I haven't looked in a mirror. I don't want to see my face.' She jerked away from him. 'Leave me alone, Jonathan. Let me do my job. Don't worry, if anyone asks, I'll keep your secret.'

'Catherine...' It was a plea. She scowled at him, and when she spoke again, it was in a tone he'd never heard from her before.

'Tell DCI Dolan I'm going to the soup kitchen. I'll stay on the street until the case is closed. Stay away from me, Jonathan.'

Knight stood in the centre of the room and let her go. As she passed, he closed his eyes. He knew what he had to do, but did he have the courage? Could he admit the truth? He had accepted the help of a career criminal, however pure his reasons.

Could he risk destroying Catherine's career as well as his own?

Chapter 30

Rafferty saw Catherine Bishop immediately. She sat at a table with two other women, dipping a piece of bread into a polystyrene cup. Catherine didn't turn her head, but one of the women she was sitting with spotted them and made a comment. Catherine did look then. There was no reaction as she recognised Zaman and Rafferty.

There were several volunteers around, wearing plastic aprons. Rafferty approached the nearest, who was clearing a table.

'Excuse me,' she said. 'We're looking for Joel Rushford?' She took out her warrant card and held it out. The woman, seeing Rafferty was a police officer, put her hand to her mouth.

'He's in his office. I'll show you.'

She trotted across the room, eager to help, obviously dying to know what was going on. Rafferty and Zaman followed, Zaman still uneasy. He hadn't made eye contact with Catherine Bishop, hadn't wanted to. The best way to protect her was to treat her the same as everyone else in the room – as if they didn't exist. It wasn't easy.

-

'They're coppers, I can smell it a mile off.' Jasmine watched Rafferty and Zaman cross the room. She drank the last of her soup. 'I'm off. Not hanging around with them here. Coming?'

Ghislaine stood, crumpling her cup. Catherine pushed back her chair, glad her tears had stopped. If she ignored the fatigue in her bones, the tic under her eye and the crawling sense of dread in her sluggish brain, she could kid herself she was okay. She had to do this. She owed it to John McKinley, to the people she'd met. To Ghislaine and Jasmine.

They weren't the only customers of the soup kitchen who had decided to beat a hasty retreat. Once again, Catherine marvelled at the fact that police officers were so easily recognised. Rafferty and Zaman were smartly dressed, but they could have been anyone – salespeople, church representatives. All right, Rafferty had displayed her warrant card, but Catherine had noticed several people leave as soon as the two officers had appeared, before any identification had been shown. She felt vulnerable. If Rafferty and Zaman were obvious, why wasn't she? She was no actor. There was more to being homeless than chucking on some grubby clothes and hauling a bag of belongings around, yet she seemed to have been accepted. She followed Ghislaine and Jasmine out of the door. She was deceiving them, and it bothered her, more than she had admitted even to Knight.

In the street, Jasmine checked her phone.

'I'm off. See you later, ladies.'

'All right, Jas,' Ghislaine said. Jasmine sauntered away with a wave.

Catherine could see Ghislaine was troubled, but didn't want to pry. Still, she had to if she wanted to make more headway.

'See she's got her rucksack with her again.'

'Maybe it's surgically attached.' Ghislaine tried a smile. 'Though I've been robbed enough times to know it's sensible to keep your stuff with you. People will always steal, even if they know you don't have much.'

'I'll keep it in mind. Listen, what they were saying about Jasmine and Danny Marshall last night – is it true?'

Ghislaine took a step backwards, instantly defensive. 'Why do you want to know?'

'No reason. I had an appointment with him yesterday, and I didn't know what to make of him.'

'I wouldn't take too much notice. It was only Lee and the others having a laugh. Jasmine loves the attention, which means she won't deny anything.'

'You don't believe it?'

'Danny would have to be totally stupid.'

'You don't know Jasmine well then? Aren't you best friends?'

Ghislaine gave a short laugh. 'Jasmine knows loads of people.'

'Will she be going to see one of her mates?' *Careful*, Catherine told herself as Ghislaine glanced away.

'Don't know. Anyway, I'm going to head off as well.' She raised a hand and walked away.

Catherine stepped back, leaning against the church's rough stone wall. Ghislaine was in a hurry, rushing along in the same direction Jasmine had taken. Catherine watched, intrigued. Was Ghislaine following her friend? And if so, shouldn't she investigate?

Chapter 31

Joel Rushford's office wasn't large, but the vicar had furnished it comfortably. A tall pine bookcase filled most of one wall, with Rushford's desk, a small leather sofa and two straight-backed wooden chairs for visitors crammed into the rest of the space. Rushford himself sat in an expensive-looking leather office chair, with a small oil heater, the only source of heat in the room, Rafferty noted, close to it. Rushford waved Zaman and Rafferty into the wooden chairs which, Rafferty soon realised, were as uncomfortable as they looked. Rushford smiled, looking from one officer to the other, and back again.

'Good to see you again, DC Zaman. And you've brought a colleague with you today.' He widened his smile, his eyes travelling over Rafferty's body. 'Pleased to meet you.'

Rafferty remained stony-faced. If Rushford was hoping to provoke her or, more nauseatingly, charm her, he'd have to do much better. Zaman shifted in his chair, and Rafferty knew he would expect her to have a quick retort ready. Instead, she sat back and crossed her legs, making herself as comfortable as it was possible to be in the unforgiving chair. She made eye contact with Rushford, whose smile had dimmed a little.

'Are you sleeping with Jasmine Lloyd, Mr Rushford?'

The effect on the vicar was immediate. His mouth opened and closed a few times.

'I beg your pardon? I'm a married man, DS Rafferty, and I resent the implication.'

Rafferty smiled. 'And we all know married men never have affairs, don't we?' She leant forward. 'So if a witness had informed us you and Ms Lloyd were, shall we say, more intimate than the average vicar and parishioner, the witness would be lying?'

Rushford swallowed. 'Yes. It's totally untrue.'

'Hmm.' Rafferty raised a hand, touching her index finger to her lips. Rushford watched the gesture, his face red. 'And if we were to tell you we had several witnesses, all repeating the same allegation about your relationship with Ms Lloyd, *all* of those witnesses would be lying?'

'Yes, they would. Who's been telling you this? I don't... If my wife hears these rumours...' Rushford managed to sound indignant.

'Embarrassing. Unfair, too, since you're innocent.'

'Can I ask, Sergeant, what exactly you want to talk to me about? What have these baseless lies to do with anything? They're hardly a matter for the police.' Rushford spoke theatrically, but with more conviction, confident he was regaining the upper hand.

'No, extramarital affairs are none of our business. Unless...' Rafferty dragged the word out, studying her fingernails.

Rushford frowned. 'Unless?'

'Unless they're linked to a crime, a serious crime. Murder, for example.'

Rushford gave a strangled laugh. 'Murder? What the f... What are you talking about?'

'Careful, Father.' Rafferty laughed.

'Reverend, not Father,' Rushford said automatically.

She smirked. 'My mistake.'

Rushford looked from Rafferty to Zaman. 'Whose murder are you talking about?'

'John McKinley's.'

'Mackie was murdered?' Rushford appeared genuinely confused.

'We believe he was.'

'But why? He was harmless.'

'Perhaps because he knew something he shouldn't?'

Rushford gave her a cold stare. 'What are you insinuating, Sergeant?'

'Nothing at all. We'll see ourselves out.'

—

Danny Marshall was at home, he told them on the phone. His house was in the centre of a row of terraces, cars parked nose to bumper on both sides of the street, even in the mid-afternoon on a weekday.

'Nowhere to park here either,' Zaman grumbled. As they approached a corner shop, a vehicle pulled away from the kerb, leaving a space big enough for Zaman to shuffle his car into.

As they made their way towards Marshall's house, Rafferty stopped.

'Are you sure this is the right address?' She nodded at a BMX bike leaning against the front hedge of what they believed to be his property. 'Seems a strange thing for a man of Marshall's age to ride.'

'Maybe he has a visitor?'

Rafferty thumped on the door, and Marshall opened it immediately.

'Is this your bike?' Rafferty demanded.

'Bike?' Marshall raised himself onto his tiptoes, peering out. 'No, it belongs to the kid next door. He's left school, hasn't managed to find a job yet. He rides around on his stupid BMX all day, when it's not spoiling my hedge, of course. Come in.'

Marshall showed them into a small living room, dominated by a huge TV displaying some sort of army-themed video game. He picked up the remote control and switched off the set. 'I had a client not arrive for a counselling session, and I had some free time. Decided to come home and relax for a while.'

'Looked like you were doing well.' Zaman gestured towards the screen. Marshall grinned as he waved them towards the sofa before perching on a bean bag.

'Mr Marshall, did you offer counselling to John McKinley?' Rafferty asked.

'You know I did. I explained to the other officers.'

'Jasmine Lloyd too?'

'Yes. Jasmine, Ghislaine, Lee – all of them.'

There had been no reaction on Marshall's face when he had mentioned Jasmine's name. They knew it meant nothing. Marshall would be used to keeping his face impassive during his work. A good poker face would be essential.

Rafferty asked, 'What about Jake Pringle?'

'Jake?' Marshall's face darkened. 'Why are you asking about him?'

'Please answer the question, Mr Marshall.'

'Yes, I talked with him. Counselling is offered to everyone who stays at Phoenix House. Part of the conditions of them being offered a bed is they talk to me, so I can confer with Maggie about how best to help them. You know all this.' Marshall sounded frustrated.

'And how did Jake Pringle react to you? Was he receptive?'

'He was, at least at first. We helped him find a GP who could assist with his medical needs. As far as we knew, he'd stopped injecting. Then he disappeared.'

'After stealing money.'

Marshall's fists clenched. 'If you know, why are you asking me?'

'Mrs Kemp told us you'd helped Jake find a job. What happened?'

'In retrospect, it was the wrong placement. A kitchen is a high-pressured environment, even in a local pub. Jake didn't cope well with stress, and of course there was cash around, plus stuff he could sell, like bottles of spirits... It was my fault, I know.'

'Your fault Pringle couldn't control himself?' Rafferty stood, wandered over to the window.

Marshall scowled. 'Jake had problems, DS Rafferty. He came from an abusive home; he was a product of the care system...'

Rafferty snorted. 'We get it. Horrible childhood, poor unloved, badly-done-to Jake: stealing, drink, drugs. Inevitable, not his fault and we should all be sorry for him. Correct?'

Marshall was shaking his head. 'I'm not sure if you're trying to provoke me, Sergeant, but it won't work. You don't fool me – you don't believe a word of what you said.

You understand what difficulties people face, and you care.'

Rafferty turned away. 'What I care about is finding the person who killed John McKinley. What can you tell us? You know the people at Phoenix House, past residents as well as the present ones. Help us out, Danny. Who might have murdered him?'

'Murdered him? Seriously?'

'We have reason to believe John McKinley was deliberately killed.'

'But...' Marshall's mouth gaped. 'He was completely harmless. Who would have murdered him?'

Rafferty noted Marshall had said Mackie was harmless, as Joel Rushford had a short time before.

'Someone who knew about drugs, and knew where to buy them,' she said.

Marshall rallied, visibly pulling himself together. 'Anyone could get them, Sergeant. I bet you'd know where to go if you wanted to. You can't work in the environment we do without picking up a few tips.'

'Point taken,' Rafferty said. 'In your counselling sessions, no one's said anything suspicious?'

'Not at all.'

'Would you tell us if they had?'

Marshall looked at her. 'I would. There might be confidentiality issues, but not with murder. Mackie was... I only spoke to him once or twice, but he was different.'

'In what way?' Rafferty asked.

'He'd seen it all. He knew the streets, knew how to survive. The others kept their distance because they knew it was what he preferred, but at the same time, he was there to give advice. Where to sleep safely, places to avoid. He'd been there and done it.'

'If we were looking for a motive, a reason for someone to kill him, it could be because of something Mackie knew? Something he'd seen, or heard?' Zaman asked.

'It wouldn't take a huge leap of imagination, would it? It makes sense. People talked to him. And homeless people, they see things. People don't notice them, don't even realise they're there half the time. But they are, and they're aware. Trying to get some rest on the street makes you hyper-aware of your surroundings.'

'It sounds like you're speaking from experience,' Rafferty said softly. Danny Marshall gazed at her.

'I am. I was on the streets for a few weeks after university. It wasn't too bad, but it leaves a mark. I see it on the people I work with.'

—

In the car, Rafferty sat back, stretching out her legs. 'He wasn't completely honest.'

Zaman checked his rear-view mirror. 'About what?'

'I don't know. It was the impression he gave. Not lying exactly, but...'

'Not telling the whole truth?'

'Yeah. Especially about Jasmine Lloyd.'

'Maybe we should talk to Jasmine next.'

Rafferty took out her phone. 'Later. First, Mary wanted us to speak to Lee Collinson. I'll phone him.'

—

Collinson was in a pub, an old, traditional place by the castle. Rafferty strode inside, her eyes scanning the bar. The place had recently been refurbished, the sharp scent of paint still in the air. Zaman spotted Collinson, who acknowledged them with a wave. He was sitting by the huge stone fireplace, a half-drunk pint of bitter in front of him, warming his hands. Collinson had a thin, angular face and watchful brown eyes. He shifted in his chair as if ready to escape at any second. Zaman had seen the same nervousness in ex-prisoners before. In some cases, being constantly alert to danger was the only thing that had allowed them to serve their sentence relatively unscathed.

'Can I get you another?' Rafferty gestured towards Collinson's drink.

'Cheers,' he replied. Zaman found some spare chairs as Rafferty returned to the bar. 'She your boss?' Collinson asked.

'One of them.'

'Can't be bad. Very decorative.'

Zaman ignored him, and Collinson smirked. 'Don't tell me you haven't noticed.'

Again, Zaman said nothing. Rafferty returned with a tray, set a full pint on the table in front of Collinson. He smiled at her, a gold tooth glinting at the back of his mouth. Rafferty handed Zaman a bottle of lager, and took the second bottle for herself.

'Thanks, love.' Collinson took an appreciative sip, smacking his lips together. 'One of the things I missed when I was inside, a decent pint.' He leered at Rafferty. 'I'm sure you can guess the other thing.' He leant forward, blatantly ogling Rafferty's chest. She ignored Collinson's performance, poured beer into the glass she'd brought with her and drank half in one gulp. Collinson watched, impressed. 'Looks like you were ready for that, darling. Not sure I approve of drinking on duty, mind.'

Rafferty set her glass on the table. 'It's alcohol-free.'

He laughed. 'Spoilsport.'

'How did you know John McKinley?'

Collinson stared. 'You what?'

'John McKinley. Mackie. We've been told you'd known him for a long time. Years, our witness said. Not what you told our colleagues in uniform when you made your statement, was it?'

Collinson's cheeks reddened. 'Who's been talking?'

'We speak to everyone, Mr Collinson, as you should know,' Rafferty told him.

He laughed. 'And poke your noses in everywhere, don't you?'

'If we have to. How did you know him? When did you meet?'

Collinson stuck out his chin. 'Does this mean you're finally taking his death seriously?'

'Sorry?'

'Everyone's saying he died of an overdose. Blackening his name.' Collinson lifted his beer. 'Made me sick.'

'He had used drugs before,' Zaman said mildly.

Collinson snorted. 'Says who? He never did when I knew him.'

'Which was...?' Rafferty brought him back on track.

'He was a mate of my brother's when we were young. They were older, my brother didn't want to be seen dead with me, but John was all right. Let me go fishing with them, join in. When I heard he was dead... Well, I wanted to see if there was anything I could do, maybe try some poking around of my own.'

Sipping her drink, Rafferty gazed at Collinson over the rim of her glass. 'You didn't trust the police?'

'Why should I? You were treating his death as accidental.'

'No. No, we weren't.'

Collinson took a long swallow from his glass. 'Not how it looked to me.'

'What do you know?'

'How do you mean?'

'You said you'd been poking around. What can you tell us?'

'Bloody rich coming from you.' Collinson laughed. 'Aren't you supposed to be detectives?'

'Come on, Lee. You're not stupid.'

Collinson leant back in his chair, gazing into the fire. 'Some people might not agree.'

'You made a mistake. You served your time.'

'I killed a man.'

Rafferty sighed. 'We know you did. You hit another car head-on when you were answering your phone, a call from your ex-girlfriend to say your son was seriously ill. Meningitis, wasn't it?'

'He... Yes.' Collinson's shoulders hunched, as if to ward off a blow.

'And your son died, didn't he, Lee?'

Collinson raised his head, his eyes bright with tears. 'Yeah. The judge only gave me two years. Felt sorry for me, I reckon. He shouldn't have done.'

For a few seconds, no one spoke. With an impatient movement, Collinson dashed his hand across his eyes. 'Anyway, we're not here to talk about me.'

'So tell us.'

'About Mackie's death? I don't know anything. Tell you what, though. Everyone staying at the shelter has a secret.' Collinson tapped his nose.

'We all have secrets,' Rafferty said.

'True. You'll have spoken to them all, I suppose?'

'We have.'

'You have,' Collinson repeated. 'Do you know why Mackie was killed?'

Rafferty shook her head. 'Come on, Lee. We're asking the questions.'

Collinson tipped his head to the side, mock-hurt. 'And we were getting on so well.'

'Why might Mackie have been murdered?'

Collinson finished his first pint and drank a third of the one Rafferty had bought before replying. 'People talked to Mackie. I don't know why he was killed, but I do know this: people confided in him. Even back when I was a kid, I could see it. He always had a girl on the go because he knew how to listen, and he knew how to talk to people.' Collinson swallowed more beer. 'What about your colleague?'

'Can you be more specific?' Zaman asked.

Collinson lowered his voice. 'The one who was stabbed. Did you know there's a bloke on the market who sells second-hand phones?'

Rafferty nodded. 'We've spoken to him.'

'Right.' Collinson ducked his head.

'Mr Collinson? Do you have information?' Rafferty was stern.

'No, no. Wanted to mention it. Should've known you'd have it covered.'

Rafferty gave him a long stare. 'If you wanted to get out of Phoenix House at night, could you?'

Collinson rubbed his chin, considering it. 'You could do, I suppose. I've never done it, mind.'

'But it's not impossible?'

'Impossible?' Collinson met Rafferty's eyes. 'No. I'd say easy.'

Chapter 32

Jasmine had disappeared, lost in a laughing, jostling crowd of students, and Catherine had lost sight of Ghislaine too. So much for her undercover investigation – she hadn't been able to follow them for more than ten minutes. Pathetic.

Catherine stood back, close to the water's edge, allowing another group of people to pass. They were older, more her own age, and she remembered the night she'd spent with Ellie and her colleagues in the city. It was less than a week ago, but it seemed much longer. She hadn't phoned Ellie again, not even to update her on Anna's condition. She should have done, she knew, but the reluctance had returned. Ellie deserved better than her.

She zipped up her jacket, hunching her shoulders against the cold. She was by the water, at the side of the Brayford Pool. There were restaurants, bars, even a cinema. It was an area where Catherine had felt comfortable, enjoyed visiting. Groups of friends, couples, all of them out for a good time. Had Jasmine even passed this way? It was doubtful she had the money for a night out, but it was possible. She could be meeting someone, one of the men she had been teased about the night before perhaps. Catherine considered it, but dismissed the idea.

Too public. They weren't far from the bus or train station here – it was possible Jasmine had left the city centre altogether.

Catherine rubbed her hands together, the cold biting at them. It was mid-afternoon, but the sky had darkened, threatening rain. She knew she had been lucky to have a bed at the shelter. The lack of privacy, of comfort, had been nothing compared to what she would have had to endure if she had slept out on the street. Not for the first time, she considered how people survived this life. At least she would go home eventually. For Ghislaine, for Jasmine and the others, there was no such certainty. No one should have to live like this. She remembered reading that the average life expectancy for a homeless man in England was forty-seven years, forty-three for a woman. After only two days on the street and one night at the shelter, Catherine could see why. She was already struggling.

She had enough money to go inside one of the bars, grab a drink as she had the previous evening. The prospect held no appeal, alone as she was. Even Rafferty's company would be preferable. She remembered the previous evening, Rafferty's unexpected appearance in the pub. Catherine still wasn't sure why Rafferty had arrived to see her in person. Perhaps they were keeping an eye on her? They could track her movements, but not her actions, or state of mind. Perhaps her mental health was what they were worried about. Rafferty hadn't been friendly, but her manner had been less cold than on their previous meetings. She had confided a little about her personal life, even admitted to being tired. Perhaps Rafferty was human, after all.

Catherine knew she should be talking to people, searching for clues about Mackie's murder, about Anna's stabbing. Instead she was hiding here, her heart thumping, her hands trembling, wanting nothing more than to turn her back on the city and run.

Taking her phone, her personal mobile, from her bag, she selected a number, ending the call before it connected. She knew she had been too harsh when she'd spoken to Jonathan Knight earlier, but what had he expected? He'd treated her like a wayward child, trying to ferry her back to headquarters as if she were incapable of thinking for herself. She smiled. Perhaps she was. Over the past few weeks, months even, she had felt herself slipping away. Now, the decline was welcome, almost comforting. She wouldn't fight it.

She took a few breaths, attempting to steady the tumble of her thoughts, and lifted the phone to her ear again.

'Catherine?' His voice was quiet, as if he didn't want to be overheard. She didn't speak, staring out over the expanse of water. The churning mass of dread crawling through her body couldn't be described, not in any words she was familiar with. 'Are you there?' Knight asked. 'Where are you, Catherine?'

'Brayford Wharf,' she managed to whisper, though he would be able to find her if he wanted to. He had earlier.

'I'm coming. Stay where you are.'

She pushed the phone into her jacket pocket as she stumbled towards a nearby concrete bench. Why had she called him? Only a few hours before, she had told him to leave her alone. Knight couldn't help her. He had his own problems, his own concerns. She wrapped her arms around her body, her gaze fixed on the ground. Behind her, people hurried by, chatting and laughing. Catherine was oblivious. Dragging her focus away from the torment of her own mind was, in that instant, impossible. She felt as though she had been tied to a post and left to wait for high tide, as if she were watching the waves ebb ever nearer, slowly eroding her intelligence, her personality. Whatever made her the person she was, or had been.

He didn't speak at first, but sat beside her, taking both of her hands in one of his own.

'Shall we get you out of here?' Knight asked at last. She couldn't reply, but she got to her feet and he followed. Her legs were leaden, her mind blank, as if she were watching the scene unfold without being part of it. Knight took her arm, supporting her as they walked. He had parked as close as he was able, a multi-storey car park by Brayford Wharf. When they reached his car, Knight opened the passenger door, and slowly, carefully, Catherine climbed inside. Knight slammed the door, got into the driver's seat and put on the heater.

'Catherine, you need to go home,' he told her. 'This can't go on.'

'One more night,' she said, barely opening her lips.

'Rafferty and Zaman are due in the incident room soon,' Knight told her. 'Why don't you come back with me? There's a briefing in an hour. Talk to DCI Dolan again. They may not need you out here now. She did say you didn't have to do this any more.'

'Fine,' Catherine whispered. Her head ached, and she leant forward, pushing her fingers through her hair.

Knight started the engine, giving her no time to change her mind.

Chapter 33

Giles Melis, Dolan's least favourite detective sergeant, was digging crisps from a packet and pushing fistfuls into his mouth as Dolan entered the briefing room. She wrinkled her nose as the stench of cheese wafted towards her from his orange-stained fingers.

'Wash your hands, Melis,' she ordered. He grinned, taking his now-customary seat at the front of the room as Dolan gazed out at the sea of officers. When everyone was seated, she gestured towards the photo of Anna Varcoe, still smiling down on them.

'Anna's hanging on in there,' she told them. 'Who has something to report?'

Melis waved his hand.

'Go on.' Mary Dolan treated him to her best hard stare.

'I spoke to a man on the phone who'd seen our e-fit in the local paper,' Melis told them. 'It jogged his memory.' He paused, turning in his chair to check his colleagues were listening.

'Get on with it,' Dolan barked.

Melis smirked. 'This gentleman recognises our suspect. He's seen him before, more than once.' He coughed, cleared his throat.

Dolan glowered. 'You're not making an Academy Award acceptance speech, Melis. Enough dramatic pauses; tell us what you know.'

'He said he's seen him begging around town.'

Dolan raised her eyebrows. 'Recently?'

'In the last few weeks.'

'He could be anywhere by now,' Dolan thundered.

'I'm telling you what he said.' Melis wasn't the least apologetic. 'Can't help it if it's not what you want to hear.'

'Not exactly the concrete evidence we're looking for. Go back to him, DS Melis. Do your job.' Dolan turned on her heel, her gaze flitting over the assembled officers. 'Anyone else?'

Shrugs, headshakes. Dolan clenched her jaw. Rafferty and Zaman were on their way back to Headquarters, but they would have nothing to contribute either. Anna Varcoe had not been their focus today. At the back of the room, Dolan spotted Jonathan Knight, and, to her fury, Catherine Bishop. Bishop looked terrible – pale and gaunt.

'DS Bishop.' Dolan waved at her. 'Come out here and introduce yourself.' Catherine looked up, confused, as Knight frowned at Dolan. 'Come on, Catherine. We haven't got all day.' She knew she was being unfair, was aware that what she was doing was cruel. Anyone could see Catherine Bishop was struggling. But Anna Varcoe was lying in hospital with machinery breathing for her. Dolan decided it was time to take off the kid gloves. As Catherine stumbled to the front of the room, Dolan said, 'DS Bishop has been our eyes on the ground over the last few days, mingling with the homeless people of the city, trying to discover what they know. What do you have to report, Catherine?'

Catherine lifted her chin, staring into Dolan's eyes. 'Nothing,' she muttered.

Dolan bared her teeth. 'Nothing. Absolutely fucking nothing. Pretty much sums up our entire case, doesn't it?'

There was silence. Officers were studying their shoes, their cheeks flushed, their eyes focused on anything but Dolan's furious face. In the front row, Melis was sitting back, legs crossed, observing Dolan's meltdown with a smirk on his face as if he were watching a particularly amusing play at the theatre.

'Get out of my sight, the lot of you,' Dolan snarled. 'Be here at seven sharp in the morning.'

There was a rush for the door. Dolan turned away, guilt descending. Catherine Bishop stood quietly as Knight approached.

'Was that necessary?' he demanded of Dolan.

'Sometimes you have to put a rocket up their arse.'

'Right,' Knight sneered. 'I'm going to speak to Detective Superintendent Stringer. Catherine's coming with me.' He took Catherine's arm, jabbing a finger at Dolan. 'You were completely out of order.'

Dolan turned. 'I'm not here to be liked.'

Melis sauntered over, hands in his trouser pockets. 'Bloody good job, isn't it?'

'Enough, Sergeant,' Dolan told him. 'Go home. All of you, get out of here.'

She walked out, shoulders slumped. Knight stared after her, still holding Catherine's arm.

–

In the corridor outside, Dolan's hands were over her eyes, her shoulders trembling. What she had done was unacceptable. She should go directly to ACC Clement, tell him she would be travelling back to Nottingham as soon as he had found a replacement for her. No doubt she was already the talk of Lincolnshire Police Force. It was difficult to care. Knight had surprised her, though. She'd only known him a day, but she was willing to bet it took a lot to break his composure. Interesting that it had taken a dig at Catherine Bishop to draw him out of his shell. Catherine was gay, she knew, but there was an obvious bond between the two which intrigued Dolan. If it wasn't sexual, what was it?

A male voice interrupted her thoughts.

'Ma'am?'

Dolan froze. 'What are you doing here, Melis?'

'Thought you might want to talk. Looks like you could use a drink, too.'

She laughed, the sound harsh to her own ears. 'Are you joking?'

'Never been more serious in my life.'

Dolan turned. Melis ran a hand over his shaved head, waiting for a response.

'I'll need to wait for Rafferty and Zaman. They should be on their way back,' Dolan said.

Melis lifted his shoulders. 'I'll go out and get some food, bring it back here. We can have a picnic.'

–

Catherine stopped, her hand on Knight's arm. 'I'm not coming with you.'

Dolan's performance had hurt, of course it had, but it had also woken Catherine from the stupor that had been threatening to drag her out of sight. She blinked a few times, taking in Knight's face. 'You go home. Spend some time with Jo, but come back tomorrow. Please don't go to Stringer. Dolan's a good officer, but she's frustrated. We all know how it feels when we've made no progress on an investigation.'

'We haven't all thrown our toys out of the pram though,' Knight pointed out. 'The case is hardly a few days old.'

'I know. She's right about one thing though. I need to be at Phoenix House. This homeless man Melis mentioned – what if his witness was right?'

Knight shook his head. 'If you're sure.'

'I am. I'll be in touch.'

Catherine walked away. Her lips trembled, but she steeled herself. Her mind might tell her to give up, to go home, but she wouldn't. She was in this until the end.

Chapter 34

Back in the smaller incident room, Rafferty and Zaman updated Dolan on their findings. Dolan listened carefully, more at ease now she was with her team. She was used to working with different officers, but she had to admit having people around her she knew, who she could trust, was invaluable.

'It's interesting Pat Kemp mentioned working with John McKinley during his early days on the force. You said McKinley told Kemp he was too late, he should have done something sooner. Did you press him, ask what McKinley meant?'

'He took it to mean McKinley needed help when he first found himself on the street, not when he'd been living rough for a while. Kemp didn't seem sure though.'

'Adil?' Dolan glanced at him.

'I'd agree with DS Rafferty, ma'am. We can't assume we know what McKinley meant, especially after Danny Marshall told us McKinley knew things, saw things. Lee Collinson said people talked to John McKinley and he knew how to listen. What if he had knowledge that made him dangerous to someone?'

'And ultimately got him killed,' Rafferty said.

Dolan nodded. 'We need to speak to his ex-wife. They were still married when John McKinley quit the force. Do we know where she lives?'

'About thirty miles away,' Rafferty told her. Dolan checked her watch.

'Go and speak to her now. It's not late. Phone later and update me.'

Rafferty and Zaman got to their feet. Soon after the door had closed behind them, Melis arrived bearing a huge pizza box.

'Dinner is served, ma'am.' He set the box on the table with a flourish. Dolan laughed, despite the dig of unease. Melis was proving to be something of a chameleon.

–

Dawn McKinley's house was at the end of a row of terraced cottages, on the outskirts of a small village. The sky was dark as they parked outside, a few street lights illuminating the gloom. Rafferty flicked on the interior light, flipped the mirror on the car's sun visor to check her appearance. She was exhausted, grubby and wished she was back in her hotel room, running a bath. Instead she was out here, hoping for a break. Zaman had been quiet on the drive out of the city, and Rafferty knew he would be regretting missing another of his young daughter's bedtimes.

'Let's do this as quickly as we can.'

Zaman smiled. 'I won't argue.'

As they approached Dawn McKinley's front door, a security light glared into action, momentarily blinding them. Rafferty squinted as she thumped on the grubby white front door. A frenzied yapping came from inside the house. Eventually, a security chain rattled. The door opened slightly and a bleary eye appeared in the narrow gap.

'Who is it?'

Rafferty held out her warrant card. 'Police, Mrs McKinley. We'd like to speak to you about your ex-husband.'

A hand appeared, snatching the identification from Rafferty's grasp. The yapping continued, now interspersed with growling, but thankfully the dog making all the racket didn't appear.

At last, the door swung open fully and a short, plump woman appeared, dressed in a fluffy leopard-print dressing gown and huge mouse-shaped slippers.

'You'd better come in,' she told them.

The living room was small and overcrowded, with a large three-piece suite, a dresser and a vast TV crammed around its walls. In the centre of the room stood a battered coffee table, laden with celebrity gossip magazines and unwashed mugs. The TV was switched on, but muted, one of the soap operas beaming extra misery into homes all over the country. Dawn McKinley picked up a glass containing a clear liquid as she showed them into the room.

'Sit. I'll put the kettle on.'

'There's no need, thank you. We don't want to take up much of your time,' Rafferty told her.

'Don't worry. If you want to ask about John, you won't need long.' Dawn McKinley drank from her glass and wiped the back of her hand across her mouth. She settled in one of the armchairs, her gaze straying back to the TV, cradling the glass to her considerable chest.

The dog continued to bark in the background, but Dawn McKinley made no move to intervene.

'It must have been a shock to hear of your ex-husband's death?' Rafferty said.

'And to find out he'd been living like a tramp. When I first saw the officers at the front door, I thought, "Here we go, John's topped himself." He always was a miserable bastard.' Dawn McKinley drank again.

Rafferty watched. Did the glass contain gin or vodka? She doubted it was water. McKinley's words weren't slurred and she wasn't staggering, but Rafferty knew it meant nothing. If she were any judge, whatever was in Dawn McKinley's glass was a long way from being her first drink of the day. It seemed alcohol was her drug of choice these days, whatever she'd dabbled in before.

'Why did you assume John had killed himself?'

'Well, he had, hadn't he? Injecting.' Dawn rolled her eyes. 'Anyone knows it's a mug's game.'

Zaman and Rafferty exchanged a glance. Rafferty sat forward in her chair.

'Mrs McKinley, I'm afraid I have more bad news.'

Dawn McKinley's eyes were on the TV screen again. 'Oh, yeah?'

'We believe your ex-husband was murdered.'

There was a silence. To Rafferty and Zaman's surprise, Dawn McKinley laughed.

'Murdered? Give over, will you? Who'd want to murder John? From what I heard, he had no money, no possessions. He'd given up on life.' She took another mouthful of her drink, rolling the liquid around her mouth as if savouring it.

'You're surprised?' Rafferty asked.

'Surprised? I don't believe it, my love.'

But even as she said the words, her eyes narrowed as if she had a sudden twinge of pain. Her expression had changed for only a second, but Rafferty had seen it, as had Zaman.

'We have evidence, Mrs McKinley. Someone deliberately gave your husband an overdose of heroin,' Zaman told her.

'Listen, young man. After John left the police, he became depressed. He drank, he used drugs. We'd separated, but you hear things. As I understand it, he managed to get off the drugs for a while, years even. You no doubt know as well as I do if you inject after not using for a while, you don't have the tolerance you used to have. It's how overdoses happen, and it's what happened to John.' She waved a dismissive hand. 'Nothing you say will persuade me otherwise.'

'Why might someone want to hurt John?'

Dawn McKinley laughed. 'Don't be daft.'

'What about when he was a police officer?' Zaman said. 'He must have made a few enemies?'

Dawn McKinley sniffed. 'People he arrested, yes. I'm sure a few hated him. But he was always popular with his colleagues. We went out with a few of them socially at one time.'

'Can you remember who?' Rafferty seized on the statement, the first sentence McKinley had uttered that could potentially give them new information.

The dog was still barking. McKinley cast a withering look in the direction the noise was coming from, but didn't speak until she had drained her glass.

'God, I don't know,' she said airily. 'Someone called Kemp. Peter?'

'Pat?' Zaman provided. McKinley pointed an unsteady finger at him.

'Pat, and his dumpy little wife. I might have lost my looks, but she, poor woman, never had them in the first place.' She tapped her fingernails against her glass. 'Who else? Clement. There was a Clement, I remember. Or was Clement his first name? A couple of others. One's very high up now – Chief Constable, or some such. Anyway, the men had a fall-out, and we didn't see them any more.'

'A fall-out? They argued, you mean?' Rafferty asked.

'It was over a woman. An affair, I'd guess. Must have been, because they were all married. I can't remember.' Her eyes were heavy now, her head slumping.

Rafferty watched, pitying her. She suspected underneath it all, Dawn McKinley was desperately unhappy.

'Can you remember the names of the others in your group? Which Chief Constable do you mean?' Zaman asked. McKinley stared at him, as if trying to figure out who he was, and why he was in her house. She held up a wobbly hand.

'I've told you all I can remember. It was a long time ago, and I'm tired.'

Zaman sighed. 'If you do recall any more names…'

'Shut it, Sukie, for Christ's sake!' McKinley suddenly bellowed, presumably at the dog, who was still barking maniacally. Her words were slurred now too. Time for them to take their leave.

234

'That could be awkward,' Zaman commented as they got into the car. Rafferty slammed the door and put on her seat belt.

'Her mentioning the Chief Constable? Unless she was getting confused, and was still talking about Clement. He's the ACC of Lincolnshire, isn't he? Anyway, Chief Constable of where? It might not be Lincolnshire. She wasn't exactly specific – she could have been talking about anyone.'

'Best let the DCI handle it,' advised Zaman.

'I'll give her a call,' Rafferty decided. 'Pat Kemp's name was mentioned again, and his only alibi's his wife. We'll need to go back to him again.'

Zaman groaned. 'Still as clear as mud, isn't it?'

Rafferty scrolled to Dolan's number on her phone. At least they had something to report, for a change.

Chapter 35

Jasmine pushed open the door to the stairwell, and peered inside. It wasn't too late, but it was dark, and the car park was close to empty. Why they were meeting here, she had no idea. It was a new location. She knew he was careful, but this was dangerous, surely? There were still a few vehicles around, which meant people would be returning to them at some point. All right, their meetings were usually brief, but if they were seen together, they would both be at risk.

The stairs were well lit, but Jasmine still felt a prickle of unease across the back of her neck. The car park was in the city centre, close to Brayford Wharf. Though there would be people there, eating, drinking, enjoying themselves, the only sound Jasmine could hear was the thud of her footsteps as she jogged up the concrete stairs. She had been here earlier, when it was busier, so she knew where to go when the time came. What did they call it? Doing a recce. He wouldn't like it if she were late, though he had been, several times. He was in charge. She was here at his command, had agreed to do whatever he asked to pay off her debt. And now, because she had exactly what he wanted. Jasmine smiled to herself. For once, she was in control, and she was finding she liked the experience.

She hitched her rucksack further onto her shoulder as she continued to climb, more slowly now, her breath coming in short gasps. She should be fitter than this, the amount of walking she and Ghislaine did. After tonight, she would have enough money saved, and she could kiss this way of life goodbye, forever this time. Any train would do, any city. She'd find a room to live in, get a job. Put her past behind her. She would miss Ghislaine, Danny, even Maggie Kemp. But the rest of them? They could fuck off. They'd never think of her again; why should she worry about them? They had made up their minds about her, written her off – Jasmine the druggy, Jasmine the ex-whore. Jasmine the waste of space, Jasmine the fuck-up.

A movement in the shadows far below caused her to freeze. She stood, one foot on the next step, listening. There was traffic noise in the distance, but up here, there was silence. Below her, a CCTV camera was bolted to the wall, protected from vandalism by a metal cage. It pointed towards the doors of a nearby working men's club, its watchful eye not trained in her direction. Jasmine smirked, not wanting any trace of her presence here tonight. This evening, she would hit the jackpot. All the skulking around, the risk-taking, the fear, would be justified.

She'd be rich. Not lottery-winner rich or footballer rich, but there would be plenty. She could wave goodbye to this shithole city for good. People said it was pretty, historic. She supposed it was, if you were the right sort of person. For her though, one squat, one draughty doorway, one lumpy mattress in a shared room was the same as any other. She was in one of the richest countries in the world, with no home to call her own. Jasmine wasn't bitter. She had made her own choices, the wrong ones, as it had turned out. She wasn't one to bleat on about her useless mum, her absent dad. Plenty of people at school had been in the same boat, and they'd done all right for themselves. Jasmine would too, she knew. She was a survivor, and now she'd given herself a chance.

The top floor loomed above her. Jasmine checked the time on her phone. Ten minutes until they were due to meet. Perfect. She would find herself a shadowy corner and wait for him. He had held the advantage for too long. It was her turn now. He had always thought himself clever, living as he did. Now though, Jasmine had him right where she wanted him – at her mercy.

For much of her life, Jasmine had been powerless. She'd had mates of course, but all out for what they could get. No one she could trust, who didn't have one eye on what she could do for them. Except Ghislaine. Jasmine visualised her wandering the streets until Phoenix House opened its doors, curling on the settee with a book and a hot drink, as Jasmine had seen her so many times before. She deserved better. Perhaps when Jasmine had found a flat in her new city, wherever it might be, she would give Ghislaine a call. She'd been a good friend.

Jasmine powered up the last few steps and emerged onto the roof level of the car park. There were lights here and there, but the area was mainly in darkness. Despite her bravado, Jasmine felt a flicker of fear. The lights shone bright around Brayford Wharf beneath her. The moon was clouded as she walked to the barrier that enclosed the car park and peered over the edge. Far below, people scurried, all of them with a destination, and a home to go to at the end of their evening. Jasmine turned away. She wanted what they had. It was the real reason she was here. The council had been promising a flat for months, but it hadn't happened. How long was she expected to wait? How long could she dangle here, trapped between one life and the one she wanted, the one she now knew she deserved? No. Better to act, to grab her fate in her hands. And he was giving her the chance to do it.

She supposed she should be grateful.

Checking the time again, she blew on her hands. A cold wind was numbing them. Nearby, an estate car was parked up. Jasmine had no idea of the make or model, but it was huge, and would provide some respite from the biting wind. She ducked behind it, tucking her numb hands under her armpits, hoping he wouldn't be long.

Beyond the car was the lift. As she waited, she heard the mechanism move. Maybe she should move away from the car. If its owners were on their way back to claim it, how would she explain her presence here? There were no other vehicles in this corner, meaning she couldn't claim to have been confused about where she'd parked. Jasmine moved quickly, hugging her rucksack close to her chest, panic thumping through her veins. *Five more minutes*, she told herself. Five more minutes and he would arrive, their business would be complete and she would be on her way. Hotel room tonight, train out of here tomorrow.

Soundlessly, the doors slid open. Jasmine caught her breath as she recognised him. No need to panic. He was here, and was carrying a padded envelope, as he'd promised. Inside would be her cash, her ticket to freedom.

He strode towards her, confident as always, with the familiar half-smile in place. She'd come to hate it. As he approached, Jasmine backed away a few paces, aware again of how exposed she was.

'Come on, Jasmine, let's get this over with.' He held out the envelope. 'It's all here, as we agreed, like I promised. Do you have my property?'

She held out her rucksack. 'How are we going to do this?' she asked.

He smirked. 'What, don't you trust me?'

'Do you need to ask? About as much as I'd trust a rattlesnake.'

He stuck out his lower lip. 'I'm hurt. All right, if you're going to be awkward, how about this? I'll put the envelope on the ground. You pick it up, count the money, leave your rucksack in its place, walk away.'

'But I need the rucksack.'

He cupped a hand around his ear. 'Pardon?'

Jasmine stared, overcome with hatred. 'I need the rucksack. I don't have anything else to put my stuff in.'

Laughing, he shook his head. 'I should have realised. Not a matching luggage set kind of girl, are you? Fine. Take my property out of the bloody rucksack. Put it on the ground – is it in a bag?' She nodded. 'Good. Put it on the ground, then go. I don't want to see your face around here again.'

'You won't.' *Not a fucking chance, you bastard.*

He stepped forward, placed the padded envelope on the tarmac between them. 'This is ridiculous,' he muttered as he stepped away.

Jasmine watched him warily. The envelope looked thick enough, but for all she knew it was filled with blank pieces of paper. She would have to bend to reach it, and would be vulnerable. She took a hesitant step forward. He made a gesture of impatience with both hands.

'Come on, we don't have all night. Get on with it.'

He was as tense as she was. The realisation gave her comfort, and she took another step. He didn't move, didn't speak. She darted out a hand and snatched at the envelope, moving away before tearing it open.

Twenty-pound notes, used, loads of them. She looked at him, and he grinned.

'There you go. Easy-peasy. Now it's your turn.'

'Fine.'

She slid the carrier bag from the rucksack where she had kept it safe. This was her trump card, and without it she was lost. But she had her money. Time to run.

The bag hit the tarmac with a clatter, and he whipped his head around.

'Can't you do it quietly? Fucking hell.'

She tossed her hair. 'You never said. Right, we're done. See you around.'

He snorted. 'Hope not.'

She shoved the envelope deep into the rucksack as she walked away, resisting the temptation to run. Relief bubbled in her throat, tears blinding her for a second. It was happening. She was leaving, free to go wherever she chose.

'Jasmine.' Ten paces. He'd allowed her to take ten paces.

She froze, the rucksack cradled in her arms. She didn't want to turn her head, didn't want to see his face.

'Jasmine. Look.'

Cursing him in her head, she halted. 'What?'

'You won't know unless you turn around.'

Slowly, knowing she was making a mistake, she turned her head. Why was she listening? Why was she allowing him to do this?

Because she was weak. She was weak and worthless and he knew it, knew exactly how to manipulate her to his advantage. He held out a syringe. Jasmine swallowed, knowing she should run.

'What is it?' she heard herself ask.

He tutted. 'As if you don't know. Your favourite.'

She turned away. 'Not any more.'

'Come on, Jasmine. Once an addict, always an addict. You're all the same.'

'Fuck you,' Jasmine snarled.

'That's not nice, especially when I've brought you a present. Are you telling me you don't want it?'

'Yep. I'm leaving.'

He laughed. 'Come on, Jasmine. You're going to walk away from this?'

Jasmine tried to shut out his voice. *Keep going*, she told herself. *Don't listen to him.*

'Okay, your loss.'

The warmth. The delicious, luxurious warmth. Jasmine pressed her lips together, ignoring the voice in her head telling her one last hit wouldn't hurt. She wouldn't do it.

Unbidden, the memories flooded her brain. No worries, no pain. The wonderful sensation of being held, cradled. Warm, loved and secure. The outside world fading to a point well beyond anything meaningful. Beautiful, blissful absence. Jasmine slowed, hesitated. Would it hurt? Would it matter? Did any of it matter? One last time.

She could stop again, she knew. She'd done it before. She could always stop.

He was waiting, holding the syringe out to her with a smile.

'I knew you wouldn't let me down.'

Chapter 36

DCI Mary Dolan held her head in her hands and groaned.

'This is a nightmare,' she complained. The incident room was quiet after she had ordered most of the officers assigned to her home earlier. On the desk in front of her was a half-eaten slice of pizza, melted cheese greasing its way across the paper napkin. Since DS Rafferty had phoned, Dolan had lost her appetite. The list of suspects in the John McKinley case had rapidly gone from being non-existent to stretching as far as the eye could see. Giles Melis sank his teeth into his third slice of pizza.

'Want to talk about it?'

Dolan looked at him through her fingers. 'Not your case.'

'Sounds like you need all the help you can get.' He pulled a wad of tissue from his trouser pocket and wiped his hands.

'Zaman and Rafferty should be here soon, and we can work out how we're going to weather this particular shitstorm.' Dolan lifted her pizza and took a bite.

'I couldn't do your job.'

'Good thing no one's asked you to then.'

'What are those marks on your wrists?'

'None of your bloody business.'

Melis held up his hands. 'All right, keep your hair on. Looks like you've been shackled – not something you see every day. If you don't want to talk about, I'll be quiet. Maybe wear longer sleeves in future, hey?'

He stood. In one movement, he balled his tissue and lobbed it towards the bin in the corner, where it bounced against the rim and nestled inside.

'See you tomorrow.'

Dolan kept chewing, watching as he straightened his tie and collected his jacket from the back of a nearby chair.

'Good night, Melis,' she said as the door thudded behind him. She closed her eyes, as exposed as if he'd walked in on her in the shower. She was usually careful about keeping her scars concealed, though she was sure Catherine Bishop had seen them too. Luckily, there was no way either Bishop or Melis would be able to find out how she'd got them. The truth was classified – buried under many layers of bureaucracy, it had disappeared. Only the scars on her wrists and the ones in her head remained to tell the tale.

–

Zaman dove for the pizza as soon as he entered the room. Dolan watched, amused, as he sank his teeth into a slice and closed his eyes.

'Starving,' he mumbled.

'What's all this about ACC Clement?' Dolan pushed the pizza box towards Rafferty. 'Eat, Isla, for God's sake. You'll disappear.'

Rafferty took a piece, nibbling at it as she explained what Dawn McKinley had said. Dolan listened as she ate another slice of pizza.

'Interesting,' she said. 'I'm not sure I want to bother ACC Clement tonight, or the Chief Constable. I suppose I'll have to speak to him too.'

'Neither of them has mentioned knowing John McKinley?' Rafferty asked.

Dolan shook her head. 'I haven't spoken to Chief Constable Southern though.' There was a silence. 'Was Dawn McKinley serious about her ex-husband and his mates falling out over a woman?'

'She seemed to be, though she was falling asleep, or passing out, more likely.'

'We need to identify this woman. She could be important.' Dolan gave Zaman and Rafferty a hard stare. They should have come back with a name, and they knew it. Zaman looked away, blushing, but Rafferty refused to be cowed.

'I doubt Dawn McKinley knew any more than she told us, ma'am.'

'Fine. Go back to Pat Kemp, but we need to know who she is. Something triggered an argument, and I want to know what.' Dolan grabbed a pen and piece of paper. 'Now.' She wrote John McKinley's name in the centre of the page and drew a circle around it. 'Suspects?'

'Everyone associated with Phoenix House, including the Kemps, Danny Marshall and the soup kitchen vicar.' Zaman sounded exhausted.

Dolan dropped her pen. 'All right, point taken. Who benefits from Mackie's death? Obviously, I don't mean financially.'

'Maybe we shouldn't rule out a financial motive yet,' Rafferty said.

Dolan glanced at her. 'What do you mean?'

'It's been suggested McKinley was killed because he knew something. What about blackmail?'

'McKinley was blackmailing whoever killed him, you mean?'

'It's possible, isn't it?'

'Worth considering, yeah. But I'm not sure any of the residents of Phoenix House could stretch to paying a blackmailer,' said Dolan.

'You knew him, ma'am, years ago. Can you see him resorting to blackmail?' Zaman asked.

Dolan frowned. 'It's hard to say. Back then, he had a job, security. After a few years on the street, who knows.'

Rafferty glanced towards the door. 'The Chief Constable could afford to pay a blackmailer.'

'As could the ACC,' Dolan said, remembering her conversation with Clement. The information Dawn McKinley had provided threw a new, more sinister light on his warning about removing her from the case. What if Clement himself was involved? He wouldn't be the first high-ranking officer to be drowned in scandal. 'Shit. How the hell am I going to play this? We need to know more. There's no way I can talk to Clement or Southern yet.'

'You don't seriously believe...?' Zaman looked surprised.

'No, I don't, but we have to cover every angle. Clement and Southern being who they are shouldn't affect how we treat them.' Dolan hoped her voice carried more conviction than she felt. Even approaching the two men might mean career suicide – it was the stuff of nightmares. 'Let's tread carefully. We'll speak to Pat Kemp again – I'll go and see him myself. I'll ask why he didn't mention the nights out with John and Dawn McKinley, and the rest.'

'If they only went out a few times, Kemp may have genuinely forgotten,' Zaman said. 'It was a long time ago.'

'Let's hope you're right.'

As Dolan spoke, there was a knock on the door, and a uniformed officer stuck his head around it.

'Sorry to interrupt. Are you the team from Nottingham?'

Alarmed by his tone, Dolan was already on her feet.

'What's the problem?'

He came further into the room, blinking at them.

'I'm sorry, ma'am, I was told to inform you immediately. One of your witnesses has been found dead.'

Chapter 37

Two hours after the body had been found, Dolan was finally allowed to see it. There was a lift to the top floor of the car park, but it stopped working at ten p.m. Without knowing how Jasmine Lloyd and her murderer had accessed the sixth floor both the stairs and the lift had to be examined by the forensics team before access was allowed. Dolan had to wait until the crime scene manager was satisfied any evidence had been collected, or preserved. Kicking her heels before she could see the body, Dolan had sent officers to speak to the couple who had discovered the victim, and whose car was still parked on the roof level. They had been taken to the nearby county hospital, such was their distress on finding Jasmine's body. Other officers were retrieving the data from the cameras in and around the car park, which would tell them which vehicles had accessed it, since all number plates were automatically recorded. They might even catch a glimpse of the person who had ended Jasmine's life, but Dolan wasn't counting on it. Other members of her temporary team were tracking Jasmine's movements, retracing her steps. It wouldn't be easy, but it was necessary. She had also phoned Jonathan Knight, who was on his way back into Lincoln. Rafferty and Zaman were waiting to go to Phoenix House to break the news to the people who knew Jasmine, as soon as her identity was confirmed. Dolan swallowed as she gazed at the night sky. Was this latest death her fault? The investigation hadn't progressed as quickly as she would have liked. If she had kept her temper earlier, hadn't sent everyone home, would Jasmine still be alive? It was too late now, but the thought lingered in her mind. Dolan knew it would take root there.

Having struggled into one of the white crime scene suits, including a face mask, hairnet, hood and bootees, Dolan hurried up the stairs when she was finally given clearance. By the time she reached the final flight, she was breathing heavily.

On the top floor, she was intercepted by a stocky figure, kitted out in the same rustling white outfit as herself.

'DCI Dolan? Pleased to meet you. I'm Mick Caffery, crime scene manager.'

'I'm told we're in safe hands with you.'

'I'll do my best. You know of the victim?'

'We've spoken to her several times. Jasmine Lloyd?'

'That's what the bank card in her purse says. You'll be able to tell us for sure?'

'I've not spoken to her myself, but I've seen a mugshot.'

'She's been arrested before? Her prints will be in the system, should speed up the identification process. The pathologist is with her – Jo Webber.'

Dolan looked over to the far side of the car park, where several more figures in white suits were busy. A large light had been erected, illuminating the dingy corner. Dolan couldn't see the body, and presumed it was hidden behind the shadowy vehicle parked in one of the bays.

'Can I go over there now?'

Caffery replaced his face mask. 'If you keep to the footplates.'

Dolan hurried across the tarmac, careful to step on the plastic footplates Caffery's team had laid. They enabled the crime scene investigators and anyone else whose presence was necessary to move around the scene without compromising any evidence. Under the harsh glare of the spotlight, another white-suited figure crouched. Dolan approached quietly, aware as always of being in the presence of someone who had had their life snatched away. She rounded the car, saw the slumped body. The pathologist stepped back as she heard Dolan's footsteps.

'Dr Webber?'

'Pleased to meet you.' They kept their voices low, in deference to the dead woman.

Jasmine's body was propped against the steel railings which ran around the car park. Her eyes were open, staring at the wing mirror of the car parked beside her. Her mouth was closed, a tiny smear of blood on her lips. A canvas rucksack lay by her side. Dolan knew photographs would have been taken, a video recording made before the purse had been removed from the bag and the bank card checked for the name of the victim. She stared at the pitiful scene, the familiar rage building in her chest. A young woman, mid-twenties at the most, lying here dead, discarded like rubbish. Dolan felt the press of guilt again. If she had been a better investigator, would Jasmine Lloyd still be alive? She didn't know, but it wouldn't stop her worrying about it. Jasmine's death had to be linked to John McKinley's though. It was too much of a coincidence to suppose otherwise. She steadied herself. All she could do now for Jasmine was find the person who had killed her.

'What can you tell me, Doctor? How did she die?' Dolan asked.

Jo Webber sighed. 'Come on, Chief Inspector. I can't be certain, not until I've examined her properly.'

'Off the record? I'm not seeing obvious injuries.'

'Don't quote me yet, but I'm fairly sure she was suffocated.'

Dolan frowned. 'It couldn't be an overdose? I notice her left sleeve is rolled up.'

'Like John McKinley? Yes, she, or someone else, injected something into her arm soon before her death, for sure. No attempt to disguise it. Maybe we were meant to believe it's what killed her.'

Dolan leant forward, peering at the body again. 'But it didn't?'

'I doubt it. A drug overdose wouldn't cause bruising around her mouth and nose.'

'Bruising?' Dolan had missed it, much to her annoyance. Webber moved close to Jasmine's body, indicating with a gloved fingertip the marking she was referring to.

'As I see it, someone held his hand over her mouth and nose until she stopped breathing.' Webber's voice was flat, emotionless. Dolan knew Webber was detaching herself from the reality of the situation. It was the only way to cope with the horrors they saw. 'I'm guessing he waited until the drug had kicked in, and she was nice and relaxed, barely conscious. He sat behind her, put his hand over her face, and waited.'

'Jesus.' Dolan was shaken.

'I know, it's brutal. Also, the position of her body...' Webber pointed. 'The way her legs are curled under her, it's not a natural way to sit. He may have tried to lift her or move her, struggled and dropped her.'

Dolan was silent for a moment, considering it. She stepped closer to the barrier, looked over the edge. Far below was a small concreted area where a few industrial dustbins languished.

'Perhaps he was planning to throw her over,' she suggested. 'Falling from this height would do some serious damage to a body, wouldn't it?'

Webber shuddered. 'I'll say.'

'What better way to hide the evidence, if he did smother her?'

'We'd still have known,' Webber said, indicating Jasmine's body. 'Even before the post-mortem, the signs are there. Petechiae, the blueish tinge to her face, the bruising around her mouth...'

'Yeah, but it wouldn't have been as obvious, would it? Not if she fell head first.' Dolan too was switching off her emotions as she spoke. No point feeling sorry for Jasmine now; no point worrying about appearing cold. They needed to find the person who did this, and quickly. Anyone who could sit calmly while preventing someone from breathing, waiting for their victim to die in their arms, was not a person she wanted out on the streets for long.

Chapter 38

Lying on her side, her eyes open, Catherine Bishop knew she wasn't going to sleep. In the bed a few feet away, she knew Ghislaine was still awake too.

'Are you okay?' she said into the darkness. Ghislaine shuffled.

'Worried about Jasmine,' she replied. 'She usually lets me know if she's not staying here.'

'Where could she be?'

Ghislaine sighed. 'With her druggy mates.'

Catherine wasn't sure how to respond, and there was silence, broken by a knock on the door. Ghislaine turned on the light.

'I'm sorry to disturb you, ladies, but you need to get out of bed,' one of the night support workers told them. 'The police are here.'

—

Catherine watched Ghislaine's face crumple as she struggled to process the news of her friend's death. Stricken herself, she slid her arm around Ghislaine's shoulders as the younger woman sobbed into her hands. Having broken the news quietly, sensitively, Rafferty stood silent by the window in the shelter's common room. Zaman had disappeared to make cups of tea. Despite her long-sleeved T-shirt, jogging bottoms and thick woollen socks, Catherine found she was shivering.

Zaman returned, squatting in front of Ghislaine, holding out a mug. 'Here, Miss Oliver. Drink this.' His voice was gentle, and Catherine gave him a grateful glance. Ghislaine lifted her face and took the cup, her eyes already red and swollen.

'I'm sorry,' she said. 'I know you need to talk to me.'

Rafferty moved closer, pulled out a wooden chair from under the dining table and sat. 'Miss Oliver, we understand you're upset.' Catherine looked at Rafferty, narrowing her eyes, silently asking her to continue to be considerate of Ghislaine's feelings. Rafferty focused on Ghislaine. 'I'm sorry to have to ask you questions when you've heard such awful news about your friend, but if we're going to find the person who did this to her, we need to move quickly.'

Ghislaine sniffed, wiped her eyes and nose on a wad of paper towel Zaman had retrieved from the kitchen. 'I understand. I want to help, if I can.'

'Thank you. I've explained where Jasmine's body was found.'

Catherine heard Ghislaine gulp at Rafferty's words, and wished the interview could wait, but knew their questions had to be asked. Rafferty had glanced in Catherine's direction several times, but now Catherine avoided eye contact. She didn't want Rafferty's sympathy.

Rafferty was speaking to Ghislaine again. 'Do you have any idea why she would have been in the car park? Especially on the highest level?'

'No. Obviously, she doesn't have a car. I don't even know if she can drive. It makes no sense. Unless...'

'Yes?'

'I'm not sure, but... I know in the past, when she was desperate, Jas worked as an escort. I mean, I don't know how far it went, but...'

'Might she have gone there with a client?'

Ghislaine glared at Rafferty, colour rising in her cheeks. 'She wasn't a prostitute.'

Rafferty held up her hands. 'I know, I'm sorry. We're struggling to understand what Jasmine was doing in the car park.'

'What about her mobile phone records?' Catherine asked without thinking.

Rafferty frowned a warning at her, and, embarrassed, Catherine dropped her gaze to the carpet. Now was not the time to ruin her cover. More than ever, she needed to remember who she was supposed to be.

'You might be able to tell if she'd arranged to meet someone. I've seen on TV you can...' Catherine allowed her voice to trail away.

'It's in hand.' Rafferty was curt.

There was a pause.

'I'm trying to remember the names of people Jas mentioned,' Ghislaine told them.

'You're doing well, Miss Oliver,' Zaman said. 'We know how difficult this is.'

Attempting a smile, Ghislaine sipped her tea.

'When did you last see her?' Rafferty tried again.

Ghislaine explained they had eaten at the soup kitchen together at lunchtime, but Jasmine had wanted to leave quickly when Rafferty and Zaman had arrived. 'I followed her yesterday though,' she said suddenly.

Catherine frowned. She had tried to follow too, but had lost them before being rescued by Knight. She was nauseous, knowing she had failed. The question was, had her incompetence cost Jasmine her life?

'You followed her?' Rafferty sat forward. 'Why?'

Immediately, Ghislaine was defensive. 'She was acting weirdly, and I was worried she'd gone back to drugs. She was on smack before, and I... Well, I was worried, like I said.'

'Where did she go?' Zaman asked.

Ghislaine gave the address – 24 Merry Road. Immediately, Zaman got to his feet.

'Need to make a phone call.'

Catherine knew he would be ringing Dolan to tell her what Jasmine had revealed.

'Is the address important?' Ghislaine asked.

'It could be. We need to check it out,' Rafferty said.

Frustrated at being in the dark about the significance of the address, Catherine frowned a question at Rafferty, who averted her eyes. Catherine resolved to have a private word with her and Zaman before they left. She needed to know what they had discovered.

'Do you have any idea what Jasmine might have been doing at the house on Merry Road?' Rafferty asked.

'Buying drugs.' The reply was immediate.

'You sound certain.'

Ghislaine squirmed. 'Why else would she have gone there? I know what withdrawal looks like.'

'Which suggests Jasmine was using heroin regularly?'

257

'Maybe.' Ghislaine wiped her eyes. 'Like I said, I was worried. She denied it, but they always do.'

'Was Jasmine afraid of anyone? Any threats, violence against her?'

'In her past, maybe. She'd been abused in some way, I'm guessing sexually. She didn't talk about her early childhood. Jas was thrown out of home when she was sixteen. Her mum got a new boyfriend, and he said he didn't like Jasmine's "sort".'

Rafferty was bemused. 'Her sort?'

'He didn't like the colour of her skin. Didn't want her in the house, reminding him of her black dad, he said.'

'He meant the house Jasmine had grown up in?' Rafferty asked.

'Yeah. The one she and her mum paid for. Told Jasmine's mum to sling her out, and she did. Her own daughter.' Ghislaine shook her head.

'And her mum went along with that?' Catherine was sickened.

'She'd always thought more of her boyfriends than her kids, from what Jas said.'

Rafferty said nothing, but made a note. 'We'll need to contact Jasmine's mum anyway, as next of kin. Don't suppose you have an address?'

'No. Jas hadn't even spoken to her for a few years. Why would you?'

Zaman returned to the room and sat. When Rafferty looked at him, he gestured with his head, nodding to one side to indicate they needed to leave.

'Catherine, I need a quick word with you too. Can we go into the bedroom?' Rafferty asked.

When the door closed behind them, Catherine demanded, 'Where did Jasmine go? You obviously recognised the address.'

Rafferty strode over to the window, gazing into the street. Catherine was willing to bet she used it as way of distancing herself from her witnesses and colleagues. Using the space between them as a physical barrier.

Rafferty ignored her question. 'You realise you could be in danger? Jasmine's murder means you need to be even more careful about your safety than you have already.'

'Will you tell me whose house it is?' Catherine was increasingly frustrated. If they were concerned about her safety, why wasn't she on her way home?

Turning back, Rafferty ran her hands over her face. 'We were going to speak to Jasmine. If we'd gone to her first instead of Lee Collinson, if she'd had a chance to tell us where she'd been, even if Ghislaine had... We were too late.'

Uncomfortably, Catherine studied her shoes. If Rafferty had been someone else, someone more approachable, she would have put a hand on her arm, even hugged her close as she had Ghislaine. However, she knew Rafferty would not welcome an attempt to comfort her. Catherine bit back another demand to know who lived at the address Jasmine had visited. If Rafferty didn't share the information soon, she would phone Dolan herself. How could Catherine keep herself safe, Ghislaine too, if they didn't know where the danger lay? Rafferty's face was grey, the shadows beneath her eyes darker than they had been the previous evening. Was Rafferty experiencing guilt because she believed she and Zaman could have prevented Jasmine's death if they had spoken to her sooner? Catherine was in no position to be sure the assumption was true, but she did understand the corrosive nature of guilt. It could destroy from the inside, worrying at your mind until you submitted. Catherine should know; she'd spent enough time living with it over the past months, both professionally and in her personal life. Thomas was experiencing guilt because he was fine and Anna was not, and Knight... Catherine didn't know. Did Jonathan Knight lie awake at night, remembering his actions and regretting them? Wishing he had taken a different turn, trodden a different path? It was impossible to guess.

Rafferty turned her engagement ring around on her finger.

'You can't blame yourself,' Catherine told her. 'Whatever's happened, it's not your fault. DCI Dolan makes the decisions.'

Rafferty's eyes narrowed. 'You're saying it's Mary's fault Jasmine's dead?'

Catherine took a step back. 'It's no one's fault except the person who killed her. We're sure she was murdered?'

Rafferty explained how Jasmine had died. Catherine listened, horrified. 'He sat there holding her, preventing her from breathing?'

'The post-mortem's not until early tomorrow morning, but Dr Webber told Mary she's confident her findings will prove her theory.'

'Not like Jo to comment before the PM.'

'I think she was rattled.'

'Not surprised.' Catherine took a second to erase the images her imagination was producing of Jasmine's last moments from her brain. What thoughts had hammered

260

around her head? Perhaps none. Maybe there had been nothing more than a growing darkness. The heroin may have shielded her, cradling her as her life was extinguished. Catherine found it hard to believe, but it was a crumb of comfort. 'It's a shit-awful way to die. She didn't deserve it.'

'Who does?' Rafferty was brisk again. The moment of vulnerability, fleeting though it had been, was over.

'Are you going to tell me who lives on Merry Road?' Catherine folded her arms at Rafferty's tone. If she wanted to be dismissive, let her. If she wanted to build a wall around herself, to be unpleasant and snappish, fine. Catherine had no patience with her.

Rafferty glanced at her watch. 'Stay here, Catherine. We'll be in touch in the morning.'

'Can't I come back with you? I want to help find who did this,' Catherine heard herself plead. She wasn't going to beg, not to Rafferty, but she wanted them to know how she felt. Sidelined, shunted out of the way. Where was Jonathan Knight? Why should he be involved when Catherine wasn't?

Rafferty shook her head. 'Mary said we still need you here. Adil and I need to get back. DCI Dolan's organising a search warrant.'

Catherine smothered a scream. 'A search warrant for where?'

'The property on Merry Road.' Rafferty said it as if surprised Catherine hadn't guessed, as if it were obvious. 'Danny Marshall's house.'

Chapter 39

Pat Kemp's phone was ringing, but he wasn't answering. Dolan cursed, slamming her own mobile onto the desk as Kemp's voicemail kicked in yet again. It was after eleven p.m., and she shouldn't be calling at all, but she believed Kemp knew much more than he had shared with Rafferty and Zaman. She was irritated her two junior officers hadn't returned with more information, but she knew during an investigation you often needed to know the right question to ask. Returning to witnesses and suspects and questioning them again was a necessary, if frustrating and time-consuming, aspect of the job.

'Kemp's no doubt in bed.' Jonathan Knight was in the chair beside hers, his legs crossed, his handed folded loosely in his lap. Dolan rounded on him.

'I know it's late, but we need to speak to him. He could be key to this whole case.'

'Try him again in the morning. He won't go anywhere tonight.'

'We hope.'

'What do you mean?'

'Well, John McKinley's dead. If Kemp knows about whatever McKinley was involved in, he could be at risk too, especially since we've been sniffing around. Maybe we should go out to his address anyway, to be sure.'

'Knock on his door to check he's okay before battering him with questions, you mean?'

Dolan pulled a bottle of water from her bag, unscrewed the cap and drank. 'No. I'm not intending to speak to him. I want to make sure there are signs of life at the house. Look, I'm sorry I dragged you back here tonight. Dr Webber had to come, but you didn't.'

'It's not a problem. Jo's going to perform the post-mortem first thing?'

'Yes.' Dolan rubbed her eyes, the image of Jasmine's slumped body vivid in her mind. Though she knew from spending only a few minutes in Jo Webber's company that she would be as gentle and respectful as possible in her work, the indignities inflicted on a body during post-mortem were unavoidable, however sensitive the pathologist. 'Jasmine's death changes everything.' She would find him, this man who had casually, callously, ended Jasmine's life, and she would make sure he was punished. 'Jasmine knew something, she must have. She might have injected herself with the heroin, though no syringe or tourniquet was found this time. He wanted us to think McKinley's death was an accidental overdose, but since he made sure Jasmine was dead by smothering her, it didn't matter if he took the drug paraphernalia away with him. He knew we'd soon see she didn't die accidentally.'

'You're certain her death is linked to the John McKinley case?'

'Too much of a stretch to otherwise.' Dolan looked at him. Knight smiled, rubbing a hand over his chin. 'You don't agree?'

'It's worth keeping an open mind,' Knight said. 'We still don't know who attacked Anna.'

'Jasmine had met McKinley, but didn't know Anna. Both Jasmine and McKinley were injected with heroin, had both spent time at Phoenix House. Danny Marshall had spoken to them during his work. We need to have a poke around his house.' Dolan wriggled in her seat. 'No chance of our search warrant until the morning either. He could dispose of anything incriminating in the meantime.'

'You mean you don't have someone watching him?' Knight grinned.

Dolan tapped her nose. 'No comment.'

'Jasmine was out on the street every day. Who's to say she didn't have information about who attacked Anna?'

Dolan scrubbed her hands over her eyes. 'She might have. She might have information about all sorts of people, all sorts of crimes. Until we speak to Pat Kemp and get into Danny Marshall's property, we're guessing, as we have been for nearly a week.'

Knight was scribbling on a piece of paper. Dolan shifted in her chair, scanning it. He'd divided the page in half with a wobbly vertical line, 'Anna' at the head of the first column, the other labelled 'John McKinley/Jasmine Lloyd'.

'Didn't you want to keep an open mind about McKinley and Lloyd's deaths being linked?'

'True.' Knight tapped his pen on his teeth. 'I thought this would help organise my thoughts.'

'I tried the same earlier,' Dolan said. 'Didn't work for me. My biggest concern,' she glanced over to be certain the door was closed, 'my biggest concern is the mention of Assistant Chief Constable Clement.'

'Why?'

'Dawn McKinley mentioned him by name, which suggests she remembers him clearly. ACC Clement's already told me if I don't have the case tied up by this time tomorrow he'll replace me as SIO.'

'I see.'

'He's going to speak to the Chief Constable about it. We need to check who the others in the group were with Pat Kemp. What do you know of Chief Constable Southern?' Dolan asked.

'Never spoken to him.'

'Me neither, though I saw him when we did the press conference. He did most of the talking; only to be expected. He's confident, assured, charming. If he's involved... Well, let's not consider it unless we have to.' She swiped the screen on her phone. 'Bloody Kemp's not going to call back, is he?'

'Doubtful.'

'All right, let's call it a night.'

Knight stood, buttoned his jacket. 'What about the post-mortem?'

'I'll be there. Seven sharp. Coming?'

'Okay. Then Pat Kemp?'

'He can't avoid us forever.'

—

Sleep was even less likely after Rafferty and Zaman's visit to Phoenix House. Catherine lay on her back, staring into the darkness as Ghislaine wept quietly. The news had shocked her, made her even more aware of the precariousness of her own situation. And Dolan wanted her to stay here? Catherine had promised Knight one more night at the shelter only, and she intended to keep her word.

'Ghislaine? Are you okay?'

'I told Jas to be careful. She never listened, always knew best.'

'Careful of what?' Catherine turned her head towards Ghislaine.

'The police said I shouldn't talk about Jasmine dying. They want me to make a statement tomorrow morning,' Ghislaine worried.

'It'll be okay; tell them exactly what you tell me. It might help to talk about it.' Catherine made her voice gentle, though she was desperate to hear what else Ghislaine knew.

'Well, Jas has been acting off recently.' Ghislaine sniffed. 'I was worried. The night the police officer was stabbed? Jasmine was out late, nearly missed being allowed a bed here.'

Catherine's stomach lurched. 'You're suggesting Jasmine was involved?'

Ghislaine flicked on the light, leaning on her elbow, turning towards Catherine. Her eyes were swollen, her face blotchy. 'No, please don't misunderstand me. She'd seen the crowd, heard someone had been stabbed. She was...' There was a pause as Ghislaine fumbled for the right word. 'She was excited, I suppose. It sounds terrible, especially now, but it was like when people slow to look at a car crash, you know? It's sick. Staring at someone else's misfortune, glad it's not you. Only this time, it is. Jasmine's the victim now.' She wiped her eyes with her duvet.

Catherine pulled herself into a sitting position, her arms wrapped around her own body, chin on her chest. She needed to call Dolan or Rafferty. This could be the breakthrough they were waiting for. Could Jasmine have seen something? She couldn't be the attacker, not based on Thomas' evidence. Catherine knew he had been definite the person he'd seen stab Anna was male, as had the other people who had been robbed.

'Can you imagine Jasmine blackmailing someone?'

'Definitely. Can't you?' Ghislaine forced a laugh. 'Jas was my friend, but she wasn't an angel. She loved to know secrets, liked to tease. Yeah, I'd say she'd see blackmail as a good laugh, as well as a way of making a few quid.'

Catherine remembered the rucksack Jasmine had guarded so jealously. Had it been found with her body? If it contained a large sum of cash, her assumption about Jasmine possibly being a blackmailer could be substantiated. It would also explain why she had been overly protective of the bag.

Ghislaine turned off the light and they lay silently for a while. Catherine's eyes were sore, scratchy. She needed to sleep, but she wanted to stay awake to creep into the bathroom and text Dolan and Rafferty.

Catherine couldn't have said how long they lay there, she and Ghislaine in their lumpy single beds, Ghislaine mourning a friend and Catherine regretting the loss of another life. Though she'd barely known her, she'd liked Jasmine. She remembered Rafferty's moment of vulnerability, when she had worried she could have done more. Catherine was considering her own actions, though she knew it was a waste of energy. Guilt again.

Ghislaine was quieter now, but she wasn't asleep. After another few minutes, Catherine heard her shuffle, a rustle as she slipped out from beneath her duvet. Catherine held her breath as Ghislaine crept closer, hesitating at the side of her bed.

No words were exchanged. None were needed. She pulled back her duvet and Ghislaine crept into the narrow bed beside her. Turning onto her side, Catherine relaxed as Ghislaine settled her head on the pillow, the younger woman trembling. Catherine reached behind her for Ghislaine's hand, holding it high against her chest so Ghislaine nestled against her back. They lay quietly, each drawing comfort from the other. It wasn't sexual; the embrace was as innocent as siblings huddling together while their parents argued downstairs. Catherine closed her eyes, Ghislaine's breath warm against the back of her neck, and waited for sleep.

The investigation could wait for a few hours.

Chapter 40

A cold, grey, miserable morning. The weather suited Dolan's mood as she and Knight left the hospital, having endured most of the post-mortem performed on the body of Jasmine Lloyd. Emerging from the sterile white mortuary into radiant sunshine would have been all wrong.

They hurried across the car park and bundled into Dolan's vehicle. Inside, Dolan rummaged in her shoulder bag before holding out her phone in triumph.

'A voicemail from Pat Kemp.' She turned the key in the ignition as Kemp's voice echoed around the car, informing them he wasn't going to work because of the horrible weather. 'What a shame. We'll have to call on him at home.' Dolan was gleeful. 'Shall we call him and check it's convenient, or arrive unannounced?'

'He said he'll be there all day.'

Dolan nodded as her phone rang.

'Good morning, ma'am... Mary,' Isla Rafferty said. 'I have the search warrant.'

Dolan cheered, lifting both hands from the steering wheel for a second. 'Excellent, Isla. Thank you.'

'We're waiting for the search team to arrive. When they're here Adil will bring Danny Marshall in for questioning.'

'The station in the city centre, remember. No cosy room in Headquarters for Mr Marshall.' As Dolan swung the car around a sharp corner, Knight automatically grabbed the armrest on the door. 'And make sure no one mentions Jasmine's death to him. I'm hoping he hasn't heard. Better still, he might pretend he hasn't.'

'Yes, ma'am.' Rafferty hesitated.

'Spit it out, Isla.'

'DS Bishop wanted to know when she could leave Phoenix House.'

Dolan considered. 'Today, I'd say. I'll let you know, or I'll call her myself.'

'Okay. What happened at the post-mortem?'

'Nothing we didn't already know. I'll update you later.'

As Rafferty ended the call, Knight thumbed a text to Catherine, asking how she was. After spending time with Jasmine Lloyd, no matter what the pretext, the young woman's death would have come as a shock. Catherine could be in danger, a fact Knight hoped she had been alerted to. There was no certainty in her current state Catherine would realise for herself. Within seconds, Knight's phone was ringing.

'Can you ask DCI Dolan to call me when you see her?' Catherine yawned. 'I've tried her twice but her phone's going to voicemail.'

Knight explained where he was, and on speakerphone, Catherine shared the information Ghislaine had provided about Jasmine's behaviour the evening Anna was stabbed. Dolan and Knight listened in silence.

'You're suggesting Jasmine was blackmailing someone? We've been considering blackmail as a motive for John

McKinley's death,' Dolan said. 'Can you let Isla and Adil know about this?'

She explained to Catherine what was happening – the search warrant and questioning of Marshall. When Catherine had gone, Dolan drummed her fingers on the steering wheel.

'Making progress,' Knight said.

'We hope. Maybe ACC Clement won't be throwing me off the case after all.'

Knight laughed. 'Especially if it's him we have to arrest.'

–

'Maggie's not going into work today either,' Pat Kemp told them as he handed out mugs of coffee. 'The news about Jasmine hit her hard.'

Dolan raised her eyebrows. 'How did she hear?'

'Someone phoned, late last night.'

'Me, for one.'

'I'm sorry, Chief Inspector. I went to bed early with a headache, didn't hear your messages until this morning. It was late…'

Dolan sat back, the wooden dining chair creaking as she shifted. They were in the Kemps' kitchen, a large, homely room, cluttered but clean. 'You know how it is, Pat. We don't clock off at five.'

'No, but I do. Before, if I can.'

'Privilege of being your own boss.'

Kemp drank deeply from his mug. 'I'm not sure what else I can tell you.'

Dolan set her cup on the table, finalising in her mind what she was going to ask him. Kemp looked relaxed, she noted. He sat with his legs stretched in front of him, one elbow leaning on the arm of his chair, resting his cheek on his hand.

'Tell us about your friendship with John McKinley.'

'I wouldn't call it a friendship. I saw him around the station. We exchanged a few words if we were on the same shift.'

Dolan threaded her fingers together, tipping her head to one side. 'Come on, Pat. You sent us to Dawn McKinley. You must have realised she'd mention your nights out.'

'Nights out?'

'You, your wife, Dawn and John McKinley, Assistant Chief Constable Clement and the Chief Constable himself.'

Kemp drew in his legs. 'We had a few drinks together occasionally, yes.'

'Mrs McKinley said there was an argument over a woman, and you all fell out?'

Kemp closed his eyes. 'Jesus. An argument? She's no idea.'

Dolan spoke softly, persuasively. 'Tell us, Pat. What happened?'

Getting to his feet, Kemp turned to rummage blindly in a cupboard. He withdrew a bottle of whisky, three-quarters full, and a glass. After pouring a generous measure, he sat again.

'I haven't spoken about this for years, not even to my wife,' he told them. His mouth trembled as he set his jaw. 'Seems I have no choice now. John deserves justice.'

Dolan waited. Knight was silent, studying the wooden flooring, his face impassive. Kemp swallowed another mouthful of whisky.

'In the early days, we were all young lads in uniform. Me, John, Eddie Clement and Russ Southern.'

'We're talking about the Chief Constable and Assistant Chief Constable of Lincolnshire Police? Russell Southern and Edward Clement?' Dolan wanted to be certain. Kemp stared at her, and she regretted the interruption.

'They are now, yes. Back then, they were constables, bobbies on the beat. That's when we went out with our wives a few times. You realise,' Kemp fidgeted, 'you realise this could backfire? If you go poking around into Clement and Southern's past, they won't thank you for it. This particular skeleton has been safely hidden in their cupboards for years.'

'We're talking about murder, Mr Kemp,' Dolan reminded him. 'If the ACC and Chief Constable are implicated in the death of John McKinley, I'm not going to baulk at telling the world. They'll be treated the same as any other suspect.'

Kemp held up a finger. 'Not both, Chief Inspector. One of them, maybe neither. I don't know enough about it.'

'Wait a minute, you said…'

'Let me tell you what I know. What you choose to do with the information is up to you. I don't want any more to do with this. Keep my name out of it.'

'You know I can't guarantee that.'

'I understand I'll need to make a formal statement, even give evidence, if it comes to it. But when you talk to Clement and Southern, *if* you do, don't mention me.'

Dolan shook her head. 'You want to see the person who killed John McKinley go down for it, don't you?'

'Which is why I'm talking to you now. Listen, Chief Inspector. When we were on the beat, plain old police constables, there was an incident. It was a Saturday night, and we were called to a disturbance in the city centre.' Kemp took another sip of whisky. 'Southern, Clement and a few others were already there when John and I arrived. It was a fist fight, nothing more, but there were about twenty people involved. A brawl. Men and women, kicking lumps out of each other. By the time we got there, a few bottles had been thrown at the police, a lot of verbal. You know how it is.'

'Sounds like any other Saturday night,' Dolan said. It didn't, but she wanted Kemp to keep talking.

'Maybe where you're from. We'd retreated a little, protecting ourselves until more back-up arrived. By then, the crowd was dispersing. Terrified of being arrested once their mates had run off. Back at the station, we chucked them in the cells for the night. Pissed out of their minds, most of them. I had a guy who was trouble – making threats, throwing his weight around. Took three of us to get him into a cell.' Kemp paused again, drank the last of his whisky.

'What happened, Pat?'

'It was at the end of the shift. John came to me, and his face… I don't know. He was furious. It had been a difficult shift, no doubt about it, but there was more. I asked him what was wrong. He stared at me, spat out two names.'

Dolan said, 'Clement and Southern.'

'Yes. There was a woman, a girl. She was in a cell on her own; she was the only woman brought in. She was homeless. I'd seen her on the street before, even given her a few coins. She'd obviously taken a few blows to the face

– black eye, bruising. But she wasn't shouting abuse like the rest of them. I don't even know if she'd been involved in the fighting. She was silent. Her eyes were blank, her clothes torn. I didn't know what had happened, didn't want to know. And I… I walked away. Went off shift, got on with my life.'

'This was when?' asked Dolan.

'Years ago. Twenty, give or take.'

'Ten years before you left the force?'

'And ten years before John did.'

'What triggered you leaving? You said you were disillusioned.'

'I was. I was an inspector, uniform, not CID. John called me one day, out of the blue. He wanted to see me. We met in a pub, had some food and a few beers. Clement was a DCI, as I remember, and Southern was about to be promoted to Superintendent. John said a woman had come into the station, wanted to talk to Southern. Said she had a crime to report. It was the woman from that night.'

'And?'

'Southern spoke to her, got rid of her, maybe paid her off. I don't know. John saw her leave, in tears. He asked for my advice, wanted to know if he should find her, talk to her. Something had happened in her cell the night she was arrested. John wanted to know what.'

'Why would she wait ten years to come forward though?' Dolan asked.

'I don't know. Maybe they paid her to keep quiet. I told John to keep his nose out, said he was doing himself no favours getting involved. He had his career to consider, his family, his pension.' Kemp looked at Dolan. 'I'm not proud of it. But so much time had passed… John left the force. I didn't know why, hadn't spoken to him. For all I knew, John was involved in whatever happened to the woman. We lost touch again. I didn't see him until he turned up at Phoenix House.'

'Still doesn't explain why you left too.'

Pat Kemp rubbed his hands over his face. 'I heard on the grapevine a complaint was going to be made about me. I didn't know the specifics, but I'd be stupid not realise it was tied in with what went on that night. It was gossip around the station; threats weren't made directly. No names were mentioned, but I quickly came to understand if I didn't jump, I'd be pushed. Someone worked hard to ensure I got the message, turned my back on my career. Luckily for me, it turned out better than I could have imagined.'

'You weren't approached directly? No one came and said, "If you know what's good for you, get out of here"?'

'No. Everywhere I went, people were whispering. I was hounded out by someone who was worried about what I knew.' Kemp leant forward, set his empty glass on the pine dining table. 'Or two people.'

Dolan's mind was racing. 'Do you know this woman's name?'

Kemp shook his head. 'Never asked. Didn't want to know. You should be able to find out though.'

–

As they walked back to the car, Dolan checked her voicemail. Suddenly, she grabbed Knight's arm, halting him. He watched as she listened, her eyes widening.

'What is it?' he demanded.

Dolan blinked. 'The rucksack Jasmine Lloyd always carried, the one found with her body? Mick Caffery found a knife inside it, wrapped in a carrier bag. A knife with traces of blood still on the blade.'

Chapter 41

'Jasmine can't have stabbed Anna,' Knight said. 'Everyone who's seen the attacker says he's male.'

'She was in the right area that night though.' Dolan glanced left and right as she pulled out of Kemp's drive. 'She could have seen what happened, found the knife wherever the attacker disposed of it. This adds weight to Catherine's theory about Jasmine dabbling in blackmail. Seems you were right to keep an open mind about Jasmine's death being linked to Anna's stabbing, not McKinley's murder.'

She said it lightly enough, but Knight caught her frown. Being proved right gave him no satisfaction.

'Have they confirmed the blood is Anna's?'

'Not yet. There are no fingerprints on it, though. We've applied for Jasmine's mobile phone records, and Danny Marshall's. Should have the data later today. John McKinley didn't have a phone, as far as we know. When we have Marshall at the station, I want Thomas Bishop to come and have a look at him. We'll take a mugshot around to the other people who were robbed too.'

Knight gazed out of the car window as they headed back towards the city centre.

'Why would Marshall turn to robbery, though? He doesn't have a drug habit to fund.'

'As far as we know. We'll have a nosey into his financial records too, if we can. I doubt he's well paid. He could have a gambling addiction, be a compulsive shopper.' Dolan glanced at Knight as she negotiated a roundabout. 'You don't think it's him, do you.' It wasn't a question.

'He needs to explain why Jasmine visited his house. We have to follow the evidence.'

Dolan's expression was grim. 'Which is pointing to Danny Marshall.'

–

Marshall looked bewildered when he was led into the interview room. His blonde hair was uncombed, his cheeks shadowed with stubble. An unsmiling constable offered water as Marshall sat and gazed around. The interview room had grey walls, hard chairs. It wasn't the worst, but it could never have been described as welcoming either. Warily, Marshall's eyes passed over the recording equipment, the video camera perched high on the wall. In the observation room next door, Dolan watched him.

'I'd like you and Adil to question him, Jonathan. DS Rafferty's at his house while the search takes place. The search team are there now, and Isla will feed back anything we should raise in the interview.' She set her hands on her hips. 'He's said he doesn't want a solicitor.'

Knight followed Zaman into the interview room. Once Zaman had readied the recording equipment, taken his place in the chair beside Knight's and introduced them, Marshall asked, 'Why is there a vanload of people searching my house? What do you think I've done?' His voice was plaintive, like a confused child's. He slumped in his chair, his elbows resting on the table between him and Zaman and Knight.

'You should have received an explanation from the search team,' Knight told him. 'Were you shown the search warrant?'

'Yeah. They even gave me a copy. I still don't understand.'

'Let's see if we can help you out,' Zaman said with a smile. 'Jasmine Lloyd is a resident at Phoenix House, the homeless shelter where you're employed as a counsellor, correct?'

'You know it is.'

'We have a witness who saw Jasmine Lloyd visit your home at 24 Merry Road the day before yesterday, at around three thirty in the afternoon. Can you explain why she came to see you?'

Knight watched Marshall's face as he absorbed Zaman's words. He appeared genuinely bemused.

'Jasmine came to my house? How does she even know where I live?'

'We were hoping you'd be able to tell us, Mr Marshall. What's the relationship between you and Ms Lloyd?' Zaman raised his eyebrows.

'Relationship?' Marshall swallowed. 'There isn't one. I talk to her about her drug use, try to help her. I'm not sure how much she takes in, if I'm honest.'

Zaman made a note. 'You're her counsellor. There's no more to it?'

Marshall blushed. 'What are you implying?'

'Nothing, sir. But since she visited your home, it seems unlikely your association was purely professional, wouldn't you say?' Zaman tapped his pen on his notepad.

Marshall gritted his teeth, his expression thunderous. 'I don't know who's been feeding you this rubbish. Jasmine's never been to my house, I promise you. I wasn't even at home that afternoon.'

'Where were you?'

'I went to the supermarket, the big Tesco on Wragby Road.' Marshall glanced at the video camera. 'You'll be able to check, won't you?'

'Did someone go with you?' Zaman asked. 'Did you speak to anyone who might remember seeing you?'

'Only the woman who served me, but why would she remember? Won't there be CCTV footage? I didn't keep the receipt. I paid in cash.'

Zaman ignored him. 'What time did you arrive at the supermarket, Mr Marshall?'

'I don't know exactly. How do you expect me to remember?'

'It's less than forty-eight hours ago,' Knight said.

Marshall glared at him. 'I didn't make a note of the time. How was I to know you'd drag me in here and interrogate me about it?'

'It's hardly an interrogation.'

'There are people searching my house – what do you expect me to call it?' Marshall flung himself back in his chair.

Knight placed his hands on the table. 'Danny, you may not have heard.'

Marshall looked from Knight to Zaman and back again. 'Heard what?'

'Jasmine Lloyd was found dead last night.' Knight was deliberately blunt. Marshall's mouth gaped as his eyes widened. A sound emerged from his throat, a strangled yelp of pain. 'Danny?' Knight said. 'Can I get you some water?'

Marshall had his hands over his face. 'You're lying.' His voice was thick with tears.

'It's true, I'm afraid.' Knight folded his arms.

'What do you mean, she's dead? How? An overdose?' As Marshall struggled to control himself, Zaman pounced on his question.

'Why would you say that, Danny? We know you spoke to Jasmine about her drug use.'

'She told me she was clean. I believed her. She was turning her life around.'

'Was she?' Zaman smirked.

Marshall glared. 'She meant it. What do you know?'

'I know if you're lying to us and Jasmine was in your house, we'll find proof.'

'You won't because she was never there. Wait a minute, all this is because Jasmine's dead? But... Fuck, someone killed her, didn't they? Like Mackie.' Marshall raised a hand to his face, covering his mouth, his eyes bulging. 'And I'm a suspect.' He laughed, though tears were flooding his cheeks. 'I want a solicitor,' he managed to choke out. Zaman's face was grim as he announced the suspension of the interview for the recording.

–

Dolan had her phone pressed to her ear. She turned away as Zaman and Knight appeared. Zaman headed for the water dispenser, handing a plastic cup to Knight before filling one for himself.

'Cheers. Your impressions?' Knight asked him.

'He didn't know Jasmine was dead. If he did, he should be on stage. How about you?'

'I agree. He had no idea.'

'Marshall didn't like the idea of his house being searched though. Not sure what they're hoping turns up.'

Dolan approached, grinning widely. 'They've found plenty already, as it happens. When Marshall's solicitor arrives, we're going to have an interesting chat.'

Chapter 42

Isla Rafferty drove a bland silver car, spotless on the outside and unnervingly tidy inside. Catherine, still in her Phoenix House clothes, hoped her trainers were clean as she climbed in. Rafferty, smart in black trousers and a cardigan with a shimmering silvery top underneath, turned to look at Catherine fastening her seatbelt.

'Where do you live?'

'Northolme.'

Rafferty clicked her tongue. 'I need your address.' She pointed towards the built-in satnav. 'Type it in there.'

Catherine leant forward to obey. 'Why are we going to my house?'

Rafferty pulled away from the kerb. 'To get your warrant card. And you can have a shower, change your clothes. You've finished at Phoenix House.'

'Have I?'

Catherine was surprised to find herself saddened. Though she hadn't spent long in her undercover role, the people she had met had made an impression. She would have liked to have said goodbye, to Ghislaine especially.

'The DCI has an urgent action for us,' Rafferty said.

'Both of us?'

'Apparently.'

Rafferty's voice was cool, as if disappointed Mary Dolan wanted Catherine back in the fold. Catherine smiled to herself. If Rafferty wanted to take umbrage, let her.

'Is there a problem?' she asked.

'Not at all.'

Catherine stretched her legs, forgetting her worries about the cleanliness of her shoes. If she was going to be trapped in Rafferty's car for the next half an hour, she may as well be comfortable.

'Is this about Jasmine's death?'

Saying the name made her throat tighten. When Catherine had woken, alone in the bed, there was no sign of Ghislaine. Carl Baker said she'd left early, not mentioning where she was going. After all that had happened, Catherine was uneasy. Still, where Ghislaine went and what she did was her business. Catherine had to get on with her job. Nevertheless, she pulled out her phone and sent her a text. No harm in being friendly. How Ghislaine would react when she realised Catherine was a police officer remained to be seen. Catherine swallowed, hoping she would understand.

'Not about Jasmine's death, no. McKinley's,' Rafferty said. Succinctly, she told Catherine about the information given to Knight and Dolan earlier by Pat Kemp. 'We need to find out who this woman is, and speak to her.'

Catherine blinked. 'There's a chance the Assistant Chief Constable could have killed McKinley? Or the Chief Constable himself? I don't know. It's difficult to believe.'

Rafferty shrugged. 'They're people like anyone else, capable of who knows what, same as the rest of us.'

There was a silence, Catherine wishing Dolan had sent Zaman to partner her. Jonathan Knight, even Dolan herself, would have been preferable. Instead, she was stuck with Rafferty, with no idea how she was going to keep conversation going for the next twenty-five minutes. She smothered a groan, realising she would have to invite Rafferty into her home, offer her a drink when they arrived. She knew Thomas wouldn't have been spending much time in the house, but she hoped he'd left it tidy. Not, she reflected as she turned back to the window, watching as the sun tried to muscle its way from behind a cloud, that she cared what Rafferty thought.

'What about the investigation into Anna's stabbing?' Dolan had already spoken to Catherine about it, of course, but it was a way to allow Rafferty to fill the silence.

She should have known better. After mentioning Marshall had been brought in for interview and telling Catherine about the search still ongoing at his property, Rafferty fell silent. Catherine was racking her brain for another topic when eventually Rafferty said, 'You won't have heard about the knife? DCI Dolan phoned as I was leaving Danny Marshall's house.'

Catherine turned. 'The knife?'

'No fingerprints, but the blood on the blade is A – the same as Anna Varcoe's. It'll take a while longer to confirm it's definitely her blood.'

'Where was it found?'

Rafferty took her eyes off the road for a second, glancing at Catherine, who then knew for certain.

'You're saying Jasmine had it?'

'In her rucksack.'

'Shit. I knew I should have tried to look inside it.'

'Could you have done?'

'I suppose not. She had it in bed with her, even took it to the bathroom.'

'Your brother's seen Danny Marshall, heard him speak – he doesn't recognise him.'

'But we're still questioning Marshall, searching his home?'

'Jasmine was there. He hasn't explained why. It feels as though we're going in circles, I must admit.'

'DCI Dolan does seem worried.'

Rafferty came immediately to her boss' defence. 'Mary's under some pressure.'

'She's an SIO, there's always pressure.' Catherine was dismissive. The humiliation of being forced to stand in front of a crowd of her colleagues and admit her undercover investigations hadn't borne any fruit still rankled.

Rafferty glanced over again. 'She shouldn't have dragged you out to the front like she did. I'm sure she had her reasons though.'

'She was pissed off, frustrated. I was an easy target.'

'Yeah, well, you're not any more, are you?' Rafferty pointed out. 'Information you provided led us to Marshall, as Mary knows.'

She said it casually, as if it were no big deal. Catherine felt a blush stain her cheeks. 'You'd have had to speak to him again eventually.'

'Maybe. Maybe not.' Rafferty cleared her throat. 'Mary's the best DCI I've worked with though. I'm sure she would have soon made the connection.'

And all at once, Catherine understood. She watched the scenery rush by through the window, seeing none of it as she considered the implications of what she now believed she knew.

As they stopped outside Catherine's house, Rafferty gave an approving nod.

'Do you own it?'

'Had to buy my ex out, but yeah, I do now. Pay the mortgage, anyway.'

'I... We looked at new builds. Didn't find the right one. Still renting.'

Catherine released her seatbelt. 'It's okay. You can hear your neighbour three doors away closing their kitchen cupboards or having a wee, but...'

Rafferty gave the now familiar quirk of her lips that indicated amusement or acquiescence. 'I'll keep it in mind.'

Inside, the house smelled stale, but was clean and reasonably tidy. Catherine sat Rafferty in the living room with a cup of tea and the TV remote before rushing upstairs. As she shampooed her hair, relishing being in her own bathroom, she remembered Ghislaine. There had been no reply to the text she had sent. Where was she? More importantly, was she safe?

Catherine dressed quickly, pulling on a pair of dark trousers and a sweater. She dried her hair, pulled it back into a ponytail, and hurried downstairs. Rafferty hadn't turned on the TV, preferring to sit and stare at her phone instead. She looked at Catherine as she entered the room.

'Welcome back,' she said.

Catherine laughed. 'It's only been a few days.'

Getting to her feet, Rafferty said, 'Let's get back to Lincoln. We need to find our mystery woman. By the way, DI Knight and Adil are resuming the interview with Danny Marshall. Some interesting items have been found in his house.'

Chapter 43

Now accompanied by his solicitor, Marshall was pale and obviously nervous, shuffling in his chair as the police officers came in. The solicitor, a sharp-suited man already drumming his fingers on the table in impatience, looked at his watch.

'Can we get on with it, officers?' he asked. 'My client has already been here over three hours.'

'Plenty of time left before we need to charge him.' Zaman smiled.

The solicitor ignored the comment, but Marshall's face was panicked.

'Charge me?'

The solicitor shook his head at Marshall, attempting to calm him as Zaman ran through the formalities.

'We all know why we're here,' Knight said. 'Mr Marshall, we'd like to talk about certain items recovered during the search of your house earlier.'

Marshall hesitated. 'No comment.'

'Scales were found, quantities of tin foil, plastic bags. Do you want to explain why those items were in your home?'

'It's not a crime to have scales in your house, is it?'

Marshall was openly terrified now, his eyes shifting from side to side, the metal leg of the table clinking as his foot repeatedly tapped against it.

Knight smiled at him. 'Usually, no. The issue is what those scales were being used for. They'll be forensically examined now, you know. Traces of any substance that has been in contact with them will be found. Anyone who's touched them will have left fingerprints. Our forensics people will find them.'

The solicitor stretched his back. 'This is extremely interesting, Inspector, but...'

'I've never touched them,' Marshall said quickly.

'We'll have to wait and see, won't we? If you've never touched them, how did they get into your house?'

'They're... They're not mine. They were in the house when I moved in.'

Zaman snorted. 'Yeah?'

'I swear they were. Load of stuff was left in the kitchen cupboards.'

'You realise how this looks?' Knight demanded. 'We have two victims: John McKinley and Jasmine Lloyd. Both of whom you knew, both displaying evidence of heroin injection. And we find scales in your house.'

'I've told you...'

'Doesn't look good for you, does it? No one better placed to supply them with drugs than the man who knew all the juicy details of their habits. Pretending to help them, when in truth you were feeding their addiction for your own financial gain.' Knight forced himself to stay calm. He wanted the truth from Marshall, but losing his temper wasn't going to help.

Lazily, the solicitor said, 'Do you have any actual questions to ask my client, Inspector, or are you going to entertain us with baseless supposition all day?'

Knight watched Marshall's eyes roam the room. 'Who lives with you, Danny?' he asked suddenly.

Marshall stared. 'Lives with me? No one. I live alone.'

Knight shook his head, tutting. 'Not what I hear. Our search team found plenty of evidence of another person. A sleeping bag, a toothbrush. We've seized them, of course. Lots more DNA evidence to collect.'

'I don't know what you're talking about,' Marshall muttered.

'Who are you protecting? Was it Jasmine?'

His solicitor was frowning now. Marshall clearly hadn't been entirely honest with his legal advisor about who lived in his house.

'I told you, Jasmine has never been to my house. Had, I mean.' Marshall's mouth trembled. 'I can't believe she's dead.'

'Where were you last night between the hours of nine p.m. and eleven p.m.?'

'At home. Playing my video game again.' Marshall smiled at Zaman, trying to garner some sympathy, but Zaman's face remained expressionless.

'Can anyone confirm that?' Knight asked. They would soon know, when they received reports about Marshall's mobile phone. Marshall's movements, or to be more precise, the movements of his mobile phone, would have been tracked each time his phone 'pinged' a telecommunications mast.

'No. As I've told you several times, I live alone.'

'We know you're lying.' Knight folded his arms, watching Marshall steadily. 'Are you willing to take the rap for whoever you're protecting?'

'Must be someone important,' Zaman said. 'Or else they know your secrets.'

There was a tap on the door and Dolan's head appeared.

'A word please, DI Knight.'

She was holding a few sheets of paper. Marshall craned his neck, trying to see what was printed on them. Knight stood and slipped out of the room after Dolan. In less than a minute he was back.

'We have some new information,' he told them.

The solicitor raised his eyebrows. 'And are you going to share it with us?'

'Mr Marshall, we now have your mobile phone records.'

'Right...' Marshall was wary. Knight handed him a photograph.

'Do you recognise her?'

'No. I've never seen her before.'

'Are you sure?'

'Yeah, I told you. Who is she?'

'Her name is Anna Varcoe. She's a police officer.'

Marshall dropped the photograph as if it had burst into flames. 'She's the woman who was stabbed a few nights ago.'

'You know the name.'

'I saw it on the news. Why are you showing me her picture?'

'My client has already said he doesn't know this unfortunate woman, Inspector. Can we move on?'

Knight retrieved the photograph, setting it back on the table. 'Anna Varcoe is still fighting for her life,' he told them. 'Her boyfriend and parents have barely left her side for the past two days and nights.'

'A shame, but I don't see...'

Interrupting the solicitor, Knight held up a hand. 'Can you tell me where you were on Tuesday evening, Mr Marshall?'

'I... I was at home. Playing—'

'Your video game, yes.' Knight sighed. 'And I suppose they'll be no one to corroborate your statement, since you live alone?'

Marshall flushed. 'No.'

'You were at home all evening? Between the hours of, say, seven and ten?'

'Yes.' Marshall stared at Knight, the colour on his cheeks deepening further. 'You're not trying to pin the stabbing on me now?'

'We know where you were, Danny. You were in the city centre.'

'What? No, I was at home.' Marshall turned to his solicitor. 'He can't do this. He's lying. I was at home all night.'

'I'm guessing the inspector believes he can prove your whereabouts, Mr Marshall. Am I correct?'

Knight nodded. 'As I've told you, we have the data from your mobile. You were close to the street where Anna Varcoe was stabbed, at the time the incident occurred.'

Marshall gaped. 'Listen, I... My phone was stolen.'

Zaman let out a guffaw. 'How convenient.'

'No, it's true, I swear. It went missing a while ago. I had to buy a cheap one, couldn't get out of my contract.'

'Did you report the theft? Do you have a crime reference number?' Knight asked, sure he already knew the answer. Marshall looked wretched.

'No, I didn't report it,' he mumbled. 'What would have been the point?'

'It wasn't insured?' Zaman asked.

Marshall gave him a baleful look. 'No, strangely enough, it wasn't insured.'

Knight leant his elbows on the table, linking his fingers and resting his chin on them. 'Here's how it looks, Danny. You're low on cash. The counselling job can't bring in much money. You hear a name through your work, you contact them, agree to deal drugs for them.'

Marshall was shaking his head, his eyes wide. His solicitor tried to intervene.

'Inspector...'

Again, Knight raised his hand and continued. 'Eventually, you hit on another way to make some cash. You stole phones, wallets and purses at knifepoint. You recruited Jasmine Lloyd to help, promising her drugs as payment.'

Marshall let out a strangled gasp. 'No, no...'

Knight was relentless. 'And when you realised your crimes were being investigated, you killed Jasmine and planted evidence on her body, hoping she would be blamed for your actions.' Knight knew it wasn't true. Thomas Bishop had been certain – Danny Marshall hadn't stabbed Anna.

But he knew who had.

Marshall was sobbing. 'I'm innocent. You've got to believe me.'

'Then tell us the truth,' Knight bellowed. 'Tell us who you're shielding.'

Marshall's mouth worked desperately. 'I can't.'

Knight stood, pushed back his chair. 'Then we can't help you.'

He turned and strode towards the door, Zaman on his heels.

'Wait.' Marshall's voice was little more than a whisper.

Knight stopped, turned his head. Marshall gazed at him, as if willing him to understand, his face wet with tears. Knight turned away.

'We'll speak again soon, Mr Marshall,' he said. 'Perhaps your solicitor can talk some sense into you.'

Chapter 44

Rafferty shoved back her chair, her expression triumphant. 'Got it.' She waved a slip of paper towards Catherine and leapt to her feet, grabbing her handbag.

'You've found a name and address?' Catherine asked as she hurried after Rafferty, who was now crossing the room towards Dolan's desk.

'Yeah, both,' Rafferty said over her shoulder. 'You won't believe this.'

Catherine wanted to ask what she meant, but Rafferty was already halfway across the room. Dolan was reading a report, but she paused as Rafferty held out the piece of paper.

'I've found her, ma'am.' Rafferty gave Catherine a sideways glance. 'I mean, we've found her – the woman Pat Kemp told us about.'

'Stop calling me ma'am, Isla, for the billionth time.' Dolan took the paper and studied it. 'Bethany Oliver.' Catherine raised a hand to her mouth as Dolan frowned at the name. 'Oliver as in...'

Rafferty was more animated than Catherine had seen her before. 'As in Ghislaine Oliver. Bethany is her mother. Gives Ghislaine a pretty good motive, wouldn't you say?'

Dolan chewed her pen as she considered it. 'Only if John McKinley attacked her mum.'

Rafferty refused to be discouraged. 'She could be planning to kill the other men involved too. Kemp, ACC Clement and the Chief Constable – Russell Southern.'

Whipping her head around to check who was listening, Dolan hissed, 'Quietly Isla, for God's sake.'

Catherine's mind reeled as she tried to process what this latest piece of the jigsaw could mean. Could Ghislaine have killed John McKinley? Could she have murdered Jasmine Lloyd, her best friend? Catherine recalled the night before – Ghislaine's vulnerability, her tears, her body trembling as she fell asleep. She didn't believe it, and yet she had been wrong before. Catherine knew her judgment had been impaired on previous cases – by lust, by loyalty. Was the fogginess in her mind, the aching heaviness of her limbs, blinding her now?

'Doesn't Ghislaine have an alibi for the night John McKinley was killed?' Catherine asked.

'She arrived at Phoenix House at nine thirty, went to bed at eleven and left at eight thirty the following morning,' Rafferty said. 'Since we've established it would be easy to sneak out of Phoenix House at night, plus the time of death for McKinley is wide open, I can't see the alibi matters at this stage.'

Catherine wanted to ask why the possibility of Ghislaine's involvement hadn't been considered before, but decided against it. She would gain nothing from antagonising Dolan, and she knew little of the leads officers other than Rafferty and Zaman had been following. The case had been vague and undefined, the attack on Anna muddying the waters further. If they came to the correct conclusion, the one they could prove in court, did the route they took to get there matter?

'Go and speak to this woman, see what she can tell us,' Dolan said. 'We'll have Ghislaine Oliver brought in.'

Catherine cleared her throat. She remembered Ghislaine's words, the catch in her voice as she told her about Jasmine's actions on the night of Anna's attack. Had she been telling the truth? Catherine wasn't going to confide in Dolan or Rafferty about sharing her bed with Ghislaine. Innocent as it had been, she didn't want them to know, especially if Ghislaine had been deceiving her all along.

'Ghislaine left the shelter early this morning,' she said. 'No one seemed to know where she'd gone.'

'Great,' Dolan groaned. 'You two, go. We'll find Ghislaine. I'll update DI Knight and Adil. Maybe the person Danny Marshall is protecting wasn't working with Jasmine after all.'

Rafferty was driving again, more urgently now, nosing out of junctions and not always adhering to speed limits. Catherine watched her change gear, frowning as she concentrated. Stuck with Rafferty again. She would sooner have questioned Marshall, believing the shock of discovering Catherine was a police officer could work in their favour. Instead, she was spending the day as Rafferty's assistant. She sighed as Rafferty sped across a roundabout. May as well have stayed at Phoenix House.

'Ghislaine mentioned her mum to me once,' Catherine said, to break the silence. 'I'd asked if she was okay and she complained I sounded like her mum. She said, "My mum wouldn't give a shit."'

Rafferty made a sound of exasperation, rolling her eyes. 'And you didn't mention it?'

'Are you serious? It was a throwaway comment; it meant nothing.'

'Based on what we've discovered today, it might.'

'Forgive me for not being psychic.'

Catherine turned away, hunching her shoulder to provide a barrier between herself and Rafferty, furious. What right did Rafferty have to speak to her as if she were stupid? Catherine closed her eyes. Every right, if Ghislaine had been fooling her.

'Sorry,' Rafferty said.

'Forget it.'

'The last thing we need is another suspect.'

Catherine turned, surprised. 'What do you mean?'

Rafferty shook her head, frustrated. 'We're questioning Danny Marshall, having searched his house, but we know he didn't stab DC Varcoe. We've spoken to different people, most more than once, about John McKinley's death, and we're no nearer to the truth.'

'They're not straightforward cases.'

'True. And they involve homeless people, which complicates matters.'

Catherine felt a sting of resentment. 'Why?'

'Their mistrust of the police. The transient nature of the community. The drug and alcohol problems.'

'Stereotyping, aren't you?' Catherine forced herself to keep her tone civil.

'I'm talking about the people we've questioned, not everyone.'

'Sure?'

Rafferty glanced at her. 'Catherine, I don't have a problem with homeless people. I want this mess sorting out. We should have protected Jasmine Lloyd, and we didn't.'

'We weren't the only ones,' Catherine said, remembering Ghislaine's comments about Jasmine's mother. 'Has Jasmine's mum been to identify her body?'

'Earlier. Made a lot of noise about how she'd had to take time off work, the cost of the train ticket. Didn't seem in the least upset. Maybe the grief will hit her later, though I doubt it. Lovely woman.' Rafferty's mouth twisted.

'Let's hope Ghislaine's mum is more helpful.' Catherine visualised her own mother: homely, kind, keen to be involved in her children's lives but not interfering. Catherine's elder brother Richard had died before she was born, and she supposed it could have been easy for her parents to allow their understandable grief and heartbreak to colour the rest of their lives. Catherine had never spoken to her mother or father about how Richard's death had affected them, she realised. She had been selfish, still playing the part of a child though she was now an adult. It was easy to imagine parents as all-knowing, fearless, when you were young. It took time to realise they were as frail as children, with the same doubts and fears. She resolved to speak to them about it next time she visited them.

'Nearly there,' Rafferty said. They were driving through a village large enough to support a row of the usual shops — butcher, bakery, hairdresser — as well as a supermarket. As they passed a primary school, hordes of children charging around the playground, Rafferty cleared her throat.

'How do you want to play this?'

'You're asking me?' Catherine was surprised.

'You know Ghislaine better than I do. Bethany might confide in someone who knows her daughter.'

'But we know she and Ghislaine aren't close. Why don't we meet her first, see how she responds to us being here?'

Rafferty had slowed the car as they approached a council estate. She eased over a speed bump before replying.

'Agreed. There's the house.'

Number seventeen was in the centre of a terrace, with two houses to either side. Unkempt privet hedges divided the small front garden of Bethany Oliver's house from those of her neighbours. Rafferty nudged the car against the kerb. As they climbed out, they could hear music pounding from the open window of number fifteen, the thumping bass rattling their teeth.

'Relaxing,' Catherine said.

Rafferty twitched her lips, waving Catherine ahead of her. The concrete path was cracked, the square of lawn a sickly brownish-green. Mindful of the row emanating from the adjoining house, Catherine hammered the white-painted front door a few times with her fist. Shuffling her feet, she waited.

Nothing. Catherine tried again. Eventually the door was yanked open and a short, skinny woman appeared in a waft of warm air and cigarette smoke. She drew heavily on her roll-up before pulling it from her mouth.

'Yeah?'

'We're looking for Bethany Oliver?'

'And you are?'

Catherine flashed her identification, introducing herself and Rafferty, who was hovering behind her. The woman squinted at them and replaced the roll-up.

They followed her into a gloomy hall, the music from next door clearly audible through the wall. Catherine made to take off her shoes, but the woman snorted. 'Shouldn't bother, love. Beth isn't house-proud, as you can see. Bloody music.'

Catherine looked around. The stairs were in front of her, the walls painted a faded magnolia. A spider dangled from the light fitting above her head. Underfoot, a gritty brown carpet languished.

'Do you live here too?' Rafferty asked.

The woman shook her head. 'No, thank Christ. I'm Beth's oldest sister, Wendy. I drop in now and again, make sure she's still alive, bring her some shopping.'

She waved them into a square living room, sparsely furnished. A two-seater settee dominated one wall while a dining table and four chairs stood under the window. There were no books, no TV, no photographs.

'You may as well sit. I'll ask if she'll see you, but I doubt she'll want to,' Wendy told them.

Rafferty lowered herself onto the sofa. 'Is Miss Oliver ill?'

'Yes and no. Her problems are all up here.' Wendy pointed at her own head. 'Agoraphobia, depression, anxiety – you name a mental illness, Beth's got it. And she's diabetic.' As an afterthought, she added: 'What do you want her for?'

'A chat about her daughter.' Catherine gave what she hoped was a reassuring smile.

Wendy didn't look convinced. 'Ghislaine? Selfish little cow. Time she came home to look after her mother.'

It was a strange comment from someone who could be expected to care about Ghislaine's welfare. Ignoring the remark, Catherine perched on the sofa beside Rafferty, though she was reluctant. It brought them even closer than they had been in the car, which made her uncomfortable. Rafferty inched away, obviously feeling the same.

Wendy left the room, thumping up the stairs. They heard a door open, voices. The music still blared, the room stuffy and too warm. Catherine's vision narrowed. She blinked, bile filling her mouth as the walls lurched and span. The urge to escape was back. She wanted to run, to get out of this horrible house, to leave Rafferty and Wendy far behind. Setting her palms on her thighs, she took some deep, calming breaths.

'Can you come here?' Wendy's voice cannoned down the stairs, easily heard above the blaring music. No mean feat.

Catherine and Rafferty exchanged a glance. In the hall, Wendy was already zipping up a thick padded jacket.

'She's having a bad day, won't come out of her room. She doesn't bite.' She nudged Catherine hard in the ribs. 'Well, not as far as we know. You don't need me, do you?'

Without waiting for an answer, she disappeared through the front door.

Upstairs, thankfully, the music wasn't as loud. There were three doors off the landing, two closed and one ajar. Catherine stepped closer and tapped on the latter.

'Miss Oliver?'

'Come in.'

Pushing open the door, Catherine moved into the room, Rafferty behind her. A double bed filled most of the floor space, with the shadowy shapes of a wardrobe and chest of drawers looming beyond it. The curtains were drawn, the air thick and humid. Catherine smiled at the woman in the bed. Even in the gloom, it was easy to see she was Ghislaine's mother. The resemblance was unmistakable. They had discovered Bethany Oliver was thirty-eight, which meant she had been seventeen when Ghislaine was born. An idea struck Catherine. Why hadn't they seen it before? Rafferty might have noticed when she found the record of Bethany Oliver's arrest, but she hadn't said so.

With a sigh, Oliver rubbed her eyes and pushed herself into a sitting position.

'What's this about? Is Ghislaine okay?'

'She's fine. I saw her last night,' Catherine said.

'She works too hard.'

Catherine and Rafferty looked at each other, confused. Rafferty took another step towards the bed and stood beside Catherine.

'Works too hard?' she asked.

'She's a student. Graduating this year.'

Catherine hesitated. 'She… You must be proud of her.'

'I am. She's always been a clever girl.'

'Miss Oliver, we'd like to talk to you about an incident that occurred some years ago,' Rafferty said. Oliver gripped her duvet with both hands.

'An incident?'

'You were arrested after a disturbance in Lincoln city centre.'

305

Pushing back against the headboard as if she wished she could disappear through the wall, her eyes searching their faces, Oliver whispered, 'My sister said this this was about Ghislaine.'

'A friend of Ghislaine's has been murdered,' Rafferty told her. 'We believe there could be a link between her death and your arrest.'

'Why should there be? I don't understand.'

'Does Ghislaine know you were arrested?' asked Rafferty.

'No, I never told her. I wanted to forget. It's hardly something to be proud of.' Oliver twisted the duvet cover between her fingers, clearly distressed. Catherine felt sorry for her, but they had to know.

Catherine said, 'What about her father?'

The reaction was instantaneous. Oliver's mouth opened and a tiny whimper of distress escaped. She blinked rapidly.

'Her father... He's not around.'

Catherine squatted by the bed, laying her hand on the duvet, but not touching Oliver.

'We know what he did to you, Bethany.'

Rafferty frowned, not fully understanding. Bethany Oliver was silently weeping.

'How about some tea?' Catherine suggested. 'Would you mind, DS Rafferty?'

Rafferty looked as if she might protest for a second, but she left the room.

Catherine went out to the landing, found the bathroom and brought back a roll of toilet paper. She handed it to Oliver, who took it with a tremulous smile.

'Take all the time you need,' Catherine told her.

She didn't want to hear the details until Rafferty was back in the room, but she recognised this was going to be another ordeal for Bethany Oliver. Tea helped, gave a person a distraction as they talked, something to do with their hands. Taking a sip allowed them to pause when they needed to, Catherine had learnt early in her career.

'I know she's not a student,' Oliver said.

'Sorry?'

'Ghislaine. She walked out one day. I always wanted her to go to university, and I've kidded myself she did. It's been… I don't know where she is. She's phoned a few times, but from a mobile.'

Catherine said nothing. It wasn't her place to tell the woman her daughter had been living on the streets less than ten miles away. Ghislaine was an adult, free to make her own decisions.

Oliver asked, 'Is she… Is she well? Happy?'

Catherine thought quickly. 'She's obviously distressed about the death of her friend.'

'She never had many mates. Poor Ghislaine. I wasn't much of a mother.' The tears welled again, and Oliver pressed the tissue to her eyes.

Catherine willed Rafferty to hurry, knowing they both needed to hear what she said. Oliver continued to sob while Catherine waited, wanting to offer comfort. She knew there was nothing she could do other than listen.

Eventually, they heard the stairs creaking and Rafferty came in with three mugs. Holding her drink close, Bethany Oliver wiped her eyes and nose.

'How much do you know?'

'You were arrested, taken back to the station. Later, in your cell…'

Oliver raised her chin, gazing into Catherine's eyes.

'I was raped.'

Although they had guessed, to hear the confirmation was shocking. Oliver said the words without emotion. They tumbled into the room, stark and indisputable.

'Who?' Rafferty asked. 'Who was it?'

Oliver ignored the question. 'I hadn't been fighting, you know. I was living on the streets in those days. I'd been in my sleeping bag, trying to get some rest, when I heard the fighting. I was trying to get away when they grabbed me.'

Catherine forced herself to remain patient, knowing Oliver needed to tell them in her own way. Beside her, Rafferty shifted and Catherine placed her hand on her colleague's arm, silently asking her to stay quiet. Rafferty tensed, but didn't speak.

'I tried to explain I hadn't been involved, screamed as loud as I could, but no one listened. At the station, they dragged me into the cell and left me. All around, men shouting, threatening each other. Hammering on the doors, throwing up...'

She paused to sip her tea. Catherine waited, watching Oliver's face. She realised she was still holding Rafferty's arm, and relaxed her grip. Rafferty threw her the briefest of irritated glances as Oliver continued her story.

'Soon, they came in.'

'They?'

'Four of them. Four men and me, in a tiny prison cell.'

'What happened?' Rafferty asked the question.

Oliver closed her eyes, cradling her mug. 'At first, they yelled questions at me. One of them, they called him John, he left after a few minutes. I didn't see him again. The others... One backed me into the corner. He was tall, thin, with gingery hair.'

Clement, Catherine told herself.

'He kept shouting at me, but he knew I couldn't tell him anything.'

Oliver swallowed, rubbing her hand across her mouth.

'You're doing well, Bethany,' Catherine told her.

Oliver glared. 'You're police as well, aren't you? How do I know you believe me?'

'We do,' Rafferty said. 'I can promise you that.'

'I tried to report it before,' Oliver retorted. 'Ten years it took me to pluck up the courage, but no one would listen. They sent out this officer—'

'The man who raped you.' Catherine couldn't help interrupting. The Chief Constable. Cruel, calculating bastard. Climbing the career ladder, shaking the right hands, kissing the right arses. All the time, keeping his filthy secret hidden and making sure his mates did too.

Killing to maintain the silence.

But Bethany Oliver shook her head.

Chapter 45

He ignored the first call, continuing to drink his coffee, but when his phone immediately chirped again, Jonathan Knight knew he would have to answer. His ex-girlfriend was not someone who would be ignored.

'What is it, Caitlin? I'm waiting to go back into an interview.'

'Interviewing? Sounds more like you're in the pub.'

'It's a canteen. What do you want?'

'Don't you want to hear about the baby? Had you forgotten she'd been born?'

Knight closed his eyes for a second. He hadn't forgotten, of course not, but he'd pushed the fact to the back of his mind all the same. Caitlin in London, raising the child who may or not be his own daughter. Until he knew whether he was the baby's father, he wasn't going to allow himself to remember she existed.

'Have you done the paternity test?'

Caitlin sniggered. 'A little tricky for me to, wouldn't you say?'

Knight bit back the curse trying to push its way out of his mouth. 'You know what I mean. Has your boyfriend done it?'

'Not yet. It's been less than a week since the birth, Jonathan.'

'So why are you ringing?'

'God, do you have to be like this? I wanted to tell you her name.'

Knight turned away from the hubbub of the canteen. 'I do. You know I do. I'm sorry. Is she okay?'

'She's fine. Feeding well. Screaming half the night, but Jed's a natural with her.'

Twist the knife, Caitlin, Knight thought. Zaman stuck his head around the door, eyebrows raised. Knight lifted a hand, acknowledging him. Hopefully, Danny Marshall was ready to talk. 'Caitlin, sorry, I'm going to have to go. I'll call you back.'

'Jonathan? Her name's Olivia.'

Knight blinked, the room blurring for a second. 'Olivia. Lovely.'

'I'm glad you agree.'

–

Marshall sat with his back straight, his fingers laced together on the table. As Knight and Zaman entered the room, Knight looked at him, suddenly weary. Two people were dead, one of his own officers was still clinging onto her life in hospital and he was here, playing games with a man who could give them at least some of the answers they needed. Procedures had to followed, and he respected them, but there were times when he wished he could lunge across the table and grab a suspect by the throat.

Knight took his seat, surprised and shocked by his own thoughts. He wasn't a violent man, never had been. Perhaps the conversation with Caitlin has rattled him more than he'd realised.

When the preliminaries were over again, the solicitor cleared his throat.

'My client would like to make a statement.'

'About time too.' Zaman folded his arms.

Danny Marshall took a deep breath, blew out his cheeks. 'You need to find Jake Pringle,' he told them.

Chapter 46

'I'll get the DCI on speakerphone.' Rafferty opened the car door.

Catherine fastened her seatbelt, feeling as dazed as Rafferty sounded. They had their answer at last, and it wasn't the one she had been expecting.

The sound of the phone ringing filled the car, followed by a clunk and Dolan's voice, tense and businesslike.

'Isla? Where are you?'

'Leaving Bethany Oliver's house. Ma'am, we—'

'What have you found out? We've not located Ghislaine Oliver yet.'

Rafferty swung the car into the traffic. 'Miss Oliver told us who attacked her in her cell that night. She told us who raped her.'

'And?' Dolan yelled.

'It was Pat Kemp.'

There was a silence. Catherine pressed her hands to her cheeks. Rafferty hurled the car into the traffic, prompting a lorry drover to raise his finger and mouth abuse as she veered in front of him.

'Kemp?' Dolan said at last. 'Pat Kemp? Are you sure?'

Rafferty opened her eyes wide. 'Bethany Oliver is. She heard the other men call him Pat. We had an old photograph of him, from his days on the force. She's prepared to give evidence. It was him, ma'am.'

'There is a way to confirm it,' Catherine said.

'DS Bishop? What do you mean?'

'The rape resulted in Bethany Oliver's pregnancy,' Catherine told her. 'Ghislaine Oliver is Pat Kemp's child.'

'Fuck. Fuck, fuck, fuck. But Pat Kemp told us to go to Dawn McKinley. He must have known we'd catch up with him eventually. Did he murder John McKinley?'

'We believe so,' Catherine said. 'Ghislaine knows nothing about her mother's rape. She's always been told her dad was killed in a motorbike accident before she was born. She has no motive.'

'Unless John McKinley told her.'

'He didn't, ma'am. She'd have told me,' Catherine said. 'She's innocent.'

Dolan said nothing.

Rafferty cleared her throat. 'Kemp got away with rape for years. He no doubt imagined John McKinley's death would be judged accidental. McKinley knew too much, especially as he'd met Ghislaine. It wouldn't have taken him long to work out she was born nine months after Kemp visited Bethany Oliver's cell.'

'Still doesn't explain why he'd tell us to go to Dawn McKinley. What about the Chief Constable and ACC Clement?'

'They were in the cell for a while, but they left Kemp alone with Bethany. Whether they knew, or suspected, only they can tell you.'

'But Kemp said Southern got rid of Bethany Oliver when she came to report the crime. I know it was years later...'

'It didn't happen like Kemp told you it did,' Catherine said.

'What do you mean?'

Rafferty said, 'Kemp made most of it up, presumably to confuse us, to throw more suspicion on the Chief Constable. Bethany spoke to some young constable who told her she didn't have a case. She left the station in tears.'

There was another silence. 'Kemp's a conniving prick, as well as a rapist and murderer.' Dolan was furious. 'I'll get his disgusting arse brought in. Not surprised he left the bloody force… And you two, good work. Back here, and get a move on. I want you ready to question Kemp when he arrives.'

Chapter 47

'Jake's been staying with me ever since he left Phoenix House,' Danny Marshall said.

Zaman stared at him. 'You mean since he stole their money and ran?'

Marshall flushed. 'Yeah.'

'Why didn't you tell us this before?' Knight asked. 'We've wasted time, Danny.'

'I know, I'm sorry. I didn't know about the drug dealing, I swear. And Jasmine...' Marshall covered his face with his hands. 'Does this mean Jake killed her?'

'If she wasn't coming to your house to see you, she must have been visiting Jake.'

'But she did visit me.' Marshall's voice was tiny.

'What?'

'We were in a relationship. Jake realised. I agreed to give him a place to stay until he sorted himself out, if he kept his mouth shut about me and Jasmine.'

'And that's why you didn't want to tell us he was living with you.'

Marshall hung his head. 'I'd lose my job. He told me he was looking for work. I didn't know about the drug dealing, I swear.'

Knight formally ended the interview.

'What happens now?' Marshall asked fearfully.

'Now? We find Jake.'

Dolan massaged her temples. 'Jake Pringle's behind the robberies, the attack on Anna Varcoe.'

'Yes, ma'am,' Zaman said quietly.

'What an afternoon.' Dolan mustered a laugh. 'DS Rafferty and DS Bishop will soon be in the interview room, having a chat with Pat Kemp.'

She explained before sending Zaman off to organise the hunt for Jake Pringle.

'He's not at Marshall's house, and there were no drugs on the premises. No cash either. Pringle's done a runner.'

'He could be anywhere by now. If Marshall had spoken up sooner...' Knight frowned.

'Well, he didn't. We'll find Pringle. Can you check with Thomas Bishop, see if he can confirm Pringle's the man who stabbed Anna? We'll have a mugshot. Should have looked more closely at him before, but everything pointed to him being long gone.'

'Will do.'

Dolan rubbed her hands together. 'Get them both brought in, interviewed and charged, and we might get home early tonight.'

'Yes,' Thomas said. 'I'm sure it's him, the fucker. Let me hear his voice and I'll know for certain.'

'We'll need to find him first,' Knight told him.

'Why didn't someone realise? He's got a criminal record, hasn't he?'

'Not for robbery. Everyone said he'd left the city. It's not an excuse; we should have tried to find him.'

Thomas looked at Anna. 'Bastard. Roaming around while she's lying here.'

'How is she?'

'The same. No worse, but no better. I don't know, they talk in riddles.' Thomas ran his hands over his face, obviously exhausted. 'Do you know where Catherine is?'

Knight nodded. 'I'll see her later.'

'Ask her to phone me, will you, please? I'd like to see her. This course she's been on seems intense.'

'It's over. She'll be home soon.'

Thomas unzipped his jacket, took something from the inside pocket. 'And I'd like her opinion on this.' He held a small blue box out to Knight, who took it, opening it to reveal an engagement ring.

'It's for Anna,' Thomas said unnecessarily. 'If she ever wakes up.'

Chapter 48

Pat Kemp had answered the door himself when the uniformed officers arrived, already wearing his coat. He said farewell to his dog, kissed his wife goodbye, climbed calmly into the waiting car. When Catherine and Isla Rafferty entered the interview room, he greeted them. Rafferty announced the time, date, location, and introduced herself. Catherine said her own name, then asked Kemp to state his. He spoke clearly, his expression resigned. He smiled at Catherine.

'You were a copper all along. Maggie told me about you. You had her fooled.'

Catherine dipped her head, embarrassed, although she had no need to be. 'It was necessary.'

'You know what I've done. Listen, I don't want a solicitor, nor any fuss. I'll tell you what happened; you can charge me. No need for a search warrant.'

They ignored him – Kemp might be co-operating, but he was a rapist, and a murderer. The case against him would need to be watertight.

Rafferty said, 'Tell us about John McKinley.'

Kemp studied the tabletop. 'I'm sorry about John.'

Catherine laughed. 'You're sorry?'

'He was a mate, a good mate back in the day. Everything I told you before was true.'

'Except *you* raped Bethany Oliver. You, Patrick Kemp. Not John, not Edward Clement or Russell Southern.' Catherine glared at him. 'Did you honestly believe we wouldn't find out?'

'No. I wanted you to. It's been a burden, all these years.'

'A burden? A fucking burden? How do you think Bethany Oliver feels? You destroyed her for your own gratification, your own... Why? Why did you do it?'

Kemp swallowed, shocked by Catherine's rage. 'I never meant to. I went in there to question her. She wouldn't answer, I lost my temper, grabbed her, she struggled. I don't know why, how I could. I still can't believe it.'

'She didn't answer your questions because she hadn't done anything.'

Catherine was half out of her chair. Rafferty shot her a look, and taking a shuddering breath, Catherine made the effort to calm herself.

'Did John McKinley know about the rape?' Rafferty was perfectly calm.

'He suspected. He wouldn't speak to me, didn't want to know me.'

'And the other two officers – Clement and Southern?' Deliberately, Catherine didn't give their current rank. She wanted Kemp to tell the truth, and if it meant Clement and Southern were dropped in the shit, so be it. She was sick of this case, of the lies and deceit.

'Nothing was said, not at the time,' Kemp said. 'I left the force in the end. I wasn't dismissed, but like I said, I was aware I should jump or be pushed.'

'But you can't tell us who made the threat?'

'I told you, there were whispers, rumours, gossip. Nothing more. Enough to make my position impossible, not enough for me to make a complaint. How could I?'

'Why did John leave?'

'He guessed what I'd done, and the fact I was getting away with it made him sick.'

'Why weren't you charged?'

Kemp stared into Catherine's eyes, a curious smile on his lips. 'You sure you want me to answer?'

'I wouldn't have asked otherwise.'

'All right. There were men in positions of power who believed their own careers, their reputations, would be damaged if the truth came out. When she tried to report the crime, they panicked, got some new lad to tell her to get lost. They got rid of me and hoped nothing more would come of it.'

'And you went? Didn't put up a fight?'

He shook his head. 'I'm guilty.'

Catherine imagined Dolan and Knight watching the interview unfold. Where would they go from here? How would they proceed? It was a mess – a huge, sickening mess.

'What about more recently?' Rafferty asked. 'What happened between you and John?'

Kemp rubbed his forehead. 'Cards on the table time. John saw me at the shelter, at Phoenix House. I'm there occasionally – meetings, collecting Maggie if her car's in the garage.'

'He recognised you?'

'It wouldn't have been hard to put two and two together. He saw Maggie if he stayed at the shelter, but he didn't often. He'd only met her a few times, years before.

But when he saw me, even though it'd been a while, he recognised me.'

'What happened?'

'I was doing a gardening job in the city centre. John turned up, drunk. He didn't make much sense at first. He told me he knew what I'd done.' Kemp shook his head. 'I didn't admit to anything, but I agreed to give him some money.'

'He blackmailed you.'

'Not exactly. It was more a favour, helping out an old mate.'

Catherine sniffed. 'Call it what you like.'

'He was going to tell Maggie. I... I said I'd meet him, give him the cash. When I got there, he was drunk, off his face. I had the heroin, and I shoved it in his arm. He'd used in the past. I was certain it'd be judged accidental death.' He gave a tired smile. 'Shows what I know. His life was fucked anyway, he'd soon have been dead, but I couldn't take the risk.'

'You put him out of his misery? It was a mercy killing?' Catherine didn't attempt to hide her contempt.

Kemp squirmed. 'No. I killed him because I was terrified he'd ruin my life. All right?'

'Like you ruined Bethany Oliver's?' Catherine couldn't resist.

Kemp bowed his head. 'Believe me, I know what I've done. And now everyone will know.' He lifted his face, tears on his cheeks. 'Should have confessed, told Maggie, called John's bluff. Too late now.'

'Where did you get the heroin?' Rafferty was calm, her face impassive.

Kemp shook his head. 'Does it matter?'

'You know it does.'

'Want to arrest the dealer too? I'm not telling you.'

Rafferty folded her arms. 'We'll find out.'

Kemp gave a bitter laugh. 'Yeah, no doubt.'

'What time did you meet McKinley?' Catherine asked.

'Eleven. In a shitty alley where he'd slept a few nights.'
He confirmed the name of the street. 'Are you searching
my house?'

'As we speak.'

He rubbed his eyes. 'Maggie.'

'She'll be okay.'

'She wants to help. Every lame duck, every waif and
stray, everyone other people have given up on. She's a
saint. Pity she married me.' Kemp sniffed.

Catherine was unmoved. 'We'll talk again soon, Mr
Kemp.'

When they arrived back in the incident room, Dolan
was standing with Jonathan Knight.

'Well done in there, you two,' she said as Catherine and
Rafferty approached. Catherine managed a smile. She still
hadn't forgotten the way the DCI had humiliated her, but
she was willing to let it go. All she wanted now was to go
home, have a soak in the bath and spend the night in her
own bed.

'What are you going to do about what Kemp told us?
The ACC and Chief Constable?' Rafferty asked.

Dolan scowled. 'It's all there, on tape. I'm going have to
speak to Professional Standards. What choice do I have?'

Catherine froze, knowing Dolan was right, but also
aware of her own vulnerability. On a previous case,
Knight had placed her in a difficult position, and if Professional Standards were going to be sniffing around... She

had done nothing wrong, but it could still mean the end of her career. She looked at Knight, who smiled. No hint of worry, no trace of guilt. Not for the first time, Catherine wanted to confess. To tell the truth about what had happened, and fuck the consequences.

She wouldn't, out of loyalty to Knight, misguided though it might be. She had trusted him since their first meeting, though she'd never been able to explain why.

Rafferty nudged her. 'Your phone's ringing.'

Catherine pulled it out of her bag and checked the display.

The caller was Ghislaine Oliver.

Chapter 49

'Ma'am, did we locate Ghislaine?' Catherine raised her voice to be heard above the chatter of the incident room.

Dolan shook her head. 'We don't need to now. We haven't found Jake Pringle either, the slippery little bastard.'

Dolan might not agree, but Catherine certainly needed to speak to Ghislaine again. Confess who she truly was, perhaps suggest Ghislaine talk to her mum? They didn't know why Bethany and Ghislaine's relationship had fractured, but surely there was hope for it? Catherine wanted to believe it, though it was none of her business. Her mobile was still ringing.

'Hello, Ghislaine?'

'Catherine? I need your help.'

Catherine's heart leapt. She turned to Rafferty, grabbing the other woman's arm, alarmed by Ghislaine's tone.

'What's the problem, Ghislaine?'

Dolan heard the change in Catherine's voice – Knight too. Catherine pressed the button for speakerphone, and they moved closer, circling Catherine as she gripped the handset.

'Ghislaine? Talk to me, please.'

'You know where Jasmine was killed?' Catherine heard Ghislaine swallow, her voice tight as though terrified. 'There. He says you should come alone.'

'He? Who do you mean?'

But Ghislaine had gone, the call ended abruptly.

'Fuck.' Dolan had gone pale. 'I'm sure we can all guess who she's talking about.'

They could. Jake Pringle.

Chapter 50

Catherine hunched in the back of the patrol car, Knight beside her, Rafferty squashed next to him. In the front, Dolan was berating Zaman as he tried to wind his way through the traffic.

'Come on, Adil. Get out of the fucking way!' she bellowed, giving a delivery driver the finger. Her phone bleeped. 'The helicopter's been mobilised; hopefully they'll be able to fly over the car park and see what's happening. Listen, Catherine, there's no way you're going up there, do you understand? Pringle killed Jasmine, he's got Ghislaine and he'll chuck you off the car park too if he gets a chance.'

'Ghislaine asked for me,' Catherine said, her voice shaking.

'I don't bloody care if she asked for you, the Queen and Mother Teresa, you're not going. A negotiator is on his way.'

'From where?'

'Does it matter?'

'It does if we want Ghislaine safe and Pringle arrested this side of Christmas.'

Dolan's face was purple. 'You're staying in the car.'

Catherine said nothing, staring out of the window. Zaman thumped the steering wheel as traffic hemmed them in on all sides. They weren't using the siren or lights, not wanting to alert Pringle. This seemed pointless to Catherine if the helicopter had been mobilised, but what did she know?

If this had been a normal car, she could have opened the door since they were at a standstill, and made her way to the car park on foot. No chance in a patrol car – the back doors wouldn't open from the inside. Maybe Dolan had thought of that. Knight nudged her.

'Okay?'

'Okay?' Catherine swallowed. 'No.'

'Caitlin's called the baby Olivia.'

She stared at him, speechless at his timing. 'Great, Jonathan.'

'Sod this, let's get moving,' Dolan said. The siren screeched into action; the lights whirled. Finally, cars began to move.

'Right, shift your arse, Adil.' Dolan peered through the windscreen, arms folded.

'Doing my best.' Zaman's jaw was clenched in concentration.

Soon, they stopped beside the car park, the siren silenced again, the lights off. Dolan turned to the three officers in the back.

'Now, we wait. I've requested an armed response team as well as the helicopter, but it's going to take time to get them here and into position.' Catherine protested, but Dolan silenced her with a look. 'Pringle has a hostage. He could be armed. This is a busy city centre. I'm not taking any risks, not with your safety, Catherine, or anyone else's. Understand?'

'But I want to...'

'Not your decision.'

Closing her eyes, knowing further protest was futile, Catherine had no choice. She took her phone out of her pocket, willing it to ring again. Dolan squinted at the huge structure in front of them.

'Anyone spotted him?'

No one had. They were too close to see the top floor in any case. In her hand, at last, Catherine's phone was ringing again. She fumbled, nearly dropping it into the footwell.

'It's Ghislaine again.'

'Answer it,' Dolan snapped. 'And put it on speaker-phone.'

'Ghislaine, where are you?' Catherine said. There was laughter – male laughter.

'She's here with me, safe and sound. Come on, Sergeant Bishop. Join the party.'

'Send Ghislaine out first.'

'No chance. You've got five minutes.'

'And if I don't?'

He laughed again, the sound echoing around the car, taunting them.

'Ghislaine will be coming down to see you. And I don't mean using the stairs or the lift.'

He ended the call.

There was silence for a second before everyone spoke at once. Dolan clapped her hands.

'Quiet. Let's...'

'You heard him. He's going to throw Ghislaine over. Let me out of this fucking car.' Catherine pounded on the door, her knees thumping the back of Dolan's seat, hard.

'All right, DS Bishop,' Dolan barked. 'Boot my seat again, and I'll kick your arse. Now listen. It seems we have no choice. He's obviously seen us arrive.' She tried to look at the sky. 'No sign of the fucking helicopter. Catherine, I hate to do this…'

Knight said, 'You're not seriously going to send her up there?'

'What choice do I have?'

'He's a fucking maniac, he'll…'

'I'm going, Jonathan. We can't let him hurt Ghislaine.'

Knight snatched at Catherine's arm. 'She could already be dead. Listen to yourself, Catherine. You don't need to do this.'

She shook him off. 'I do. It's my fault she's there.'

'What? You're being ridiculous. Why put yourself in danger?'

Dolan opened her door. 'DI Knight, we have no choice. Go on, Catherine. Ring my phone, keep the call connected and hopefully we'll hear what's happening. We'll follow.'

She opened the door for Catherine and she tumbled out, sprinting towards the car park's entrance. There were stairs and a lift – she'd be more vulnerable if she took the lift, because Pringle could attack her as soon as the doors opened. But if she took the stairs, even though she considered herself fit, she'd be out of breath by the time she arrived at the top. It would have to be the lift.

She thumped the button, relieved when the doors immediately slid open. Hammering the button for the top floor, she leant against the wall. Why had Pringle asked for her? Because she was Ghislaine's friend, and he guessed she would come if Ghislaine was in danger? He must know Catherine was police, though how, she'd no idea.

The lift clattered and hummed, the number for each floor flashing as she passed it. With a clatter, it halted and the doors opened.

Catherine looked around. Several cars, plenty of empty parking spaces, but no Ghislaine. No Jake Pringle either. She stepped out of the lift, her blood thumping in her ears. Silence. There was no movement, nothing to indicate they were even here. Had Pringle been bluffing? A few seconds passed before realisation dawned.

Her phone. He was waiting for her to break the connection with Dolan. He must have tried to ring her again, and got the engaged tone. Slowly, she removed the handset from her pocket and ended the call to Dolan, holding it out so Pringle could see what she was doing, wherever he was. Immediately, Ghislaine's name lit the screen.

'Better,' Pringle said. 'Don't want any interruptions, do we? Now walk forward.'

Catherine did as she was told, her eyes scanning the area. Still she couldn't see them. She didn't know exactly where Jasmine's body had been found. If Pringle was expecting her to be able to come to them, he was in for a disappointment. She hoped he wouldn't take it out on Ghislaine.

Warily, conscious of every movement, she kept walking, the phone pressed to her ear. She could hear him breathing heavily, as if excited. No doubt he was. Having her and Ghislaine here at his mercy was bound to be a massive turn-on.

'Where the hell are you?' Catherine demanded, tension tightening around her chest. He laughed again, and this time she heard him properly. He was close.

'Leave the phone on the ground. Stand slowly, keeping your hands where I can see them.'

Catherine rolled her eyes. She did as he said, wondering if he'd said the same to Thomas and Anna the night he stabbed her. They stepped out from behind a car, Pringle dragging Ghislaine, hugging her to his chest, a knife under her throat. Ghislaine's mouth was taped shut now, but her eyes, wide and desperate, found Catherine's.

'Good afternoon,' Pringle said, as if they'd bumped into each other in the street. 'Fancy seeing you here.'

'What do you want, Pringle?'

He simpered. 'How rude. Maybe you should be polite, since your little friend here's at my mercy.'

Catherine had a second to decide how she was going to play this. 'My friend?' There was a sneer in her voice. 'What are you talking about?'

Pringle's smirk faded a little, but he rallied. 'I know you're mates. I've seen you together.'

Catherine laughed, harsh and mocking. 'I was under-cover. I wanted to get close to Ghislaine to find out what she knew. I pretended to be her friend, yeah. Doesn't mean I give a shit what happens to her now.'

As she spoke, she maintained eye contact with Ghislaine, hoping she would realise Catherine was lying. If she hadn't cared, she wouldn't be within a mile of this place. She held her breath as Pringle hesitated, hoping she hadn't signed Ghislaine's death warrant.

'You're bluffing.' He gave another laugh. 'Why would you come, if you didn't care?'

'To talk to you, Jake. You've had us all confused. We'd never have found you if you hadn't asked me to come here.' The words filled her mouth with bile, but they were necessary. She was banking on Pringle's ego being larger than his brain.

'Led you all on a dance, haven't I?' Pringle adjusted his arm, the blade scratching at Ghislaine's throat. She whimpered behind the gag, her eyes pleading. Catherine knew she had to keep him talking, give Dolan's back-up a chance to arrive – the helicopter, a marching band. Anyone who could help, who could rescue Catherine from a situation she had no idea how to manage.

'You have, Jake. You've been clever.' The word stuck in her throat.

'How's the policewoman? The one who got hurt?'

Got hurt? She didn't want to tell him about Anna. 'She's okay.'

'Still alive? I didn't mean to do it, you know. The knife... I waved it around, had to make them believe I was serious. All at once, she was bleeding all over me. Silly bitch.'

He was lying. She could see he'd known exactly what he'd been doing. Catherine clenched her fists, hating him. Pringle saw the movement and smiled.

'What about Jasmine?' Catherine demanded. 'Her death wasn't an accident.'

'Poor Jasmine.' He cackled. 'You must think I'm stupid, after all.'

'Why bring me here?'

'One hostage is good, two's better, especially if one's a copper.'

'How did you know who I was?'

333

'I guessed. I've been watching, following you. You went to the Headquarters, more than once. I knew you couldn't be a suspect.'

'I still don't understand why I'm here.'

'You're going to drive. Here.' Loosening his grip on Ghislaine for a second, he fumbled in his pocket, retrieved a bunch of keys and flung them at Catherine. 'Black Ford Focus, over there. Start her up.'

Catherine didn't move. 'I can't, Jake.'

'What?'

'I can't drive.'

His eyes widened. 'You're lying.'

'I honestly can't. Don't you think I would if I knew how to?'

'They wouldn't have a policewoman who couldn't drive.'

Catherine was worried she was going too far. It had been a stupid idea, born out of desperation. 'They can't discriminate, Jake.'

Ghislaine stared, her eyes questioning what Catherine was doing. Catherine had no idea.

'Jake, tell me about Jasmine. Was she blackmailing you?'

Pringle's eyes darted left and right as he tried to figure out what to do. 'She found the knife, when I stabbed that woman. Devious cow. Wanted money, drugs, or she'd grass me up.'

'Meaning you had to kill her.'

'Yeah, she was bleeding me dry.' He giggled at his joke. 'Wait a minute, you smart-mouthed bitch, you can't talk your way out of this. I know you can fucking drive; pick up the keys and let's go. Otherwise…'

'Otherwise?'

'Say goodbye to your girlfriend here.' He gave Ghislaine's hair a savage twist. She squealed as the knife bit into her neck.

Catherine threw herself onto her knees, snatching at the keys. 'All right, I've got them. Don't hurt her.'

Pringle was laughing as Catherine unlocked the car and climbed inside. He had to be off his head on something. As she turned the key, Catherine considered her options. She could floor the accelerator and smash into him, but Ghislaine would be killed too. Catherine had no way of knowing how badly Pringle had cut her, but at least Ghislaine was still alive. And could she bring herself to do it, to purposely plough into him? Catherine was out of ideas.

'Bring the car over here, get out and open the back door,' Pringle called. 'Ghislaine can sit on my knee. She'll enjoy it, won't you sweetheart?'

Gritting her teeth, Catherine slid the car into first gear and eased it forward. She stopped beside Pringle, climbed out. As Catherine opened the door, Pringle jerked Ghislaine again, pressing his mouth against her ear.

'You know what, I've changed my mind. You can stay here.' He stroked the knife against Ghislaine's throat, smiling at Catherine. 'It'll be easier to handle one hostage, and the copper's more valuable than you are. Maybe I'll cut your throat now and get it over with.'

Catherine froze as Ghislaine let out a muffled scream. Pringle suddenly thrust her away from his body, keeping hold of the knife as Ghislaine tumbled across the tarmac.

'Fucking hell, the dirty bitch has pissed herself...'

Catherine didn't see where the shot came from, but she heard Pringle scream as the bullet entered his body. The knife fell from his grasp, clattering away, blood blooming on his shoulder, the front of his shirt. As Catherine fell to her knees beside Ghislaine, Pringle crumpled to the ground.

Chapter 51

'What a fucking baby,' Dolan said.

Catherine laughed. 'He had been shot, to be fair.'

'Yeah, in the arm. All that whining and snivelling – pathetic.'

'How did the armed response team arrive so quickly?'

'They were training nearby. I may have pulled in a few favours.'

Catherine blew out her cheeks. 'Thankfully.'

'You saved Ghislaine's life, not me.'

Catherine waved the statement away. 'Any one of you would have done the same.'

'But we didn't.' Knight was beaming.

'How's Ghislaine?' Catherine asked. She was sitting in a cubicle in Accident and Emergency, having arrived by ambulance despite protesting she was fine. The paramedics muttered about shock, and kept smiling at her.

'She fine,' Dolan said. 'Shaken, of course. They've stitched the wound on her throat. She should be able to go...' Dolan blushed. 'She should be able to leave later tonight.'

'Can I see her?'

'Don't see why not.' Dolan checked her watch. 'I need to leave. See you at Headquarters soon. I'll send a car.'

She marched away with a wave. Alone in the cubicle, Catherine and Knight looked at each other.

'You know you took a massive risk?' Knight said.

'More than one. But what choice did I have?'

'Look, Catherine, about the Paul Hughes case. I've spoken to Professional Standards.' Catherine opened her mouth, but Knight kept talking. 'It's okay. I told them what happened, that I had some help from outside the force. I didn't mention your name, kept you out of it.'

'And?'

'And it's all right. I told them everything. There was overwhelming evidence against the accused, as you know. They killed him, and they're doing the time. You can forget about it.'

'Promise?'

He smiled. 'Promise.'

She exhaled. 'All right.'

'Catherine!'

Thomas burst into the cubicle, grabbing his sister. 'What the hell have you been doing? Someone phoned, told me you were in here.' He held her at arm's length, examining her. 'You look all right to me.'

Catherine laughed, the tension of the day leaving her as she threw her arms around her brother. Thomas scrubbed his eyes with his knuckles, and Catherine turned to Knight.

'Can we go? I want to see Ghislaine.'

Knight cleared his throat. 'You're not supposed to walk out...'

A nurse stuck her head around the curtain. 'You can leave when you're ready, Sergeant Bishop.'

Catherine grinned. 'It's as if they're listening. Thank you!' she called.

Ghislaine was in a bay at the other end of the department. Lying on a trolley with her eyes closed, wearing a hospital gown and covered by a thin green blanket, she looked tiny. A white dressing covered the wound to her throat inflicted by Pringle's knife.

Catherine stepped closer to the bed. 'Ghislaine?'

Her eyelids fluttered. She smiled.

'Catherine. You're here. Is he dead?'

Catherine shook her head. 'No. Listen, I'm sorry I lied to you.'

Ghislaine frowned. 'Lied?'

'Said I was homeless. I didn't mean to deceive you. It was…'

'Your job. It's okay, I understand.'

There was a silence.

'Where will you go?' Catherine asked.

'I don't know.'

'I spoke to your mum. She misses you.'

Ghislaine turned her face away. 'I doubt it.'

'How do you know?'

'She hates me.'

Catherine remembered Bethany Oliver lying in her dark, half-empty house. Her hands trembling, her eyes filling with tears as she spoke about her daughter.

'I don't think she does, Ghislaine.'

'Did she tell you why I left?'

'No. I didn't ask.'

'You'll have to arrest me.'

'Arrest you? What do you mean?'

'I killed her boyfriend. Her drunken, fat pig of a boyfriend.'

The floor shifted beneath Catherine's feet. 'You… You killed him?'

Ghislaine trembled. 'Well, I don't… He used to beat her up. Her, me, his own kids. One day, I was in my room and he came storming in, pissed out of his head, ranting at me. I hadn't tidied or something. I ran. At the top of the stairs, he tried to grab me, and I stepped back. He fell, and…' Her eyes were far away, watching the incident happen again in her mind. 'We called an ambulance, they took him to hospital, but he died. They said he'd smacked his head.'

'It was an accident.'

'I felt like I killed him. Still do. My mum said I did. We had row after row, and in the end I walked out, never went back.'

'She'd like to see you.'

Ghislaine looked away. 'I'll think about it.'

Catherine knew she could do no more. She held out a piece of paper to Ghislaine.

'Here.'

'What is it?'

'My address and phone numbers. Ring me any time, or come to the house. Stay with me, if you want to. You don't have to go back to the streets.'

Slowly, Ghislaine reached out a hand. 'I haven't even thanked you. You saved my life.'

'You did that yourself,' Catherine told her.

Ghislaine laughed. 'If I'd known wetting myself would make him let go of me, I'd have done it long before.'

Catherine laughed. 'It was original, I'll give you that.' She checked the time on her phone. 'I need to go, but I meant what I said.'

'Won't I need to give a statement?'

'We'll be in touch. Don't worry about Pringle. The shot was meant to disable him, which it did. He'll soon be fit to stand trial for Jasmine's death.' She turned. 'Take care, Ghislaine.'

There were tears in her eyes as she walked.

'Catherine.'

Ghislaine was behind her.

'You shouldn't be out of bed,' Catherine scolded.

'Thank you,' Ghislaine said. 'Not only for today, but for what you've said. And for last night…'

Catherine opened her arms. Ghislaine clung to her for a second, but when she stepped back, her eyes were dry. Catherine smiled, blinded by tears again herself. She kissed Ghislaine's cheek, and walked away.

–

'Last night?' Thomas said. 'What happened last night? Bit young for you, isn't she?'

'Shut up, Thomas.' Catherine gave her brother a shove as they walked across the hospital's car park. 'You shouldn't have been listening.'

'I wasn't. I was on the phone. That's all I heard, promise.'

'She was told her friend had been murdered. I comforted her.'

'Never heard it called that before.'

Thomas was protecting her, Catherine knew, joking around, keeping her mind off what had happened.

'I'm okay, you know,' she told him.

'If you say so.'

Inside his car, Catherine put on her seatbelt, but Thomas waited.

'What?' she said. He gave a hesitant smile. 'Don't piss around, Thomas, not today. What is it?'

He fumbled in his pocket and brought out the small blue box. Opening it, he held it out for her to see. An engagement ring – a diamond set on a platinum band. Her eyes welled again, but she choked the tears back.

'Thomas, I'm flattered, but I can't accept. I'm your sister.'

He snapped the box closed. 'Hilarious. Think she'll like it?'

'Anna?'

'Yes, Anna! Who else?'

'Does this mean... Is she responding to the treatment?'

'They say she is. Her mum phoned. A slight improvement, anyway. They're hoping to wake her soon.'

Chapter 52

When Catherine walked into Lincolnshire Police Headquarters, Maggie Kemp was waiting at the reception desk. Confused, Catherine approached her.

'Maggie? Can I help?'

Maggie barely saw her. 'I want to see the Chief Constable.'

'I see. May I ask why?'

'It's about my husband. He's confessed to a murder, but I know he's innocent.'

Catherine blinked at her. 'Mrs Kemp, I know it must have come as a shock, but...'

Maggie set her hands on her hips, finally realising who she was speaking to.

'You've solved John's murder, have you, Catherine? You've arrested Pat, who can't squash a spider, Pat who cried when a bird flew into the window and died.'

'Pat who raped a young girl.'

Maggie Kemp waved her hand. 'Nonsense. She's lying.'

'Mrs Kemp, your husband has confessed. I know it's difficult to accept, but...'

'I killed him.'

Catherine stopped, stared. 'What did you say?'

'I killed John McKinley. Stuck a needle in his arm. He tried to blackmail Pat, ruin everything we've worked for. He was going to tell everyone his lies, go to the newspapers. Ruin Phoenix House, where we'd made him welcome.' She fluffed her hair. 'Now, can I see the Chief Constable or not?'

–

Dolan bought the first round, knocked back a gin and tonic and called for another.

'I didn't even get to go home early,' she said, swirling ice around her glass. 'Anyone else want to confess to the murder of John McKinley?'

'Do you think she's telling the truth?' Adil Zaman asked, swallowing a mouthful of lemonade. He was eager to get home to his family, his car waiting outside the pub.

'Who knows?' Dolan burped discreetly. 'And who cares. One of them did it, and I'll worry about which in the morning. Maybe a night in the cells will bring her to her senses.'

Catherine cradled her bottle of lager, worrying about Ghislaine. Where she was spending the night?

Knight touched her arm. 'Okay?'

'Yeah. Remembering it might have been me with my throat cut.'

'You did well.'

She shrugged. 'Is Jo coming over to celebrate?'

'No, and I'm only staying for one drink. DCI Dolan has asked me to come back tomorrow.'

'Early night with Jo then?'

Knight blushed. When Zaman and Knight stood to make their excuses, Catherine also got to her feet.

'Can I cadge a lift please, Jonathan?'

Catherine could have booked into a hotel, stayed for a few more drinks, but she didn't want to. Dolan was already talking about going back to her room, and being stuck on her own with Rafferty wasn't in the least appealing.

'Take tomorrow off, Catherine,' Dolan told her.

'We'll see.' She waved. 'Good night, DS Rafferty.'

Rafferty inclined her head and twitched her lips. As she followed Knight out into the cold, crisp night air, Catherine smiled to herself.

Some things didn't change.

Chapter 53

Later, after a bath, Catherine got into bed with a sigh of contentment. Her own home. She felt as though she'd been away for weeks.

The house was silent. Thomas was staying with Anna's parents, as their house was closer to the hospital. Catherine's eyes were open, loneliness soon creeping over her again. As strange as sharing a room with Ghislaine and Jasmine had felt, at least she hadn't been alone.

As she lay there, recalling the events of the day, a thought came into Catherine's head, something she'd recognised, but had forgotten.

She sat, swinging her legs out of bed. Pulling her bathrobe around her shoulders, she grabbed her phone.

It rang four times before a bleary voice answered.

'Have you seen the time? What is it?'

'Can I come to see you?'

'What are you talking about?'

'You,' Catherine said. 'I want to talk about you.'

–

The sky was bright, frost slipping through the air, high-lighting blades of grass and cobwebs. Catherine drove quickly, not allowing doubt to creep into her head. She was right; she knew it.

She parked the car and hurried towards her destination. She had dressed quickly in jeans and a T-shirt, her hair loose around her shoulders. As she'd pulled on her coat, she had wondered if the stresses of the day, of the week, were the reason behind her decision. She didn't care. If she didn't do this now, tonight, she would never know. What did she have to lose?

Only my self-respect. Her mood had lifted, but the darkness lingered. She would talk to Jo, go to her GP. It wouldn't beat her. This was reckless, foolish even – but so what? She could have died today. How long you could live in the shadows?

Catherine approached the door, not permitting herself to consider turning around. She raised her hand, steeled herself and knocked.

Isla Rafferty peered out.

'Are you mad?' she said.

Catherine grinned. 'Possibly.'

'You'd better come in.'

Rafferty opened the door and stepped back. The hotel was basic, but modern. Rafferty's room was tidy – no clothes thrown over the chair or empty food containers lying around. Catherine had expected no less. There was a double bed, a sofa and a desk with a chair. Rafferty was wearing casual clothes: jeans and a navy-and-white striped sweater. Her hair was damp, the scent of shampoo and shower gel lingering. She sat on the bed, clearly confused and not a little pissed off. Catherine perched on the sofa, leaning forward, her elbows on her knees. Now she was here, she may as well get on with it.

'I'm sorry to turn up like this.'

'What do you want, DS Bishop?'

'Where's DCI Dolan's room?'

'The floor above somewhere. Why?'

'I wondered.'

Rafferty shook her head, frowning. 'I don't understand.'

'Does Dolan know?'

'Know what?'

'That you fancy the pants off her?'

Rafferty blushed. 'What are you talking about? I'm engaged.'

'Are you?' Catherine sat up straight. 'So why aren't you rushing back to your fiancé every night, like Adil does to his wife? Any chance he has, Adil goes home. And you? You sit in your hotel room, wishing you had the courage to tell your boss how you feel about her.'

Rafferty turned away. 'You don't know what you're talking about.'

'But I do, Isla. I've seen how you look at her, how you defend her. How you call her "ma'am" when you speak to her, even though she hates it, because you're afraid of giving yourself away if you're less formal. I *know*, Isla. I've been there myself.'

Rafferty's shoulders were shaking. Horrified, Catherine ran to her. 'Come here. It's okay, honestly.' She sat on the bed, wrapping her arm around Rafferty. 'You don't have to live like this, Isla. You don't have to hide, to keep pushing people away.'

Rafferty was holding back tears. 'It's not what you think.'

'But...'

'Okay, yes, you're right. I had a crush on Dolan – who hasn't? I saw the way you looked at her too.'

Catherine glanced away, her cheeks flaming. 'Bugger. I hoped no one noticed. It didn't last long.'

Rafferty managed a laugh. 'I even bought myself this stupid ring to stop people asking when I was going to get a boyfriend. I had to say he was a paramedic, so he couldn't come on nights out, tell them he didn't mind me working late because he always was too...'

'You bought yourself an engagement ring?' Catherine couldn't help it. She laughed. 'What did the people in the jeweller's say?'

'I got it online. Anyway, that's why I was such a cow to you for the first few days.'

'Because...?'

'Because you were living the life I've never let myself have. You're gay, and you don't care who knows it. And me – I'm Rafferty the bitch, Rafferty who never smiles, never lets anyone close. I'm awful with Adil, selfish and difficult, keeping him at arm's length in case he guesses. He doesn't deserve it. You were closer to him five minutes after you met than I've managed in a year of working together. I resented you.'

'But you don't have to live like this – sell your bloody engagement ring for a start.'

Rafferty pulled off the ring, stared at it. Slipped it into her pocket. She shook her head. 'It's not so simple.'

'It is, Isla. Live your life. No one's bothered, honestly. I'm not saying it's easy. You don't come out once, you come out every time you meet someone new. But if you don't... If you don't you'll never be happy.'

'But my career...'

'You're worried you won't be promoted because you're gay? Would it even matter? When I'm old, looking back at my life, will I care whether I made DCI, or would I sooner have someone by my side, reliving the memories with me? You've got a chance, Isla, a chance to find happiness. Lots of gay people in the world still don't.'

Rafferty said nothing. Catherine stood, turned away, knowing she had said her piece. 'I'm sorry, Isla. I should go.' She moved to the door. 'Maybe we'll work together again one day.'

'I'll be civil next time.' Rafferty got to her feet, hands in her pockets, her eyes fixed on the floor.

Catherine laughed. 'I'll look forward to it.'

'Thank you for coming back, for what you've said. I know you're right. I...' She couldn't finish the sentence.

Catherine opened the door, embarrassed. 'I'm sorry I barged in here, Isla. It's none of my business. Good night.'

–

She was pressing the button to summon the lift when Isla's bedroom door opened.

'Catherine. Catherine, wait.'

Slowly, she turned. Isla walked towards her, held out her hand. Catherine took it, not smiling now, or wondering what was right.

Inside the room, the door closed behind them with a click. Slowly, tenderly, Isla raised her hand to Catherine's face, frowning as if about to ask a question. Catherine touched her lips to Isla's forehead, to her cheeks. She hesitated, not wanting to push too hard. Gently, she pulled Isla closer, closing her eyes, savouring the moment.

Then Isla was kissing her, their hands caressing, exploring, and the world ceased to exist. When Isla eventually pulled away, there were tears in her eyes. Catherine took her hand, kissed it and led her across the room.

As Isla sat on the edge of the bed, Catherine knelt between her knees, arms circling her waist, holding her close. She pressed her lips to Isla's throat, kissed her ear, felt her shiver.

'Are you sure?' She whispered. Isla beamed. Not her usual quirk of the lips, but a genuine smile. There was no doubt in her eyes, no hesitation. Catherine saw only tenderness and trust. She unfastened the buttons on Isla's sweater and lifted it over her head, knowing for the past few days, they had both been waiting for this.

And Dolan? Dolan had known, sensed it, pushing them together until they realised themselves. As Isla moved closer to kiss her again, Catherine sent the DCI a silent message of thanks.

Acknowledgements

Once again, there are many people whose help I have been extremely grateful for during the process of writing this book.

My wife Tracy believes in my work even when I don't, and I will be forever grateful for her support and faith in me. Thank you to my son, Mum, Grandma, Paul and the rest of the family for their constant encouragement and support. A mention too for my furry writing companions, Evie, Poppy and Alexa.

Thank you to Britt Pflüger, who offered advice and encouragement from the first day I contacted her, when I hadn't even finished a book.

Thank you too to the wonderful friends, who have shown me so much support since the first book was released, and who continue to do so. I won't mention names for fear of accidentally missing someone out, but I hope you know who you are, and that I'm hugely grateful.

A huge thank you to everyone who bought and read *On Laughton Moor* and *Double Dealing*. It means so much to know people are reading your work, so special thanks to those who have taken the time to email me to say they've enjoyed the books. It's a dream come true.

To the amazing team at Canelo – thank you.

My website is www.lisahartley.co.uk.

Thank you for reading *From the Shadows.* Catherine Bishop and her colleagues will return soon.

Detective Catherine Bishop